"*Turtle Season* is a lovely and wise book."

—*Katherine Forrest,* author of *Curious Wine* and the Kate Delafield mystery series

"I loved the trajectory of the story of Anna's transformation toward her authentic self—from the dreary, deadened woman we meet at the beginning of the book to the enlivened, self-accepting, and passionate person we come to know at the end. . . . A totally absorbing novel full of humor, rich detail and authenticity. I was sorry it had to end."

—Linda Garnets, PhD, co-editor of *Psychological Perspectives on Lesbian, Gay and Bisexual Experiences*

"With economical and precise prose, Miriam Ruth Black paints a believable portrait of a woman on the verge of total disintegration who catches herself in time to find new life and love where she least expected it."

—Magazine editor and author Michele Kort is co-editor of *Here Come the Brides! Reflections on Lesbian Love and Marriage*

"This funny, moving novel about a woman's struggle to find the right life for herself in late middle age grabs the reader's attention and doesn't let it go. A good story that hasn't really been told before, *Turtle Season* is full of delightful surprises and honest emotions. I loved reading it."

—Alice Bloch, author of *Lifetime Guarantee* and *The Law of Return*

"Sweet joy and bitter anguish of a woman's journey towards self, true independence, and exploration of sexuality. Beautifully written, tender, and heartfelt. Ms. Black manages to convey Anna's inner life, doubts, regrets, and desires magically."

—Roz Sohnen, professor, digital filmmaking, the Art Institute of NYC

"*Turtle Season* is a beautifully written story that pulls you in right from the first line. Anna is so real, she's someone you'd want to have as a friend, and you don't want the friendship to end when you put the book down. Black's inside view of Anna's metamorphosis is compelling and engaging."

—Barrie Levy, author, psychotherapist, and adjunct professor, UCLA

"Miriam Ruth Black has created a memorable and recognizable character in Anna as she struggles—as we all must—to see herself anew and decide which elements of her past to keep and which to let go."

—Terry Wolverton, author of *Stealing Angel*

"In this emotionally rich novel, we follow Anna, widowed and living alone, as she moves out of depression and, bit by bit, engages with the world again—meanwhile reexamining her relationship with her late husband. A coming-of-age story when the age is well beyond adolescence."

—Mary Whisner, reference librarian, University of Washington

Turtle Season

Turtle Season

Miriam Ruth Black

BEAVER'S POND
PRESS

ISBN: 978-1-59298-548-7
Library of Congress Control Number: 2012917154

Cover design by Emily Mahon
Book design by Ryan Scheife, Mayfly Design
Typeset in Minion
Author photo by Andy Lessin

Printed in the United States of America
First Printing: 2013

17 16 15 14 13 5 4 3 2 1

Beaver's Pond Press, Inc.
7108 Ohms Lane
Edina, MN 55439-2129
(952) 829-8818
www.BeaversPondPress.com

To order, visit www.BeaversPondBooks.com
or call (800) 901-3480. Reseller discounts available.

For Emmie Russell,
who makes me laugh and gives me a home in the world.

Acknowledgments

This book wouldn't have happened without Mary Carroll Moore, teacher and editor extraordinaire, and Alice Bloch, great writer and cherished friend. For your belief in me and your wisdom, I give thanks. Adde Russell, my niece, wise beyond her years, was always available to help me with a laugh, a link, or a zinger.

Kelley Benyo, Gail Gardiner, C.J. Michurski, Suze Rutherford, and Judy Sigler, my "listeners" honored me with their attention and appreciation—for hours! Their grimaces, laughter, and tears guided me on my journey.

Katherine Forrest, with her deep experience and keen insight, challenged me to a ruthless revision—thank you for your honesty and generous spirit.

The talented Patricia Boiko provided technical assistance on documentary film making. Careful readings by dear friends Barrie Levy, Jane Matteson, and Jane Ross often gave direction when I lost my path—thank you all.

Susan Whitaker Duncan, Linda Garnets, Sylvia Gravrock, Jerry Sadoff, and Esta Soler—thoughts of your enthusiasm and support sustained me on gray days. Elise Asch, Joan Drury, Ronni Felicetti, and Mary Whisner, great friends, provided many helpful suggestions.

Due to one of those synchronistic weirdnesses that dot our lives from time to time, I reconnected with Mike Conley, a North High School classmate. He generously cheered me on and introduced me to his publishers, the excellent people at Beaver's Pond Press. Amy Quale, managing editor, provided consistent helpful guidance while the editorial skills of Jennifer Manion and Angela Wiechmann enriched whatever they touched.

A special thanks to the Loft in Minneapolis, the Madeline Island School of Art, and NANOWRIMO—all create wonderful climates for writers to blossom.

Finally, the memory of five special people lived in my heart as I wrote. Each in their very unique ways fostered my writing: Thom Negri, Bob Bua, Gale Kaplan, Chuck Borgman, and Paul Black.

Chapter 1

Her skirt flapped against her knees in the wind. Anna felt encumbered. Wanted to rip off the skirt and her blazer and her underwear. Maybe she would leave her clothes strewn across the beach, slowly scatter the contents of her purse along the shore as she disappeared into Puget Sound.

Of course, the big diamond Mort had given her for their twenty-fifth anniversary would go down with her. Someday a lucky swimmer would come across a few karats wedged between knuckle bones.

She rolled her eyes at her own melodrama as she imagined the headline, "Prominent Widow Drowns in Puget Sound. No Foul Play Suspected."

Anna pictured herself diving into the freezing cold waters of the sound, struggling for air, salt stinging her skin, water rushing up her nose. Disgusting. No way. She didn't want to die, not really.

She just didn't want to live. Up until that afternoon, no one had noticed she had become a ghost in her own life. Who paid that kind of attention?

Apparently, her students had. Her face flushed as she replayed her meeting with the dean earlier that afternoon. Anna Simon, the woman who had designed the hospice curriculum, one of the most respected instructors at Seattle Community College, was now on probation. Formerly respected. No longer.

As far as Anna could see, no horizon. Only gray. Seattle gray. The clouds blended into the water of the sound. No lines, no demarcations. Overcast. As she walked along the beach at Golden Gardens, her heels sank deep and sand shifted into her shoes. She looked around the empty beach, pulled off her heels and panty hose and tossed them into her large purse. Her legs trembled as she tried to balance, first one leg, then the other.

She hunched her shoulders together, clutched her purse to her chest, and lowered her head against the wind. By the time she reached the water's edge, cold sand had seeped between her toes, covering her feet. She sank into the sand. Comforting, she thought. Cuddle up with cold sand. She might as well cuddle up with Mort in his casket, for all the warmth the sand would give her.

She knew it was her fault. She had excuses: Mort's death last year, menopause. But still, other people did not melt away, like ice cream on a hot day. Other people lost spouses. Even suddenly. Prematurely. And lots of women complained about menopause, but they still functioned.

She wrapped her arms around her body, turned away from the wind, walked a short distance away from the gray water, and hunkered down behind a large driftwood log. Warmer and less windy here, but surrounded by the damp, briny smell of the sea mingled with old wood.

Anna looked north and south along the sound. Not a boat in sight, or another person. Only seagulls in the distance, gliding on the wind, soaring and then swooping.

Would that she could just fly away, she thought as she wiped the sand from her feet and put her shoes back on. Would that she could just crawl at this point, drag herself up from the fog that was her life. As she walked to her car, her mind drifted back to the meeting with the dean.

"He'll be with you in a few minutes."

Anna had sat in small reception area on a stiff armchair upholstered in some easy-to-clean vinyl. Even with the elastic, the waistband of her skirt pinched her. She had no idea how much weight she had gained. It seemed as if all of a sudden she weighed more. Her stomach ached, felt raw. She had tried to summon a tougher self for this meeting, but to no avail. She waited naked, vulnerable, and stupid.

"He'll see you now."

Dean Saunders walked toward her and shook her hand, reached around her to close the office door, gestured toward one of the two chairs at a conference table. She'd forgotten how young he looked. She was sure he knew nothing about menopause.

They both sat. Through the glass tabletop she noticed his knee bobbing up and down.

"I haven't seen you since my predecessor's retirement party. You haven't attended any of the staff meetings."

"Sorry about the meetings." She looked at his stiff face and knew there was only bad news coming.

His lips stretched across his face. "I know your husband died last year. Apparently that's been very difficult for you."

"Pardon?"

"I understand the previous dean spoke to you about the number of absences you had during the last school year." He waved a letter in front of Anna and then studied it closely. "I notice your signature on this letter after that discussion. Clearly, you read it. Of course, he understood that your husband had just died."

"I always arranged for a substitute."

He reached for another document. "I see three documented cases in which you did not." He slid some forms across the table to Anna, who shook her head.

She listened to the traffic noises outside. A siren, cars honking.

"And now this semester, a full year after your husband's death, there are other issues. Of course, we often overlook student complaints. We know students often blame the teachers. They have trouble taking responsibility. Don't you think?"

He wants me to bond with him, Anna thought. She stared at his eyebrows. Perfectly straight lines. She wondered if he plucked them. He must be one of the metrosexuals she'd read about. He wanted her to agree, but she didn't want to make it easy for him.

Saunders opened a file folder on the table, shuffled some papers, and shook his head. "But we can't ignore the kinds of things we've been hearing about your classes, particularly in light of previous warning."

"Warning?"

The dean nodded. "That's the form you signed last year. A warning."

"I didn't realize."

"That's why the previous dean got your signature. Now about the current issues..."

"Current issues?"

"Well," he said, selecting another document from her file. "Last week after your class, three of your students came to see me. They're worried about you."

"Worried? Who?"

"That's confidential." The dean adjusted the knot in his tie and continued, "It doesn't matter who came, but what they said concerns the whole department."

Anna pressed her hand down against the cramp in her stomach. She tried to smile, to look alert. She wondered what the appropriate expression might be.

"Well. I'll try to summarize the main points for you." He studied the papers in front of him again as if he were reviewing the

Magna Charta. "They said you lost the first set of papers they submitted. Apparently their midterm papers were returned with grades, but without comments. When they asked why you gave them certain grades, you told them to find partners and discuss it amongst themselves. After twenty minutes, they told me, you left the room and never came back."

Anna said nothing.

"The final is coming up, and they're anxious." Saunders glanced at the file. "You seem 'out of it' is what they said."

Anna focused on his eyebrows. She looked for tiny hairs just growing back, but couldn't see that kind of detail without craning her neck and using her bifocals. The office felt stuffy. She could smell sweat from her body.

She remembered the midterms. A bunch of stupid papers. She hadn't been able to concentrate, they were so boring. She had thought that if they showed their classmates the papers, they'd come to understand their grades. It had made sense then. Now it sounded foolish.

"Nothing to worry about." Anna lifted her chin and made eye contact. "If they've read the assigned readings and followed the discussions in class, they'll be fine. They'll all pass."

"They are worried. So am I. We have a reputation to maintain here. We've come a long way as a community college. Our degrees are worth something. This is more than a warning, Anna. I'm sorry, but I have to place you on probation."

As he spoke, Anna felt her face grow hot; her body, while actually rigid in the chair, felt as if it were collapsing in on itself. She watched the dean's fingers as they tapped against her file. Her mouth opened, but no sentences came out. She wanted to defend herself, but she knew no defense.

"We cannot tolerate more complaints from your students. If necessary, we'll find someone else to teach the class. I understand your husband died. But it's been a year. You have to pull yourself together."

She looked from his eyebrows down to his mouth. His lips were chapped. Without craning her neck, she had a clear view of his chin. He'd missed several hairs when he shaved. No clue about how to respond. As if she stood behind a Lucite wall, observing herself, but couldn't participate.

"Do you have any explanation? Is there something the department can do to assist you?"

She shook her head and looked at her fingers, the nails filed but the cuticles torn. Anna's throat was dry. "Not really. Just some women's issues..." she murmured.

Saunders didn't respond immediately. Then he coughed.

Anna looked out the window toward the main parking lot. People walked back and forth. All of them going somewhere. People got in and out of cars. Reached back for briefcases, kissed someone good-bye, loaded book bags into trunks.

"Oh. I see. We have a form for medical issues, for doctors to complete, if that's what you mean. I don't see anything in your file," he said as he sorted through the papers again. "As I understand it, you designed this course, you developed it."

Then he tilted his head and leaned closer to Anna. "You had an excellent reputation. I'm sure you want to continue to teach this course. Hospice is now a requirement for the major. We absolutely need to count on whoever is teaching the class."

He closed her file and folded his hands on it. "Perhaps you want to get that medical form completed by your doctor? Maybe arrange for a leave of absence...," he said as he stood up and stepped out from between his chair and the table.

Anna stayed seated and addressed her question to the chair he had vacated. "Would you hold my position for me if I took a leave?"

"We'd certainly try. But I can't promise. Anna, you know we

don't have a tenure system here." He gathered the contents of her file and replaced it in the cabinet behind his desk.

Dismissed. Chastised like a delinquent student. Elementary school principal Saunders. He walked toward her again, placing his hand on her shoulder. "I know this may be uncomfortable for you, but you can expect me to observe your class. It's for the good of the college." Then he opened the door to the reception area.

A flush crept along her neck as she rose and forced her eyes up to gaze directly into his. She saw no expression.

He shook his head. "Frankly, this meeting with you is not reassuring me. I'm not sure what it is. I don't know what I expected. But you're ..." He shook his head again and put his hand on her back as he guided her through the door. "Now take care of yourself."

Patronizing bastard. Young enough to be her child. Probably had been a bed wetter, Anna thought as she walked out of the office and down the stairs to the street.

Chapter 2

Pushing, cracking, breaking out into the sun. So bright she closes her eyes. She stumbles over broken eggs, falls, stumbles, and falls again, and then raises up on her thin, shaky legs and moves toward the light. On tiny feet she scrambles over others who are also struggling up. She feels them shoving, pushing, jostling her.

Her slight feet sink into the sand. She looks at her toes. They look like claws. She hears a ruckus above, caws and hoots. Squeals overhead. Large birds dive toward her. She rushes, compelled toward the deep darkness of the ocean ahead, dodging the squawking birds. Her mother calls from the darkness so far away. Wings flap above, squeaks, blood across the sand, and the birds diving. She hides near a rock and stares at the birds as they swoop toward the dark tiny shapes moving across the sand. So far she has eluded them as she scrambles to the sea.

There's Mort, sitting in a lawn chair, watching her, wearing sunglasses as he reads the newspaper. "Mort, help me," she calls. He can't hear her. "Help me . . ."

Something pushed her. Her nose tickled. Another push. Koru. Anna kept her eyes closed and tried to find her way back into the dream. Back near the rock. Were they turtles? Her concentration brought only the smell of her ripe, unwashed dog and the feel of his long fur brushing her nose. He barked and nudged her body again with his head. No more sleep. Anna sneezed and reached for a tissue. She pushed her hand against the morning ache in her lower back until it eased, then patted the bed next to her.

"Come here."

Koru did his dog circling until he settled next to Anna. She felt the heat of his body in the cold room. Still dark. No light filtered through the drapes.

Anna closed her eyes and listened to her dog's breathing. His name in Maori symbolized new life, which had seemed appropriate when Anna and Mort had found the blue-eyed husky pup nine years before, huddled in the alley. Now gray covered his muzzle.

The wind scraped branches against the window. She needed the gardener to cut them. Needed to have the furnace serviced.

"Get in touch with the furnace people. Feels like winter's here already." Mort's last words to her before his stroke. She hadn't called yet.

The butter knife slid from her hand into the pile of dishes in her kitchen sink. Mort had hated it when she went to bed leaving dirty dishes in the sink. Maybe he was turning over in his grave. She imagined his corpse—his face peaceful and his body wrapped, as tradition required, in a shroud. She wondered what he looked like now, after spending a year underground in a wooden box.

She would have to leave a directive to have herself cremated.

Anna finished her toast and poured herself another cup of coffee. She stared at her own reflection in the sliding glass doors leading to the deck: a slim woman of medium height; thick, shoulder-length straight hair parted so it drifted over her left eye from time to time. Had been a slim woman. She turned a quarter turn, the side view showing her stomach protruding almost as far as her breasts. She turned again, looked over her shoulder. Not much of a butt. She turned back to face the doors. Her olive skin and dark eyes gave her an exotic look, maybe Mediterranean.

She sipped her coffee and gazed into the darkness beyond her reflection. Sunrise not for another half hour.

She used to think night sweats were a joke. Hot flashes, too. But night sweats had her waking up in wet sheets. Hot flashes had her opening and closing windows and adding and removing layers of clothing. Anna had managed those things, but the emotional piece, the Lucite shell encasing her, was driving her crazy. She had to do something before she suffocated in her own body.

In the glass, she noticed the reflection of a small blackboard hanging next to the refrigerator. She had ignored it since the night of Mort's stroke. His small printing became clearer as she turned and walked across the kitchen. *Jam. Coffee. AA batteries.* His last memo to her.

Her vision blurred as she stared at the list. Not today, she decided and turned away. But she looked back and saw the eraser and chalk lying where Mort had likely left them. In the silence of her kitchen, she heard the thump of her heart. She raised her forearm and used it to wipe the slate. No more words.

Her fingers were steady as she picked up the chalk and wrote *furnace* and then below it, *doctor - Rx*. She hadn't wanted to consider hormone replacement. Too much risk. But at the moment, the idea of it gave her hope.

Maybe it was grief about Mort. Maybe it was menopause. Maybe both. It didn't really matter, but she needed help. Anna added another item to her list—*guest speakers*. She could get through the remainder of the quarter by arranging for speakers and movies.

In the past, her students had seen a middle-aged, well-dressed woman with a flair for public speaking and a reputation as one of the best teachers at Seattle Community College. Anna had been in the Social and Human Services Department for years, specializing in family issues at the end of life, the palliative-care field. Safe. Wise. Compassionate. Now, she imagined her students saw a distracted old lady who bumbled her way through class. Of course the dean had put her on probation.

There was a file in the den, she remembered, a folder without a name, full of thank-you cards, awards, and certificates she'd received over the years. Anna took her coffee to the den, turned on the desk lamp, opened the drawer, and removed the file.

On top lay her first honor, Children's Hospital's Volunteer of the Year Award, received after her first year as a hospice volunteer, even before she became a teacher. Along with the certificate was an article from the hospital's monthly newsletter, including a smiling picture of Anna standing with a proud Mort and the hospital president.

Next to the certificate lay a thank-you card with a picture of a serene mountain lake below a magnificent rainbow, from Marian Schiller. Her six-year-old son had died more than a dozen years before, his small face still fresh in Anna's memory. The smell of French fries had always filled his room, part of his mother's quest to help Mark eat something, anything. Before leukemia, he had loved fries, and she brought them to his room daily. Likely, he weighed less than thirty pounds when Anna met him, his head bald, his eyes huge, green, almost neon against his pale skin.

She sat on the edge of the desk chair, opened the card, and read:

Dear Anna,

I imagine you've heard by now that Mark's passed, a few days after your last visit. He came down with a sudden fever, turned out to be an infection in his lungs, which he had no strength to fight.

He told us all about the game you played with him, the I Spy With My Eye game.

You said, "I spy a superhero," and he told us he looked everywhere and couldn't find any superhero in the room. Mark laughed when he told us that you brought him a mirror and asked him what he saw. He acted it out for us that evening, saying, "She said I should look into the mirror! She said, 'There's Mark Schiller, superhero, brave and strong.'" Mark was looking forward to your next visit. He said he liked your teeth. I think he meant your smile.

I wanted you to know how grateful we are for the joy you brought to my baby's life.

Marian Schiller

Anna leaned back, closed her eyes, and imagined her children at that same age. How did a mother live through the loss of a child? The loss of a husband . . . miserable. But a child?

The twins at six. Lily with her ponytail swinging and laughter in her hazel eyes. And Larry, intense even at that age. Their rooms remained as they'd left them years ago. Now Larry was in Berkeley, married with children. He would be in Seattle over the weekend, and she'd see him briefly—not much, but something. Lily had a new job in Arizona. Far away, but still alive.

She picked up another card, then put it back and replaced the entire file in the drawer. Anna didn't want to read more about who she had been. That compassionate, alive woman was gone, lost to her. No point looking back.

Streaks of orange and pink spread slowly across the sky now. Morning. Another day. She turned on the TV and flipped through the channels. Nothing for her. She turned it off.

She'd watched *Oprah* the previous week and couldn't get it out of her mind. A happiness expert had been on the show. Anna wondered why all of Oprah's experts looked as if their day jobs were at *Vogue*. What happened to the frizzy-haired, overweight, poorly dressed psychologists she ran into?

The expert had said that even if you're dying, sick, depressed, unemployed, abandoned, widowed, fucked up—probably even on probation; surely that would qualify, too—you should make a list of twenty-five things that would make you happy, and go do them.

Simple. No problem. How stupid could you get? But this morning, it didn't seem so stupid. Maybe—maybe a list might help. Anna riffled through the old mail on the kitchen table, found an envelope with some blank space to make a list, and took a pencil from the junk drawer near the refrigerator. Okay. Twenty-five things.

Number one.

The pencil hovered over the white, blank space.

Okay, maybe she should start with number two; that wouldn't carry the weight of being the first on her list.

Maybe see her grandchildren more? But Larry made that impossible. Have her twins live in Seattle? That wouldn't happen, either. Join the Peace Corps? Get real, she thought. She'd have to go to a foreign country and would have worse indigestion. Take up pastels? Watch a lot of movies and documentaries? Volunteer again for hospice?

Teach more? But even before Mort's death, she had counted the minutes to the end of each class.

Maybe sex. But since Mort died last year, she knew she would never try it again—unless she could find an anonymous male prostitute. One marriage was enough. The sex wasn't worth it.

Anna could practically hear the voice of her son, Larry, sneering at her. "Don't tell me about how you feel. I have no interest in your first-world problems. There are people out there with real problems—they're hungry. Have no place to live. Diseases. Get over yourself."

Anna thought about telling Larry that she might lose her job. He'd say, "Sorry, Mom. But you know, someone who needs the money now has a chance." She wondered what Lily would say. She wouldn't tell either of them.

Koru barked and pawed at the back door. One of these days she'd have to have a dog door installed. Mort had never wanted one. "Too dangerous," he'd said. "Anyone could come in."

"Millions of people have dog doors. I'm the one who has to run home all the time to let him out," she had replied.

"Over my dead body."

Well, now it would be over his dead body, Anna thought as she watched Koru sniff around the fenced-in yard. She would add *dog door* to her list.

The catalogue of certificated extension courses from the University of Washington lay on the table among the catalogues from Frontgate and Chico's. She wondered if any class in the catalogue would move her applause meter. She remembered the phony visual on black-and-white TV. An applause meter. She needed some graphic representation of interest.

Anna flipped through the catalogue. Maybe a class on Shakespearean women heroes? No movement on the meter. Public speaking? She could be teaching it. Museum docent preparation—could anything be more tedious? Nada.

Nothing moved her meter until she turned to the photography and film courses and saw "Documentary Production." Then there was a slight elevation. She had always enjoyed photography. There were no prerequisites for the class, but she'd have to write an essay to apply. She hoped the meter would stay elevated long enough for her to apply. The only thing that had motivated her lately was getting through the day.

Chapter 3

Traffic along 65th stalled in the morning rush. She had the wipers on high speed but could scarcely see the streetlights in the early morning darkness. All Larry had been willing to grant her—and at the last minute—was a 7:00 a.m. breakfast.

"I can meet you at the Portage Bay Café next to University Inn on Roosevelt. I'm staying there. I've got a conference at the U."

"Why don't you stay here at home? Your room is just as you left it. You won't have to spend any money."

"The foundation is paying. Mom, don't give me a hard time. I can meet you for breakfast at seven o'clock. You want to see me? That's the only time I've got. I'll be here for only two days."

Even with the defroster on high, the windshield continued to fog. She cracked the window, but then the rain came into her car. With visibility low, Anna nearly missed the turn into the parking lot. A last-minute turn almost got Anna rear ended. As she stepped from the car, she landed in a large puddle. Clutching her

Gortex jacket tightly around her body, Anna raced into the restaurant and stood dripping in the doorway.

No Larry yet. The smell of freshly baked bread and peppered bacon filled the room. And the aroma of freshly brewed coffee. Anna selected a table in a corner where she could see the door.

She slipped off her soggy shoe and used her scarf to absorb some of the water from her wet sock. Then with her hands wrapped around the warm coffee cup, Anna leaned back and savored the rich aroma of French toast and maple syrup from the adjacent table.

Larry showed up about fifteen minutes late with another man. She couldn't hear their words from across the restaurant, but she noticed Larry's gestures inviting the man to join them. The man shook his head, but Larry grabbed his arm and pulled him toward the table.

Her son leaned down and kissed her cheek. His familiar smell settled around her heart. "Hi, Mom. Harvey Lundquist, regional coordinator for the foundation. You won't mind if he joins us." Anna noticed some white along the edge of Larry's mouth. Toothpaste. She rubbed her finger against her own mouth. Larry noticed her usual reminder and ran his tongue over the residue.

"Harvey's done amazing work, getting vaccines into Ethiopia when no one else has managed."

"Mrs. Simon. It's your son who is amazing. He's a genius at coordinating famine relief."

"Coffee?" asked the server.

Harvey nodded and turned his cup right side up. Anna raised hers for a refill. Larry shook his head. She listened as they talked about their world. Lundquist, like a Viking hero: massive, blond, blue eyed. In sharp contrast to her son, the Jewish activist: lean, intense, dark.

Larry was handsome despite his unruly hair and beard. His

long, dark eyelashes lent sensuality to his otherwise ascetic face. He ordered the winter hash, the vegan option, and green tea.

"When did you become a vegan?"

"I've been a vegan for years, Mom. What other option is there for a sane person these days?"

"Call me insane," Harvey said and ordered a chorizo sausage scramble.

"Goat cheese omelet; fruit instead of potatoes," Anna said.

"There's an extra charge of $1.50." The server looked at Anna.

"Fine."

Lundquist and Larry continued their conversation: the day's agenda, goals for their meeting, obstacles they expected to encounter. Neither addressed Anna, so she slipped on her wet shoe and excused herself. She knew the food wouldn't arrive quickly.

In the bathroom, she took off her shoe again and peeled off the wet sock. She squeezed as much water out as she could, then held the sock under the hand-drying machine. Larry would scarcely notice her absence.

He did good work in the world. Both of the twins did. She and Mort had stressed *tikkun olam*, the Jewish concept of repairing the world. Service had been a family activity: Habitat for Humanity; soup kitchens; packing boxes for refugees, famines, food banks. There was always a need somewhere.

Anna had spent years volunteering at Green Lake Elementary and Northwest Harvest before her involvement in hospice, and she had organized volunteer opportunities for the twins. As the years passed, Lily had focused on the injustices in the legal system and chose social justice law as her specialty. And Larry, always confidant that he had the answers, had become an activist. No grays for Larry. Black and white.

She remembered his little self-righteous self as a child. Larry would correct them constantly. He'd go through the recycling and re-sort it.

Where had he come from?

She folded a few paper towels and slid them into her shoe. Both kids had left home. Were busy in the world. She knew that's the way it should be. But Larry had always been difficult. She remembered a conversation—she always felt ill when she recalled it—that had occurred one night at dinner. The twins were probably fifteen or sixteen.

"Mom," he'd said. "You need to do more with your life."

"Really? For instance?"

"I've been thinking about it. Don't you think so, Dad? She just teaches about hospice. All these old people in Seattle kept alive, when there are so many real health-care crises in the rest of the world." Larry looked at his father for confirmation.

"I'm a teacher. That's what I do. There are all kinds of ways to contribute. I happen to be a teacher."

"Mom, teaching a class is important. I know that. But it's the easy part. You could be so much more useful if you focused on the people who are really suffering across the planet." Again, he glanced at Mort, who remained silent.

Anna smiled. "A bit judgmental, no?"

Lily jumped in. "Larry. You're a jerk. Just shut up. Mom's a great teacher. Her students love her."

"We don't say 'shut up' around here," Mort intervened. "Anna, any more of those potatoes?"

She could never remember what happened after that, only that she'd gone to the kitchen to get more potatoes. More than ten years later, she still had the conversation floating in her consciousness.

Larry smiled at her and kept talking to Lundquist when Anna returned. The food arrived, and their conversation turned to the previous week's presidential elections. The men competed with each other about who had the most up-to-date information, the best insider anecdotes about the hanging chads, and the ins and outs of the Florida recount.

"Katherine Harris, the Florida secretary of state, says she won't extend the recount deadlines," Anna added. Both men looked at her and smiled. Anna returned her attention to her omelet.

Lundquist checked his watch. "I'm out of here. Nice to meet you, Mrs. Simon. Larry, I'll see you soon."

Larry glanced at his own watch. Actually, it had been Mort's. Anna recognized the leather band. "Mom, I'm glad we had a chance to get together. I'm just really busy. Thanks for meeting me here."

"No problem. Great for me to get up so early in the morning, in the dark, and drive over here in the blinding rain to have you ignore me."

"Mom. Don't start with me. There's just too much going on in my life. Be happy I called you at all. I'm really busy. You just don't get it."

"Okay. You're right. I do appreciate that you called."

Larry reached over to her plate and took a piece of toast. He added some marmalade and ate it.

"More hot water for your tea? Coffee?" the server asked.

"Just the check," Larry said.

A large group of students had pushed several tables together near where they sat; they looked incredibly young to Anna. She wished there was something in the restaurant—carpet or curtains—to muffle the sound of tables sliding against the wooden floor, plates slamming down on the table, and everyone talking at once. The noise grated against her ears.

Anna took a deep breath, leaned in, and asked Larry, "Will you come back to Seattle for your birthday? Lily's coming."

Larry shook his head, "I can't."

"What about you and Naeema bringing the kids up during spring break?"

"I'm sorry. No way. It's impossible. I'm scheduled to get back to Ethiopia. It's a constant struggle to get food to the refugees."

Anna stacked the dirty dishes along the edge of the table. "Is that for sure? Can't you pull away for a few days?"

"Mom, I just got back from Ethiopia. Nearly eight million people are starving. The war with Eritrea, the drought. You can't imagine the extent of human suffering. I'm coordinating relief from the West Coast."

"Maybe Naeema and the kids could come to Seattle. Or I could fly down to Berkeley.

"They'll be in New York. She's worried about her mother." Larry looked at his watch again. "Mom, I've got to get going."

"What's wrong with her mother?"

"She's suffered so much in her life. The kids are everything to her."

"Of course," Anna said. "I understand." She wondered what she could do to earn the right to see her grandchildren. Maybe if a massive tsunami flooded Seattle. Why did she want to see them so much, anyway? She wasn't the kind of woman who carried around an album of baby pictures. She hadn't done that with her own children. Her old friend, Elise, and Elise's husband had moved to North Carolina just to live near the grandchildren. But Elise had never had a life separate from her children. Anna had. She wondered if she were desperate for grandchildren because now she had no life.

"Maybe I could fly to New York instead. I could stay in a hotel, of course, and spend a little time with the kids and help Naeema's mother if she needed it." She hated the pleading in her own voice, not that he noticed.

Larry pulled on his jacket. "I'll talk to Naeema about it. You know, on second thought, it just might confuse the kids." He squatted down next to her chair. "Mom, we want them to experience their African culture as well as the American one. We want to make sure they don't turn into spoiled American children."

Anna patted her son's cheek. "Did you turn out so badly?"

"Let's not have this conversation again." He stood. "We'll find a way for you to see the kids. I'll call you. I promise." He leaned down and kissed her forehead. Again, his scent, the slight whiff of her son, unchanged through all these years, triggered a yearning in her, a hunger to have him close again.

"When will you call?"

"As soon as I can." He walked toward the door, paused, and then returned to the table and sat down. "Mom, I'm kind of worried. You must be lonely."

Anna shook her head, but Larry continued, "Dad's been gone for a year. What about an online dating service? I heard there's a Jewish one."

"I'm thinking about taking a class, Larry, at the university. On making documentaries."

"That's great, Mom," Larry said. "A class would probably be good for you." He glanced at his watch. "But you should think about volunteer work. Probably more fulfilling for you." He paused and looked to Anna for a response, and when none came, he continued. "You've got the all that insurance money and all of Dad's investments. You don't need to work. Even with your teaching, you've got plenty of time. I'm not going to tell you what to do, but you should think about volunteering."

"Okay," Anna nodded. She had noticed some food stuck between his teeth on the left side of his mouth. She felt around her own mouth looking for crumbs that might be stuck.

Larry stood and kissed her forehead again and said, "You're attractive for your age. There are probably a lot of good men on

JDate. You might meet somebody and not feel so lonely. Will you think about it?"

Anna felt tears gathering around her eyes. She opened them wide and smiled. "I will."

"I love you, Mom. Everything will be okay. I'll call you." Larry waved as he walked toward the door and left her sitting in the restaurant. Alone with the breakfast bill.

Chapter 4

"So call me when you get this message." Anna came into the kitchen at the tail end of the voice message. Marilyn, her old friend. They hadn't talked for a long time.

She and Koru had gotten drenched during their walk around Green Lake. A Seattle mist had transformed into a downpour. Koru reeked of wet dog. She held his collar and rubbed a towel across his back before he had a chance to shake water all over the kitchen. Anna removed her foggy glasses, placed them on the counter, and pressed play to hear the whole message.

"Anna. It's me. Marilyn. I'm sure you still remember my voice. You do, don't you?"

Anna stepped out of her wet shoes, peeled off her damp socks, and walked into the powder room next to the kitchen for a clean towel. She could hear Marilyn's assertive voice in the background.

"Really, I'm not trying to make you feel guilty, but we haven't talked for a long time. You don't return my calls, and I miss you. We'd like to pick you up for Joe and Eva's anniversary party tonight. We assume you're going.

Anna towel dried her hair on the way back to the kitchen.

"Can you believe they made it to twenty-five? All that bickering, and here they are. Amazing. Anyway, you won't have to go alone. Everybody wants to see you. So call me when you get this message. We're not leaving until seven o'clock."

Anna pressed erase and listened for the quiet little whoosh that vaporized the message. It wasn't substantial to start with. Not even vapor kind of substantial. A voice flying through space and bringing with it uninvited thoughts, unwanted images—like a slide projector out of control. Marilyn with a champagne glass raised in toast to her and Mort at their twenty-fifth anniversary party. Jack as he stood with his arm around Mort. The smile on Mort's face as he spun her around the dance floor. Tables full of their friends. And then Joe with a shovel full of dirt to fling on Mort's grave. Had she seen him since? She must have.

Anna took off her damp jeans and hung them across the towel bar. No. She was not planning to go.

Koru lay stretched across his bed on the kitchen floor, already asleep.

She needed a hot bath and headed upstairs. The phone was ringing when she got to her bedroom, and Anna realized she'd left her bifocals downstairs. She couldn't read the caller ID. Must be Lily, she thought as she grabbed the phone.

"Anna. I'm glad I caught you."

Damn. Marilyn again.

"We're leaving early. We've got to stop to pick up the cake. Six thirty okay for you?"

"Canlis Restaurant doesn't have cakes?"

"Eva ordered something special that Joe likes—from some bakery on Queen Anne. She asked us to get it. What are you going to wear?"

"Marilyn, I'm standing here dripping. Got caught in a downpour across the lake. I'll call you back in a little while."

"No you don't, Anna. Yes or no. It's simple."

"Then no. I wasn't going to go."

"Anna, you've got to come. This is the perfect opportunity to see everyone. We all miss you. Just because Mort's dead doesn't mean you should stop living.

"Marilyn, back off."

"Eva and Joe will be hurt. Do you want to hurt them? The four of you used to go out all the time. Me? I'm less sensitive, but you could hurt them. Why make them feel sad on their anniversary?"

"You're disgusting. Manipulative. A bully."

"True. All true. But that doesn't change the facts, Anna. We'll take you home early if you're not having a good time. We'll come by at six thirty."

"Okay. Okay. I will come. But don't pick me up. I'll drive myself. So leave me alone. I'll see you there."

"Promise?"

"Sure, I promise." Damn. She could break her promise. Wouldn't be the first time since Mort died.

By the time Anna reached Canlis, the lot was full. She had to leave her car with the valet service, which would slow her down if she needed a quick escape. She rushed into the restaurant, her legs freezing in hose and high heels. Late because she had to have a manicure before she came. No time for a haircut. She used Lily's old curling iron to tease some shape into her thick hair and burned her thumb.

She had applied too much makeup. Eyeliner, foundation, blush, shadow—it all felt like a mask. Out of practice. She had tried on least a dozen dresses—some too sexy, some more appropriate for teaching, and some just too tight. Nothing felt right. Eventually she chose a long-sleeved wool one, drab and boring. She used to wear it with scarves or something. She couldn't remember. Now her arms itched.

She made her way through a crowd in the foyer toward the Penthouse steps. Drawn by the sound of the lounge piano, she paused to listen, to calm herself. But the maître d' hurried her past tables with men in suits, bejeweled women, clinking silverware, forks in mouths, knives scratching across plates. Past the savory aroma of steaks mingled with heady scent of rich wines. The room spun. Too hot in her winter coat. Anna reached the staircase and held on. "Thank you. I'll make it from here."

Anna leaned against the banister and stared out through the floor-to-ceiling windows. The rain had moved through the city, taking away the clouds and leaving a clear, brilliant night sky. She gazed at the lights flickering across the city. From upstairs she heard more laughter, muffled conversations, and what sounded like a jazz trio.

Anna took off her coat, placed it over her arm, and climbed up to the Penthouse. Joe and Eva stood at the top of the staircase. Apparently not that late. They were still welcoming guests.

"Anna. Anna. So happy you could come," Joe murmured as he wrapped his large frame around her and pulled her close. He swayed back and forth as he held her.

"Joe, let her go, she's suffocating," Anna heard Eva say. "Move away, it's my turn."

"After twenty-five years, she still has no patience," he whispered to Anna, loud enough for his wife to hear. Then he pulled back and took a long look at Anna. "You look great, Anna." She noticed that his eyes had begun to water. "It means a lot to us that you're here. We all miss you," he said, and he hugged her again.

Eva pulled on his arms and pried them away from Anna. Then she put her hands on Anna's face and kissed both cheeks. "Where have you been?" She didn't wait for a reply, but yelled out to the room, "Look who's here."

Anna glanced up and saw faces staring at her, their lips moving. Colors. Noise. "Hey, Anna. Good to see you. How are you? Where have you been?" A blur of teeth, eyes, and waving arms. No one person distinct.

Someone took her coat, handed it to a waiter, and pulled her deeper into the room. Marilyn. It was Marilyn. "A little late, but you made it," she muttered. Anna closed her eyes and tried to take a deep breath, but her heart raced. Her face felt clammy. Could there be sweat on her forehead?

Someone handed her a glass of champagne. Her hand shook as she held it and took a long gulp.

"We saved a place for you at our table. They're just starting to serve," Marilyn said as she pulled Anna along through the crowd. And there sat Jack. Mort's former law partner. Beside him she saw his sister Irene and her husband and two other couples. Jack stood, walked slowly toward Anna, and held out his arms. She held her eyes open wide and tightened her jaw. She let him hold her for a moment and then stepped back.

"You look great, Jack," she said. "Have you lost weight?"

He blushed. "You noticed?" He looked at Marilyn, "See, people can tell." He took Anna's hand in his own. "I sure did. After Mort died so fast. Not that he was ever fat really, but..." Jack snapped his fingers, "Just like that. Gone. Scared the shit out of me, if you'll excuse the expression."

Anna felt the blood leave her face.

"Sorry, Anna. I'm sorry. I didn't mean to upset you."

"You're an idiot, Jack," Marilyn said as she pulled out a chair for Anna.

"You're right. I'm an idiot. I'm sorry"

"Relax, Jack. I'm fine. Just a little warm in here." Anna finished her glass of champagne, which was immediately refilled by an attentive waiter nearby.

It seemed to Anna as if she hovered above the table where she sat, the only single person with four couples. Their crowd. Jack and Marilyn. Irene and Jerry. Diane and Phil and Mort's college buddy Sandy and his wife, Sue. She observed herself talk and laugh. She saw herself eat, but didn't taste the food. She answered questions about the twins. About her grandchildren. Her teaching. Like a hologram person.

There were speeches and toasts. The jazz trio left, and a DJ arrived. Eva and Joe opened up the dancing with "We've Only Just Begun." Jack extended his arm to her and leaned his head toward the dance floor. Very kind of him, she thought, but smiled and shook her head. Then he and Marilyn went off together. The other couples stayed at the table, most likely to make sure she didn't feel uncomfortable.

She heard Karen Carpenter sing, "*When the evening comes, we smile, so much of life ahead of us…*" Anna excused herself and went to the ladies' room.

She hid in one of two stalls in the restroom and studied the tile design: a mix of stone and glass in shades of charcoal and gray. She heard several women talking and realized a line had formed. She couldn't stay there for the rest of the evening. As she left the ladies' room, she bumped into a man who was vaguely familiar. Maybe Joe's brother or brother-in-law. She knew she knew him. He lived in New Jersey or somewhere back East.

"Anna, I was sorry to hear about Mort. We talked about sending you a card or something, but we were right in the middle of it then, so…"

"In the middle of it?"

"Yeah, in the middle of the divorce. Got a divorce last year." He had basset hound eyes, sad and droopy. "After thirty-two years of marriage. You know how it is."

No clue, Anna thought. Death she knew about, not divorce.

"Excuse me," a woman said, pointing through them to the restroom door.

"Sorry." The man touched Anna's elbow and directed her away from the bathrooms, toward the bar. What was his name?

"How about a drink?"

Anna looked out at the couples dancing across the room and said, "That sounds good. Perrier for me." They found two empty bar stools and sat.

"A Perrier for the lady and Macallan neat for me."

Sounded to her like he'd already had a few. Anna had no idea what his name was. She could ask, but did it really matter?

"My wife wanted a divorce. Her idea. Not mine."

"I'm sorry." Anna wondered where she could find her coat.

"I'm not. Oh, at first, man, it was hell, but now—sorry I didn't think of it myself. It's been great. I've met some fine ladies online." He smacked his lips as if he had just finished an ice cream cone. "Have you been dating? You know, since your husband died?"

Anna shook her head. His lips were dry, maybe from the airplane trip. She noticed a nick on his chin, likely from shaving.

"You're an attractive woman. You should get out there. Life is short."

"Life is short," she agreed and sipped her Perrier.

"Truth is, I was nervous, getting back on the horse…" His tongue licked at the tiny drops of moisture gathered at the corners of his mouth.

Anna couldn't imagine what that would be like, nor did she want to hear about it from him. "I've got to be going now," she said quickly. She took another sip of her water and started to slide off of the bar stool. "Good luck."

"What's your hurry? Sit. Maybe we could have dinner while I'm in town."

Anna sat, but was poised to escape. "Thank you, but I'm really booked this week."

"Well, at least stay a few minutes and talk. Everyone else is in a couple. What's your hurry?"

What was her hurry? "*What you want, baby I got*," she heard Aretha singing. The women were dancing together, not in couples. Eva, Marilyn, Sue, and several others had removed their shoes and taken over the dance floor. The husbands sat back at the tables. She thought about taking off her own shoes and joining her old friends as they danced. But the music, instead of moving her, irritated her. Too noisy.

Could she just sneak out? She needed to say good-bye to Joe and Eva first. Didn't she?

"Okay. Just a little longer," she said and sat back on the stool.

"How come you don't want to meet someone else?"

"Maybe sometime. Not yet. Not ready."

"I didn't know if I was ready, after so many years with one lady. You know what I mean? But those blue pills, man ..." He smirked.

"Blue pills?" she asked and shook her head.

"Don't shit me. You must know about the little blue pills."

Anna shrugged her shoulders. "I'm sorry. Don't know."

"Oh, man. That was stupid of me. Maybe Mort died too soon, before it got popular." He paused, swirled the scotch around a few times. "I'm digging myself a hole here." He went on. "Viagra."

She hadn't known Viagra came in blue pills. Maybe if Mort had lived. Anna sat back against the bar and looked out at the room. She couldn't believe this man's wife had stayed with him as long as she had. He just kept talking. She nodded from time to time and sipped her water. It made no difference if she commented or not. Like a radio left on. A few people were leaving. She saw them stop at a room near the steps to get their coats.

He was right about one thing. Everyone else was in a couple, whether they danced together all night or not. Couples they had known for years. Their friends. Were any of them her friends? Marilyn? Irene? Eva? Maybe. Had they ever talked about anything except their husbands, their kids, their married lives? They must have.

Eva and Joe were dancing, and by this time of night, they were grinding away like in high school. Marilyn and Jack were doing something that looked like a fox-trot. They had taken Arthur Murray lessons.

Anna finished the Perrier, put the glass on the bar, and stood. "Nice talking with you."

"Great talking with you. Listen," he said as he stood and put his hand on her shoulder, "I come in and out of Seattle for business every few months. Let's have dinner together."

It felt comforting to feel a warm hand on her shoulder, even if it was his. But she smelled alcohol on his breath. His tie was askew and jacket rumpled. Lots of hair still grew on his head, but it was colored and she could see the roots. No need to even mention his personality.

He gulped the rest of his drink and pulled out his business card. "Call me when you're ready," he said as he handed it to her.

Not in this lifetime, Anna thought as she took his card, waved, and walked away to find her coat.

Chapter 5

"Chanukah paper? Yes. We have that." The young clerk pointed to samples along the back wall. "Two kinds. The one on the left with the candles, or the one below it with toys. Then there's the plain royal-blue foil. Some people like that."

"The one with the toys. Dreidels. Probably my grandchildren would like that. Except kids always just rip it off. I wonder, why do we bother?" Anna handed her credit card to the clerk and removed her heavy winter coat.

The Bon Marché had the best wrapping department at the Northgate Mall. She knew Larry wouldn't care what kind of wrapping came with the presents or even if they were wrapped. For that matter, she wondered if he even cared that she sent the kids gifts.

She knew he didn't celebrate Chanukah. Maybe not even Christmas. Maybe they celebrated Kwanza. But she wanted her grandchildren to at least have a sliver of a memory of a Jewish holiday.

"I'll need at least thirty minutes. Come back then. There are two gifts to wrap before yours. Or do you want us to mail these packages?"

"No. Thank you. I've got some other things to add. Thirty minutes?"

"Give or take."

Anna stopped at Nordstrom's café for a peppermint mocha. Between the endless people with heavy coats, large shopping bags, and strollers, she could barely make her way through the holiday crowds. Should have shopped for the kids last month or before Halloween, she thought.

Rich smells came from the kiosks lining the center of the mall: shea butter cosmetics; lavender potpourri; candles of pine, apple spice, and cinnamon. She heard music coming from somewhere in the mass of people, something upbeat, jazzy, and warm. She didn't recognize the song muffled by the noise of holiday shoppers.

Anna wove her way through the clusters of people toward the music at the center of the mall. Seated on a platform, she saw five women about her own age, replete with gray hair and wrinkles.

They wore white shirts and dark slacks with scarlet cummerbunds. It was a jazz ensemble with a singer. As she approached, the grandmotherly singer belted out what once had been one of her favorites, "It's the Most Wonderful Time of the Year." Now the words irritated her. "*Everyone telling you be of good cheer.*" Wish it were that easy, Anna thought. Okay. Thanks for the tip. I'm all full of good cheer now. No problem.

But the musicians were certainly of good cheer. At least they looked it. One played bass, another keyboard, the third a sax, and then there was the drummer, who had a fabulous smile, actually a stunning face for a woman her age. She was vibrant. Alive. Somehow, her whole body seemed to be in motion as she sat behind her drums. Intrigued, Anna stood fascinated as the drummer rapped out the rhythms and sang along with the lead singer.

"*Ding. Dong.*" The crowd joined in the refrain. Was this a performance, or were the musicians truly engaged, happy? Enjoying what they did?

Someone poked her back, and she turned to see her next-door neighbor, Becky Clayton, wearing a hand-knit red-and-green-stripped scarf and matching hat. In her mid-eighties, she looked terrific. Decked out for the holidays.

"Aren't they something special? Heard them last week at my sister's nursing home."

"They are great. How is Dotty?"

"Hangin' in there. Hates the nursing home." Becky stopped talking suddenly, looked away from Anna, and observed people going in and out of the shops: families with children, seniors, teenagers. "But I can't take care of her," Becky added, her lips pursed.

Anna put her arm around Becky's frail shoulders and guided led her toward a quiet corner. "I know you tried. She lived with you for more than a year, didn't she?"

"Yeah. But you know, I couldn't lift her no more. I just couldn't.

Things I just couldn't do." Becky blinked several times and wiped her eyes with the tips of her fingers, her manicured nails a deep red. "It makes me mad to see her in there."

Becky shook her head as if clearing it. She resembled a tiny, sweet puppy after a bath, shaking off all the water. "But you know, Anna, you've got to go on. Life is for the living, Henry used to say. You remember Henry, don't you?"

"Sure I do."

"He's been gone now twelve years. Hard to believe. He used to say if you run into a dead end, go find another path. I can't help Dotty, but I'm still kicking." Becky sniffed and looked at the coffee cup in Anna's hands. "What's that smell, Anna? Where's that peppermint coming from?"

"It's my mocha. It's delicious. They only make them at Christmas. Come on, I'll get you one."

By the time Anna left the mall, the sun, such as it was, had set and the temperature had dropped almost to freezing. Her Subaru's heated seats made the ride home more comfortable, but not much. She couldn't believe Becky's husband had been dead for twelve years. Becky had certainly found a new path since then, including adding a solarium to her house and dating men she met at the senior center dances. Sharp guys in their eighties. One even drove a Corvette convertible, an old one from the '70s.

Mort would never return. That life was over. Very over. Her children were raised. They didn't need her. And the college really didn't need her; no one needed a teacher who no longer wanted to teach. Nor would menopause last forever, would it? Probably not. Maybe if she applied to the documentary class, she, too, might meet some guy driving a Corvette convertible. Anna thought now, as she thought whenever she saw Becky going out on a date, how amazing it was that Becky could get in and out of the thing so easily.

I'm eager to do something different, only I'm not sure what that is. My goal is to explore and discover new areas that capture my interest, attention, and engage my imagination.

Anna crumpled up the page and threw it on top of the others on the floor. Koru rose from his bed and sniffed at the pile of her discarded attempts to apply for the documentary class. Everything she wrote sounded stupid. They'd never accept her. She had no real experience.

Get over it, she thought, you're not applying to Harvard. They'd probably take anyone who applies as long as they pay tuition. She reached down, opened the last crumpled paper, and studied the sentences carefully. *Eager to do something different.* Yes. Eager? Theoretically eager. In real life, too tired to be eager. Indeed, no idea what she wanted to do, but she knew she had to do something different. The next sentence was true as well. Explore. Yes. Try to figure it out.

She wished she were religious so she could pray about it. Maybe she could pray about it, anyway. She put down her pen, folded her hands on the table, and closed her eyes.

"God, save me from self-pity. I have so much in this life. I know I have to move forward. How do I find a path?"

She could feel the tears building behind her closed eyelids. She cradled her head in her arms on the table. Anna remembered reading something by Isaac Bashevis Singer that reinforced what her mother had taught her. She couldn't remember the name of the book, but it was the same phrase: *act as if.* Imagine someone inside of yourself, someone who could help lift you out of despair. She needed to take action.

Anna filled the teapot, and while waiting for the water to boil, she dialed her doctor's office. "Yes, I need to schedule an appointment with Dr. Shaperman. As soon as possible. About general health. Well, actually, about menopause. Friday morning is perfect. Thank you."

She took the crumpled rough draft with her back to the den, booted up her computer, and completed the application.

What if they didn't accept her? What if she didn't like the class? What if she dropped dead tomorrow? Anna answered the remaining questions on the form, printed the application, added a check to the envelope, then addressed and stamped it. She'd worry about "what if" later. Just get it in the mail, she thought.

While she was at it, she typed a formal letter of resignation to Dean Saunders at Seattle Community College, promising to help them with the transition to a new teacher if they needed it. Anna knew sometimes one door closes before another opens. She put on her heaviest coat, a ski hat, mittens, wool socks, and hiking boots and took herself and Koru to the mailbox on 65th.

The walk was a short one. As she reached for the handle on the mailbox, she noticed she had missed the last pickup of the day. She could still think about it and come back in the morning. But Anna held her breath, opened the slot, and dropped both letters in. She listened for the tiny fluttering sound as the letters joined the other mail on the bottom of the box, then gently tugged on Koru's leash and headed home.

Back in the warmth of her house, Anna fed Koru, ate a TV dinner herself, and imagined her letters nestled all night in the cold mailbox. One letter closing a door on the past and the other opening one to the future.

She rubbed the tightness at the back of her neck but stopped when she felt tears building. Anna shook her head, went up to her bedroom, and studied her stash of hidden candy. She chose a See's chocolate lollipop and looked around the room for a spot that felt right to her. She needed to think.

Leaning against the headboard on her bed felt okay for a

moment, but soon she moved to a deep corner in her closet where she sat with her knees pulled to her chest. Koru followed her, circled, and settled at her feet.

Anna licked her sucker and studied her clothes. Dozens of elegant dresses, cocktail dresses, silk suits, gowns—all with matching shoes, none of which she'd worn since Mort had died. She wondered about her own life expectancy. How many years did she have left? She was in her mid-fifties. Was this it?

Each lick of the sucker filled her mouth with a rich chocolaty flavor. Foolish, but she wanted her life to taste as good as the sucker.

Chapter 6

The windshield of her Subaru steamed up, despite the defroster. Too hot inside; too cold outside. The rain came in torrents and pelted the car. As fast as the wipers beat, Anna could barely see through to the street. Red and green lights were merely suggestions as she squinted to find her way.

She knew the University of Washington campus; she had often attended meetings there. She had even memorized the parking map for Thompson Hall. Nothing appeared as she expected. After a few misdirected attempts, she found the right parking lot and building. Her wet shoes made a squishing sound that echoed along the empty halls. Did she have the wrong night?

When Anna finally found the room, there was a note on the door: the class had changed to room 302. She climbed the stairs, leaving a trail of water as she walked, scrunch, scrunch as her shoes hit the floor. Too much bother for nothing.

At the top of the stairs, she saw the room number and a class full of people. She stopped in the hall, out of breath. Through the open door, Anna watched as a man passed out some papers. Quietly, she walked in, took a seat near the back, slipped off the hood of her raincoat, unzipped it, and slid out of her wet shoes. Using her shirt, she cleared the moisture from her bifocals.

Anna's damp hair hung in limp strands around her face. Thankfully, no makeup was running; she'd worn only lipstick. But there was not another gray head of hair in the room. Except for one other woman across the room, they all looked like high school students.

She could still walk out. No one recognized her. None of her kids' friends. All strangers. She could be anyone. They wouldn't even notice if she left.

Sit still. Stay here, she insisted. Give it a try. If no one patronized her, was rude, sarcastic, dismissive, then she would stay. She didn't need to feel worse than she already did.

Anna took off her raincoat and draped it on the back of her chair. The teacher smiled and made eye contact when he handed her a stack of papers. Thirtyish, maybe forty, casual, in cords and a flannel shirt. Long hair.

Sam was his name, and he worked at a network affiliate in town—documentary producer. Her breathing slowed and her body adjusted to the rigid chair. Anna leaned forward and tried to focus.

"You'll be working on a ten-minute documentary. Everything you learn will focus on the skills you need to complete that. You're going to work with one other person in this class for the next two semesters to complete the project. Look around the room."

Anna's stomach tightened as she looked around for likely candidates. Who would want her? A major complication. She wouldn't come back next week. No way.

She heard one of the other students speak and realized they had started going around the room, with students explaining why they had signed up for the class, their expectations. She knew the routine from the other side. She knew how a teacher could look like she was listening, but would not be paying any attention. She hadn't been paying attention for a long time.

The desire to bolt increased as students continued around the room, talking about what brought them to the class.

"Want a career in video production."

"I've been freelancing in video work and need grounding in specifics."

"Majored in communications. It's a missing piece."

"Adjunct to community organizing."

Blah, blah, blah. She wondered how they'd react if she said, "Escape from menopause. Yams aren't working, so maybe this class..." Anna supposed any class would have worked as well. But somewhere, lurking, was a spark of real interest. She wanted this—there, she actually got to a number on Oprah's list.

Above the loud thumping of her own heart, she began, "Anna Simon. I was an instructor at Seattle Community College for many years. I taught about hospice care. I want to take this class—the description in the extension catalogue got my attention—maybe explore a more creative side of myself. I'm very interested in film, video. The class sounded right for me."

Her hands trembled, so she folded them tightly on her lap. Anna could scarcely remember what she'd said. A very young woman with short red hair and a face splashed with freckles sat next to her. Anna strained to hear her soft voice, almost a whisper. Maybe Anna was not the only anxious person in the class.

"Please get into groups of four. Talk about ideas you might have for documentaries in this class."

Damn. The first night. She knew small-group conversations

built community quickly, connected people. But she couldn't move. Anna's eyes slid toward the door. She could still leave.

She rubbed her clammy hands against her slacks as chairs scraped across the floor around her. The smell of aftershave drifted toward her from the left. She glanced up and found a few people had moved their desks into a circle and had included her.

She stared down at her lap, hoping no one saw how grateful she must have looked.

One was a Darth Vader–type guy. Black shirt, black jeans, deep black five o'clock shadow and probably on the older side—maybe thirty-five. Two very young ones, a boy and a girl—both with long ponytails and wrinkle-free skin. One wore a tie-dye shirt and the other a T-shirt that read Blink-182. No idea what or who that was. Anna wondered what they saw as they looked at her. Mom? Grandma? Were they mad they got stuck with the old lady?

The young boy who wore too much aftershave began. His words rushed together.

"I have a contact at the Hanford nuclear site. I could get us in. It's time someone really told the story of the nuclear waste buildup. The impact on the water table—"

"That's good," the young girl interrupted, "but what about what's been happening with the Makah tribe hunting whales? We could get up there and see if we could interview tribal people about their whale hunting tradition. Maybe we could even tape a hunt."

Darth, a.k.a. Ken, had no expression on his face, looked bored until Anna mobilized an inner actress who rattled off a long list of possible documentary topics, lighter ones, nothing intense: Seattle dog parks, swap meet regulars, Internet addicts, latte addicts.

Ken approached as she was putting on her raincoat. "You seem to have a lot of ideas; what do you say we work together?"

She looked up at his tall, strong body and knew he'd be great schlepping around the equipment, if nothing else. She must have something he wanted, although she had no clue what that might be. But she did feel less alone. Someone wanted to work with her. Maybe she would complete the class.

If they were going to work together, she'd have to start thinking of him as Ken. As in Barbie and ... but he was not that kind of a Ken. A darker kind of Ken, maybe a twenty-first-century one. Ken after Barbie dumps him. He wanted to do a doc about a friend of his, a trumpet player with HIV who played in a gay marching band. Apparently the trumpet player felt the band was as healing to him as any of the antiretroviral drugs.

They left the building together, and as Ken talked, Anna found herself actually considering the topic. A gay topic. Did he think she was a lesbian? Was he gay? She wondered if maybe she should offer another idea, maybe something less controversial. But these days, was a gay band really that controversial?

It sure used to be. She remembered one brief experience in college. She had been drunk or stoned or something after her mother died. Audrey. The woman's name had been Audrey.

He wasn't asking her to become a lesbian, only to do a doc about a group of people who played music together, who happened to be gay.

Ken continued talking as they stood in the chilly night air. She nodded and smiled while her mind wandered back to Audrey. A column of words stayed stuck in her throat. Nothing she wanted to share with this guy. Probably not with herself, either. The muscles around her mouth felt tense, and she realized she'd been holding the same smile for a long time.

"We could tape them when they practice marching at the Fort Worden retreat center in April," Ken said. "We could use their music for the video sound track. Excellent," he added and pumped his fist.

As Ken talked, Anna's mind drifted back to the late '60s. She'd shared a room with Audrey at a conference sponsored by the Hillel House after Martin Luther King's assassination.

Audrey had come from the newly established radical alternative Evergreen College in Olympia. She had expected someone with beads and a long skirt, but Audrey wore tailored slacks; oxford cloth shirts with button-down collars; and a fine, camel-hair blazer that fell across her broad shoulders like silk caressing her body.

Anna remembered the heat on own her cheek when Audrey first touched her. Not now, she thought. Say something. Anything. Pick another documentary topic. But she didn't.

Anna heard herself say, "Sounds great. Will you make the contact?"

"Sure will. See you next week."

Anna dodged large puddles of water glistening under the street lamps of the well-lit parking lot. Her cheeks burned from the cold that followed the rain. Would she ever have taken this class if Mort had lived? If her teaching career hadn't careened over a cliff?

Chapter 7

Camera skills, then sound, then lighting. Sam mapped out the first semester. Before anyone could take out equipment, they had to demonstrate they knew how to use it. And before that, they needed his okay on their script, or treatment, as Sam called it.

The lectures focused on treatment basics. "You need a beginning, middle, and an end. Think where you want to start. Where are you going? The same progression has to happen in individual shots."

During the second week of class, they had an extended Saturday session. No special lighting required outside. They met on the quad near Thompson Hall. No rain, but the temperature hovered at around forty-five degrees. Anna wore a thick fleece jacket while Ken seemed comfortable in a black synthetic windbreaker.

Sam had talked about how to start and how to exit a shot. "Don't start in the middle. Even when you shoot someone sitting in a chair, introduce it somehow. Go wide. Be creative. If someone is going to come in a door, shoot his hand on the knob. And never stop in the middle of a shot. Make sure you exit the shot."

Anna listened with the other students. Then the teams practiced. She and Ken shared a camera, took turns filming other students acting in their scenes. Then they became the subjects while others practiced. She kept blowing on her fingers to keep them warm when she ran the camera. Otherwise, she kept them in her pockets.

Make sure you exit the shot, Anna thought. She'd been in Mort's shot for so many years. She had had her own life, but it was all tied into Mort's. Their friends. Their home. Their children. Their vacations. She had had her job at Seattle Community College, but it was really peripheral to Mort's life. Her schedule was always the one rearranged. Never his. Should she have been burned on a pyre when her husband died? Had there ever been a shot that was hers?

"Let's pack it up and meet again on Tuesday in the classroom," Sam said as he slid a mic into its case. Ken had their equipment in hand before Anna gathered her thoughts.

"Some of us are going over to the Ave in a little while for a beer. Want to join us?"

"Thanks. Sounds good." She looked at her watch. "Oops, I can't. I won't have time. Picking my daughter up at the airport tonight." She wondered if she would have gone with them if Lily wasn't coming in for her birthday. They were all so much younger. Koru, happy with his new dog door, didn't need her. But Lily would be waiting for a ride.

As soon as she came out of the Alaska Airlines' door, Anna noticed Lily, elegant even as she clutched a fleece hoodie to her lean body against the cold November winds. She reminded Anna of a young Audrey Hepburn, one with auburn hair and hazel eyes, but that same lithe carriage and confidence.

When Lily joined her in the car, Anna handed her a box of pizza, still hot to the touch. "Your first birthday present, Cookie. Pagliacci's pizza with pepperoni, olive, mushroom, and garlic."

"I love you, Mom. Perfect," she said and opened the box.

"Some napkins in the back seat."

"How did you know I'd be starving?"

"What's new?"

Anna noticed that she'd lost weight. New job, new city. Mom far away. Lily had never been domestic. Anna knew she vacillated between granola bars and junk food.

"Too bad Larry decided not to come," Lily mused as she caught a sliver of dripping cheese with her finger and sucked it in. "This is the first year we've been separated on our birthdays."

"He came last year because Dad's death had been so recent."

"More pizza for me this year."

Lily gobbled down a few slices in the car before they got home. "Pagliacci's is the best." She talked most of the way from the airport about her new apartment and the cases she was handling.

Neither of the kids knew Anna was no longer an instructor at Seattle Community College. Maybe she could get through the weekend without Lily knowing anything, she thought as they pulled into the garage

"I found our old copy of *To Kill a Mockingbird*. You still want to see it tonight?" Anna asked while Lily wrestled with Koru on the floor.

"Absolutely. And let's go to Scarlet Tree for breakfast tomorrow."

"I'll make the popcorn while you get settled. Take what's left of that pizza upstairs.

Anna popped the corn, poured in butter, and tossed Koru a few pieces. She cradled the bowl in her arms as she breathed in the familiar smell and climbed the stairs.

Lily had stacked the pillows against the headboard. "Do you think Daddy was like Atticus?" She had tomato sauce on her chin. Anna pointed and Lily licked it off.

"Integrity?"

Lily nodded.

"Absolutely."

"He sure was. But that wasn't good enough for Larry. He once said, I think when we were in high school, that Daddy wasn't like Atticus at all. Atticus stood in front of jails, fighting for the oppressed; Atticus didn't mess around with corporate clients like Dad did."

Anna arranged the pillows behind her back and said, "He forgets that corporate clients paid his way through Berkeley."

Lily pressed play on the remote, and Koru jumped on the bed, circled, and settled with his face close to the pizza box. He sniffed. "If there's any left, Koru," Anna said and closed the box.

Anna noticed Lily's absorption in the film. Her daughter laughed, wiped tears away with her sleeve, yelled at the screen, and covered her face with a pillow. Anna marveled at Lily. She knew her to be a young woman who unabashedly cried at Hallmark commercials and who could also transform herself into an aggressive litigator: tough, powerful, even-keeled.

Lily swore at the bigotry and cried when Atticus visited Tom's family. Then came the last scene, the one where Gregory Peck, as Atticus, the personification of safety and strength, enfolds his daughter in his arms. Whoever shot that last scene was a genius. Anna had a new appreciation after working a camera herself. You could feel the emotion. Totally tangible. And apparently Lily felt it.

Anna was brought back to total awareness by the stillness in the room. Lily sat upright, now clutching her arms against her chest.

"Cookie?"

Lily shook her head. Her eyes were closed tightly.

"It's okay, Cookie," Anna said, gently stroking Lily's back.

Lily pulled her arms tighter around her body. She chewed on her lower lip, and Anna knew soon her daughter would be crying. Lily's arms gradually loosened. Her shoulders sagged, and her body rocked back and forth. "Why did Daddy have to die?" She turned to her mother, tears sliding down her cheeks. "I miss him."

Anna slowly massaged Lily's back. "It's okay, Cookie. It's okay."

"Once in the courthouse I saw someone who looked like Dad from the back. I followed him. I was sure it was Dad." Lily pulled away. "I knew it wasn't. I knew it. But still, I thought maybe. I can't explain it. I wonder where he is."

Lily lowered her arms and faced her mother. "Crazy things. Is he warm? Is he safe? Who's taking care of him? And then I think of him in the coffin in the ground..."

Anna felt her throat constrict as Lily talked, but she knew she needed to listen to her daughter. No one had been there for her when her own mother had died.

"I know it's stupid. I don't believe in heaven or hell. It's hard to imagine that someone you love so much just disappears. I'm sorry, Mom. I know you miss him, too. It must be awful for you. Are you okay?"

Anna nodded.

"Really?"

"I miss him, too, Cookie, but I'm okay." Anna leaned over and kissed her daughter's cheek. "Remember, I've learned the hospice lessons well. I stay busy, talk to people, and cry when I need to." Just a little lie, she said to herself. A tiny one.

Lily cuddled herself up against her mother. Anna brushed Lily's thick hair out of her face and pulled her closer. She kept her eyes open wide and tightened the muscles around her heart.

Chapter 8

"I can't hear you over Koru's howling. Someone must be at the backdoor." Anna put her coffee on the floor in the den and went to check.

"Stay back, Koru. Leave Becky alone. Stop jumping." She grabbed Koru's collar and held him down. "You're getting too old for all this jumping."

Becky had come from next door wearing her fancy Persian lamb coat and one of her many hand-knit winter-hat-and-scarf ensembles—this one a combination of orange, yellow, and red. She stepped into the kitchen carrying a covered Tupperware container with a bow on it. She placed it on the kitchen table and petted Koru's head.

"Both of us are getting a little creaky, eh?" She looked around the kitchen. "Where's that Lily? I brought her strudel for her birthday. Larry didn't come, did he?"

"No. Larry's not here. Couldn't make it this year. Lily's in the den. Never mind. Here she is."

"She must have smelled the strudel."

Anna watched as Lily, who now towered over the old woman, leaned down and kissed her check. Likely Becky was on the way to church, her lipstick, eye shadow, and blush carefully applied.

"It wouldn't be my birthday without your strudel." Lily opened the container, breathed in the aroma, and picked up a slice. "Heaven. I love this stuff. Thank you." She hugged Becky's wiry body. "You look terrific."

"Are you off to church?" Anna asked.

Becky nodded and then blushed. "Got a date after church. A new gentleman."

"What happened to the one with the sports car? I couldn't believe you could get in and out of that thing so easily."

"The car was great," Becky said, "but he was a whiner. Always complaining about something. Haven't heard a whine out of Clarence yet; he's the new one."

Anna motioned Becky to sit. "Coffee?"

"Maybe half a cup. Don't want to be late for church." She removed her scarf and placed her hat neatly next to it on the table.

Lily ate another piece of strudel and joined Becky at the table. "What's Clarence like?"

"Well," she tapped her index finger against her lips, "he's in pretty good shape, if you know what I mean." Her eyes sparkled.

Anna really didn't want to think about what that meant.

"He drives a vintage Camaro and polishes the darn thing every day, but he can dance. Met him at the senior center. Anna, one of these days you should come with me." She looked at Lily. "Your mother would love it. She loves to dance. Time for her to get back on the horse," she said and chuckled. "Seriously," she added looking over at Anna. "Lots of available guys there. They'd go nuts for you."

Anna noticed Lily looked surprised at Becky's comments. She refilled the coffee cups and joined them at the table. "How is your sister, Dotty?"

"Changing the subject, eh?" Becky said.

"Go on, Becky. How's Dotty?"

"She's hangin' in there. Still hates the nursing home."

Becky finished her coffee, reapplied her lipstick, wrapped her scarf around her neck, and picked up her hat. "Tell me if I put it on straight, will you?"

"Looks perfect."

"Well, I'm off. Don't want to be late. Happy birthday, sweetie."

Lily got up to hug Becky as she left. "Hope you enjoy your date."

Becky chuckled and left the house.

Lily picked up the dirty cups, rinsed them, and put them in the drying rack.

Anna turned off the coffeepot. "Let's get moving if you want to see your friends after breakfast. I'm going to finish getting dressed, and then we can go."

"Mom, wait a sec. Talk to me for a minute." Lily wiped her hands on a dishtowel. "I didn't think about it before Becky said something." Her eyes drifted toward the window. "I probably should have. Maybe this isn't my business." She ran her fingers through her hair, looked back at Anna, and lowered her voice, "Do you want to start dating? Seems like Daddy just died."

Anna paused at the kitchen door and shook her head. "It's never entered my mind, Cookie. I'm just not there. Probably never will be. And," Anna said and grinned, "if I do ever decide to date, I doubt if I'd be going to the senior center with Becky."

Lily laughed. "Would you tell me if you start dating?"

"I don't know. Maybe." Anna twisted her wedding ring and tilted her head to the side. "I've really never thought about it." She started up the stairs, then turned and asked her daughter, "Do you tell me about your dates?"

Lily's eyes twinkled. "Makes you wonder, doesn't it?"

Crowded as usual on Sunday morning, the foyer of the Scarlet Tree offered no place to sit, and it was too cold to wait outside. At least a dozen people in winter coats jammed into the entrance waiting for tables. The smell of fresh baked goods, bacon, and coffee only increased their desire to be seated.

Anna added her name to the list, and she and Lily squeezed themselves into a space near the door. Next to them stood two women who Anna thought were a couple, not just friends. She wondered if they might be in the marching band. Ridiculous. There must be thousands of lesbians in Seattle and probably only ten or fifteen in the band. She tried to eavesdrop on their conversation, but the noise around them made it impossible.

The crowd pushed them farther back into the corner, probably a party leaving the restaurant. Her heavy jacket provided some padding, protecting her from stray elbows.

They must be a couple, Anna thought, because…she didn't know why. A connection between them? Didn't she have a connection with Marilyn or her other friends? But she saw something different. No idea what it was.

One of the women, about thirty, had long hair in a ponytail, and the other one wore her hair very short and spikey. Maybe it was her hairdo? She wondered if she was thinking about these women because she'd be making a documentary about lesbians and gays. Or had she always had these thoughts?

"Mom, should we go someplace else?" Lily asked.

Anna couldn't see Lily's face, but hoped she could hear her over the din. "We're so close to the scones. I've been dreaming of them for days. The line usually goes fast."

"Anna, Anna, is that you?" She heard a voice calling to her from near the door. "Anna Simon. It's me Dave, Dave Bailey." Anna turned slightly and saw the very tall, lanky figure of another instructor at the community college—the one who had likely taken over her classes—maneuvering his way toward her.

Her shoulders tensed, and her eyes darted around the room. No escape. She tried to move away from Lily or block her view.

"Great to see you out and about, Anna." His voice bellowed out over the crowd.

"Hi, Dave." She kept her voice soft. Maybe she could model a lower decibel level.

No luck; his voice rumbled out again, "How are you? You look okay." Bailey leaned down toward her face. "Are you feeling better?"

Anna sensed Lily behind her trying to move forward.

"I'm fine now. Thanks," Anna answered in the same soft voice. Her eyes shuttered. His head pulled back as he studied her, as if he could read her mind and decipher why she had resigned from the college. She was relieved to see the dean had protected her from gossip.

He stood for a moment and then said, "Well, we sure miss you. Take care now." He turned and made his way toward the door.

Lily leaned in to her mother. "Who's that? What were you two talking about?"

"Just a guy I know. Did you hear that? Did they call our name?" Anna pushed her way through the crowd toward the tables.

"I think so," Lily said, following behind her.

A server motioned them toward a table next to the windows. Anna could see the sky darkening in the north. She hated sitting next to the windows in the winter, but in the crowded restaurant, she was content to just slide her chair as far from the cold glass as she could.

"Coffee?"

"Absolutely." Anna didn't bother looking at the menu. "And I'll have my usual: the early bird special, over easy with bacon. What about you, Lily? Do you want to see the menu?"

"No menu. I'll have the same."

"Can we get an extra order of scones with some marionberry jam?" Anna asked the server.

"Coming up."

"Who was that guy?" Lily asked as soon as the server left.

"Just a colleague, from the college." Anna took off her coat and wrapped it around the back of her chair. She turned sideways, her back to the windows, and focused out toward the tables across the room.

Lily reached out and touched Anna's shoulder. "Did I hear him say that they miss you, hope you feel better? What's that about?"

Anna noted a family at the next table, a young mother and father, a toddler on a booster seat, and a five- or six-year-old little girl. Just at the beginning of their story, Anna thought.

"Mom," Lily said louder. Anna turned her head and noticed Lily's brow furrow when she said, "You've got me worried. Answer me."

"Don't worry, Cookie. It's really nothing." She shifted to face Lily and smiled. "I actually lied to them. I've just been busy and, well, honestly, I didn't want to teach anymore."

"Don't be ridiculous, Mom." Lily's hazel eyes stared at her mother. "A first-year law student would toss you out on voir dire. What aren't you telling me?"

"Don't play lawyer with me. Didn't I tell you that I had resigned?"

"Extra scones to keep you busy while you wait," the server said as she placed a basket of warm scones on their table. "And you're lucky this morning. First cups out of a fresh pot." She turned their cups right side up with one hand and poured coffee from the carafe with the other.

Lily broke one of the scones in half and drowned it in jam. She swallowed it in one gulp and licked a residue of jam off her lips. "No, you did not tell me." Lily sipped her coffee and then lowered her cup with care. "Mom, this is serious. What's going on?"

Anna knew Lily wouldn't relent. She looked out the window, watched the tops of the trees across the street as they swayed in the wind. Heavy rain was expected in the afternoon, maybe frost. She felt Lily's eyes on her. She'd forgotten how noisy the restaurant could be. Chairs scraped across the floors, cutlery and dishes clattered, and the buzz of conversation and laughter filled the room.

"I must have forgotten to tell you."

"Help me out, Mom. I'm kind of lost here. What happened? I thought you loved teaching. Were you sick? Is that what happened?"

Anna folded her hands on the table. Her heart raced. Ridiculous. She could tell Lily. No reason to feel shame. But the words wouldn't come. "It's so noisy in here. Let's just enjoy our meal. We'll go home, and then we can talk."

"I'm supposed to meet Jen and the girls soon."

"Right. I forgot."

"I'll cancel."

Anna shook her head. "Don't cancel. There's a terrible draft here next to the windows," she said as she draped her jacket over her shoulders. "Are you too chilly?"

"I'm fine."

Anna breathed deep into her belly and exhaled a few times. Lily stared at her, eyes wide, jaw tense.

"I'm not sure I can explain it," Anna added. She tried to lower her shoulders from where they hovered near her ears.

She leaned across the table and lowered her voice. "The night it happened, the night your father had the stroke…he'd come in the house after walking Koru, and he said to me, 'Get in touch with the furnace people. Feels like winter's here already.' Then he went into the living room. That was the last time I heard his voice."

Anna sat back in the chair and rubbed each eye with her index finger, then spread jam on a scone.

"You never told me that before."

"Didn't I?"

"No. Why are you telling me now?"

Anna took a small bite out of the scone and put it back on her plate. "Because it took me until last week to have the furnace serviced. Way over a year. I don't know why." Anna looked out through the window at the awning across the street flapping in the wind. "And then there was menopause. Not the hot flashes or the night sweats. I could handle that, but I couldn't handle the despair, like an invisible shell covering me. I really didn't have the words."

Lily's body was still, brows furrowed, her gaze focused on her mother. Anna continued, "You don't need to hear this. I'm just fine now."

"Two early bird specials with bacon," the server said as she placed the plates of eggs, hash browns, and bacon on the table. "I'll check back with more coffee."

Anna picked up her fork and held it over the eggs. "I did not want you to worry about me." She put the fork down again and was distracted by the whining of the little girl at the next table. Screeching might be a better description.

"I hate milk. It makes me sick. Do you want me to get sick? Right here at the table?" the little girl screamed.

Lily rolled her eyes. "What a brat," she whispered.

"Just a kid, Lily, learning how to be a person." Anna poured ketchup on her hash browns and handed the bottle to Lily.

Lily added ketchup to her potatoes and ate a forkful. "I don't know what to think. You seem okay now. Are you okay?"

"I'm fine. Not to worry. I started hormone replacement therapy. That helps with the menopause stuff."

"Why did you resign? Couldn't you have taken a leave of absence or something until you felt better?"

Anna nibbled on her scone. "I suppose I could have." They continued to eat in silence until Lily asked again, "Why didn't you take a leave? They would have given it to you."

She looked directly at Lily but didn't respond immediately. She folded her hands on her lap, closed her eyes, and imagined a figure running through her brain with a flashlight looking for the right answer. The only answer available was the truth.

"Your father and I were married for thirty years. Actually, it would be thirty-one now. When he died, the air went out of the house and all the energy disappeared out of me. I don't know how else to explain it. I still don't have the right words. But you need to know that I am fine." Anna looked at Lily's plate. "Your food is getting cold. Eat."

"More coffee?" the server asked as she approached the table.

Anna covered her cup with her hand while Lily lifted her cup toward the coffee carafe.

"So, what are you going to do?"

"Actually, I started an extension class at the university, in making documentary films."

"Documentaries? A new career?"

"I don't think so. Maybe. Everything felt very dark for so long. Then one day, months ago, I saw this professor on *Oprah*." Anna raised her hand. "Don't you dare laugh."

Lily shook her head. "I'm not laughing. What happened?"

"Well, I thought it was stupid at the time, but eventually it worked. This professor said that even if you're dying, sick, depressed—she had a whole list of miseries—you should make a list of twenty-five things that would make you happy, and go do them."

"Did you make a list?"

"I tried. But nothing came. Zero. Then this catalogue came from the Extension Division at UW and I saw this class. Weird. It just appealed to me, so I applied."

"And you got in?"

Anna nodded.

"Do you like it?"

"Uh huh. I do."

"Beautiful. Good for you. Does Larry know about any of this?"

"I told him about the class. I don't think it registered. I haven't told him anything else. He's got a lot on his mind. I'll tell him later."

"Mom. Why didn't you tell me? We talk on the phone all the time. Don't you trust me? Are you trying to protect me?"

Anna smiled. "As long as I live, I'll protect you, Cookie. When you have your own kids, you'll understand."

Lily rolled her eyes. "I can't picture myself with kids. Sitting at a table, waiting for them to drink their milk."

"Right. That part is no fun. Any potential fathers on the horizon?"

Lily smiled and said nothing. She began eating her breakfast with more gusto. "Listen, Mom. It's simple—you don't talk, I don't talk."

Anna laughed. "I'm sorry, Cookie, really. I just couldn't." Anna picked up a slice of bacon, put it on a piece of scone, swallowed it, and licked her lips. "I love this place."

"Will you promise to tell me next time?"

"Next time?"

"You know, if there's a problem sometime. I know you're used to talking things over with Daddy, but . . . I'm your next best choice."

"Lily, you do not need to worry about me," Anna said, enunciating each word clearly. "Maybe you should worry about finding a father for those children—the ones who won't drink their milk."

"No future fathers on the horizon. As for worrying, okay, I'll save my worrying for when you get to be Becky's age. Okay?"

"That's a deal."

Chapter 9

A few days later, she and Ken met outside of class to write the treatment, and he had chosen the B&O café on Capitol Hill. She thought immediately of their lemon chiffon cake and the many evenings she and Mort had spent there when they had lived on the hill before the twins were born. Although this class was the first thing in over thirty years that had nothing to do with Mort and her role as his wife, she recognized that even in this university program, she couldn't avoid reminders.

She imagined the opening sequence of a film about her life. A long shot of the Seattle skyline. Then the Space Needle, Capitol Hill, rain, young couple, pregnant woman laughing as man helps her take off wet raincoat in funky coffee shop. He rubs her pregnant belly. Couple shares a big slice of lemon chiffon cake. He licks a drop of chiffon from her chin.

Lovely opening sequence for some movie, but not hers. Mort had never licked food off her chin, or rubbed her pregnant belly for that matter. They usually met colleagues and friends at the B&O. Anna and the women talked together. The men talked together. Mort never shared any dessert. He didn't like people eating off of his plate.

The crowded café smelled the same. Years of delicacies left a sweet aroma clinging to the walls. Still just a hint of smoke. All the no-smoking ordinances in the world couldn't rid the place of years of late night smokers. Anna knew she'd regret it, but she ordered the lemon chiffon cake, anyway.

Ken stuck to coffee. She wondered if people thought she was his mother. They didn't look remotely alike. He was massive. Broad shoulders. Probably six foot five. Long legs. Long arms. Shaven head. Black clothes. Always. She knew she usually looked slim, although since Mort's death, she'd been adding pounds. She excelled at disguising the layers of fat. But her features, a narrow nose and high cheekbones, were finer than Ken's. She could picture Ken attached to a plow, pulled by a horse through his fields. Rural. Farmer. Now a Goth.

She looked around the café and realized no one was looking at them. No one cared who they were, related or not.

As she savored her cake, Anna told Ken about her conversations with Kelley Wilson, the band director. They were developing their own unique roles in this partnership. Although Ken had first spoken with his friend to get the project going, Anna had taken on the talking, writing, and managing, while Ken would schlep the equipment and do most of the camera work. Not exclusive roles, but vaguely, she was the producer and he, the director.

"Did you set something up with Kelley?"

"She invited us to the first rehearsal. Three weeks from Thursday." Anna rolled the chiffon frosting around in her mouth and held back a whimper of delight. Orgasmic cake.

"We'll have the treatment ready by then and probably be checked out on all the equipment. Does she like the idea of a film about the band?"

"Understatement. She's ecstatic. She wants to use it for fund-raising—if we have no objection."

Ken shook his head. "I don't."

"Me either. Mostly she talked about why they organized. I took notes." Ken went to get another cup of coffee while Anna searched her briefcase.

"Here it is: organized because they wanted to march in the pride parade. There should be a gay marching band in the pride parade. There wasn't any. The community needed it. Want to make music and celebrate themselves. This year the parade is on June twenty-sixth."

"Might make an excellent last sequence. Music and marching. Crowds cheering."

"Good idea. Kelley said there are some leaders we may want to highlight—she'll introduce us at the rehearsal."

They determined how many "stars" they could have in a ten-minute doc and agreed they'd have to set up an interview schedule, as well as opportunities to tape supplemental or alternative footage for the documentary. Anna now knew it was called B-roll.

She listened to herself as she talked. How strange that she sounded confident. Strange that there could be a deep chasm inside of her, an empty pit, and that no one could tell. She'd started short-term estrogen replacement therapy after the class started. It was helping. The lethargy was gone. The depression less heavy.

Later, at their scheduled meeting with Sam, her stomach churned while they waited for him to read their treatment. She felt anxious and tried not to show it. Ken had no expression on his face.

Sam put the papers down and smiled. "Good work. This could be an upbeat doc. Lots of meaning built in. Your soundtrack's built in, too. Doc about a band. Good thinking. I need to check you out on the equipment. Then you'll be ready to start making your mistakes. That's how you're going to learn." He laughed and signaled for the next pair of students to come in.

"You've got a good eye," Sam said as he peered over Anna's shoulder to study the framing she created for the practice interviews. "I notice you're always a bit off center. That seems to be your point of entry. I like that—makes it more interesting. Ken, let's see what you can do."

Anna became the subject while Ken managed the camera and the interview. Sam studied the monitor as Ken set up the shot, then turned it so Anna could see herself on camera.

"Oh, dear. I look awful. My extra chin. The dark circles under my eyes. I don't look that bad in real life. Maybe I do. Do I?"

"Put the camera slightly above her. Don't shoot anyone, particularly women, from below." Sam demonstrated the technique, and Anna saw her chins diminish and her eyes look less haggard.

"She looks younger, fresher. Wait 'til we learn about lighting next week. That's the magic. Keep in mind you've got a lot of power with a camera."

Sam walked on to the next pair of students, prompting a smile from Anna and a thumbs-up signal from Ken. After this exercise they could schedule their interviews. They would be free to use the equipment and could actually start.

Anna watched Sam as he gave the signal to break down the equipment. He's a good teacher, she thought. Treats all of us the same. Male. Female. Old. Young. It made her feel as if she belonged in the class. Strange for her to be a student again after so many years. She noted all his tricks. Good teacher tricks. She knew them well, and oddly enough, they even worked on her. She knew calling people by name, being supportive, creating community were all techniques that worked, but now as a student, she understood how powerful they really were.

Actually, they were life skills. Help people believe that they belong, that they matter.

She watched Ken's back as he bent to lift the gear they had used and take it to the storage room. They'd gotten into a routine: she carried the mics, and he followed with the heavy equipment.

They never discussed equality. She was old, he young, with a youthful back, a strong one with beautiful motion. He had a flow to his movements. None of the stiffness she felt in herself.

She noticed some of the young women haul huge lights around the room and knew she couldn't do it. Didn't even try. Some of it was the conditioning of a lifetime. Men did some things, women others. Men always carried the heavy stuff. Women smiled and thanked them.

She was certainly a feminist. Whatever that was these days. She never understood how the Equal Rights Amendment had failed. As she observed students in this class, she often couldn't identify gender from behind, couldn't tell the young women from the men. The young women in particular appeared to have a natural ease she had never experienced.

She found herself studying bodies. Watching the smooth skin on young faces. Did anyone notice? She remembered her old aunt Fanny—dead now forty years. She used to touch the little kids. Run her hands over their cheeks. One could get away with that with babies, but she and her cousins used to laugh about it. Creepy.

But she understood it now. The smooth softness, like the difference between touching silk and touching canvas. Not that she was canvas. Maybe linen. And maybe she was preoccupied with bodies because she wanted to be touched. To touch. To have someone to hold. To be held. To feel the warmth of skin next to her own. It felt like forever. Maybe that had been Aunt Fanny's issue. Hungry for touch. *I'm hungry for your touch.* Whose touch? She wondered if that part of her life was over.

Chapter 10

Anna studied the clothes in her walk-in closet. What to wear to meet the band? What look? One of her work suits? Jeans? Try to look young, hip?

Ridiculous. She hated old people who dressed like teens. Get over it, she thought. Wear what's comfortable. Why are you making such a big deal about this?

She wore light makeup, wool slacks, and a large black cotton sweater over a turtleneck. She added a red-and-black Hermes scarf. Black always highlighted her dark eyes. A dramatic look. Maybe she'd look like an artist. A filmmaker. She smiled at her own image in the mirror and left to meet Ken at the church on the Ave where the band practiced.

There were about twenty to twenty-five men and women in the church basement tuning their instruments and setting up music stands. The shiny linoleum floor squeaked as Anna and Ken walked toward Kelley. Fortunately, someone had opened a window to let in fresh air, which eased the musty smell of old books shelved around the edges of the room. Ken introduced Anna to his friend Tim, the trumpet player, and then to Kelley Wilson, the band director, a stocky woman in her late forties.

Ken opened the cases containing the cameras, lights, mics, and extension cords. He focused on the equipment while Anna talked to Kelley.

"We are all thrilled. So excited." Kelley said, her voice eager and breathless in contrast to the solidity of her body. The questions came quickly. "Will the university own this film? Can we keep it? Do you and Ken own it? Will we get copies? For every band member? What do you need from us?"

Anna didn't know the answers to any of Kelley's questions. "I imagine we can work something out. We'll do some research and let you know."

Her shoulders tensed. It was one thing to practice in the classroom with the teacher there as backup. But here, the band director thought she and Ken knew what they were doing. They must have looked more competent than she felt.

Kelley pointed out the handful of band members she thought would be good for private interviews. The trumpet player, of course, and an elementary school teacher who played the sax, the drum major from Algeria, and a flute player who was a gay activist. Kelley thought their drummer, Carla Martinez, would be a key spokesperson for the band as well. She was a founding member and the oldest person in the band.

"Quiet down," Kelley said as she tapped her baton on the music stand. "I want to introduce Anna Simon and Ken Whooten from the University of Washington. These are the people we've talked about. The ones who are going to make us famous." Everyone laughed. "They'll be around for several months. Please cooperate with them—we need to keep them happy." Anna noticed some of the young men eyeing Ken.

As the band began their rehearsal, Anna and Ken each stood behind cameras stabilized by tripods, scanning the room for background shots, the essential B-roll, maybe an entertaining close-up or novel angle of an instrument. They both mined the room for a money shot—the shot that sang, that vibrated with perfection.

She hoped the band's music would improve. What she heard would not make a good sound track. Kelley had said this was the first rehearsal of the season. It would have to get better.

Anna found her camera drifting to the drummer. It took her a moment to realize she was the "It's the Most Wonderful Time of the Year" drummer, the same woman she'd seen at Northgate before the holidays. Still exciting to watch.

As she studied the drummer through the camera lens, Anna remembered Audrey. This woman was a Latina version of what Audrey must look like today. Audrey had been blond. Nordic. Lean and fit. Carla Martinez was dark, but had a similar lean, agile appearance with a stunning lived-in face, full lips, and high cheekbones.

She wore her black hair, flecked with gray, in a tailored haircut, slightly wavy against her graceful, shapely head. Crisp white blouse, tailored slacks. A furrow between her dark eyes as she concentrated on the beat. The camera caught her in a huge smile when she laughed at her own mistake. The same unique smile that had charmed Anna at the mall.

She intentionally refocused her camera toward the woodwinds away from the back corner where Carla sat. Too much attention on one subject. She let the camera roll but found her eyes shifting back. Carla was looking at her. Anna felt a pulsing in her body, at once familiar and still barely remembered. She dropped her eyes quickly back into the camera lens.

Anna approached the interview subjects as the band finished rehearsal and people started to break down their instruments. She set up appointments with each subject, and then she approached Carla. Sweat covered the drummer's flushed face, and Anna noticed a slight darkening under Carla's arms.

A blush rose across her face as she took out her calendar and looked at Carla. No need to be nervous, but Anna felt flustered as she looked into the drummer's dark eyes. Really, get a grip, Anna thought.

A welcoming smile met her approach, then an outstretched hand. "Heard someone was going to make us famous." And then a full laugh. Anna's spirit seemed to expand, to open from someplace within that she didn't recognize.

"Did you play holiday music at Northgate Mall before the holidays? Was that you?"

"Yeah. Did you see us?" Her voice, deep and melodic, lingered in the air.

"Yeah. It was great, great." Anna fumbled around for more words, but nothing came. Somehow she arranged the interview time and got Carla's phone number and email address.

As she drove home, she replayed the look, the handshake, the smile. In her mind's eye she saw Carla's long fingers lightly holding the drumsticks. Her forearms dark against the white blouse. The solid handshake. Strong. Electric.

Anna had noted Carla's hand as she held the pen, wrote her contact information. Her fingernails were short, buffed, with clear cuticles. She took care of her hands. Anna imagined they were strong. As the days crept by until the interview, Anna shocked herself when she wondered what it would feel like to touch those hands, to run her own fingers over Carla's.

The weeks slipped by. She'd received the letter she'd expected from the college accepting her resignation. Thanking her for her service to the community. Dave Bailey would teach her class. No surprise. Seattle Community College was replaced in her life by classes on camcorder use, lighting techniques, and sound management.

Her sink was still full of dishes, but now a cleaning crew came every other week and Anna stopped cleaning up for them before they arrived. She no longer sat for hours sipping her coffee and dissecting her depression. Was she happy now? Not necessarily, but different events filled her life and new paths opened in her mind.

The old paths got a rest, began to fade, while new avenues grew, stimulated by all that she was learning—specific tasks like editing, lighting, storyboarding. Her classmates said hello when she arrived and good-bye when she left. They smiled at her when they crossed paths in the halls. Darth Vader seemed to appreciate her skills more with each subject they interviewed.

At her usual place at the kitchen table, Anna sipped her coffee, an Italian dark roast with a bit of milk, and thought about Carla. She played the same scenes over and over. Carla holding the drumsticks, slowly tapping out the rhythms, active, powerful hands. Neat nails. Her warm smile. The electric handshake.

As she moved through the more familiar parts of her days—getting the mail, taking Koru to the lake, seeing the purple-and-yellow Japanese irises emerge along the shore—her thoughts often drifted toward Carla. Images of the drummer floated in her mind when Anna chatted with her neighbor, Becky, and when she listened to her children on the phone. A fresh path in her brain named Carla Martinez emerged. Peculiar, she thought, but felt relief not to think about her despair or about Mort and their marriage...or about menopause.

During that first band rehearsal, Anna had scheduled the interview with Carla as the last one on their schedule. Even then she knew she wanted time to hone her skills. Bizarre, but she wanted to impress the drummer.

Chapter 11

Anna noticed Ken's truck when she pulled up and parked in front of Carla's home. Likely inside, already setting up the lights. The house sat back behind a six-foot-high laurel hedge, along a curving street in Fremont, home to iconoclasts of all varieties. Carla lived in a bungalow with a wide front porch, which Anna imagined sheltered Adirondack chairs in the summer—cool, private, and intimate. Now, as Anna climbed the steps and looked around the porch, she saw only wet leaves and old neighborhood advertisements collected in the corners.

She'd learned through the band grapevine that Carla's lover of many years, Laura, had died after a long battle with breast cancer ten years earlier. She knew Carla had previously played the sax and turned to drums only after Laura died. Made sense to Anna, although when Mort died, she lacked the energy to lift a drumstick, let alone bang anything with it. When menopause stuck itself to her besieged psyche, all initiative left her—until the documentary class. Had Carla gone through menopause already? Probably. She was older than Anna.

The door opened quickly. Carla, wearing her usual crisp white shirt, along with jeans, greeted Anna with a melt-your-heart, warm smile. She must have been waiting for her.

Anna had seen her during rehearsals over the last month. They had exchanged smiles and waves, and Anna felt a kind of softening each time she saw her. Did Carla feel the same thing?

Carla guided Anna into the house, and Anna nodded her approval at the location set by Ken. "You did it again," Anna said to him. Over the past weeks, she had come to appreciate him far beyond his capacity as Sherpa. He had a great eye and steady hand, consistently did what he said he would do. They worked well together.

They adjusted the camera once Carla had settled into a chair and enhanced Garbo lighting until Carla looked smashing on the monitor, the laugh lines around her eyes adding depth to her mature beauty.

Although they'd interviewed other band members, something about this interview felt different to Anna. She wondered if it was the actual physical setting. Carla's home had an intimate feel, cozy without being cluttered. A deep-red sectional sofa in front of the windows, dark wood trim throughout the bungalow, and a large kilim rug in front of the fireplace where fresh flowers decorated the mantle all contributed to feeling of warmth and shelter.

As Anna rechecked the lighting and sound, she noticed a wall of photos in the dining room. She took a closer look. Two women in settings across the world. Carla and another attractive woman, probably Laura, near the Eiffel Tower, on a sailboat moored in aquamarine water, on skis against a mountain somewhere.

Carla got comfortable in a dark leather armchair near the fireplace, giving the camera a clear view into the den where her drums were visible.

Yes, this interview with Carla felt different than the others, and it was more than the warm physical setting. She was in Carla's presence, in her space, and it felt good. Anna took her place in a straight-back chair next to the camera where Ken stood.

She knew from past interviews that Ken would remain silent, trusting her to elicit whatever she could from the subject. Carla had signed the release. Anna took a deep breath and shut out all thoughts that wouldn't bring her closer to the moment. Her heart pounded as she leaned forward. "Why did you decide to play your music in a gay band? What does playing in a band have to do with sexual identity?"

"You're not messing around, huh? Okay," Carla said, looking past Anna into space somewhere and seeming to making a decision.

"No, not messing around."

"Okay, then..." Carla rested her hands on her thighs and looked directly into the camera. "I wanted to be with my own people. I wanted to march in the gay pride parade, be part of a long line of gay musicians celebrating our lives. It wouldn't be the same marching with just any group of people."

Anna heard the tremor in Carla's voice. She knew this interview could go deep. She looked at Ken and signaled for a close-up.

"I found that, for me, the only way out of shame is straight ahead—forward. I had to face my own fear and tackle it, beat it out of myself by letting it hit the light. You have to do that, no matter how overpowering the fear. That's what I've learned." Carla nodded her head slowly and moved her eyes toward Anna.

"Try to speak directly into the camera," Anna reminded her. "Was there a specific fear?"

Carla nodded her head, "Oh, yes. Rejection. I was afraid that someone would find out I was a lesbian and reject me."

"Had anyone ever rejected you?" Anna kept her back straight. She did not want to lean forward and risk impacting the flow of Carla's words. The slight drone of the camera beside her faded as the intensity of Carla's voice increased. The room felt small, as if the three of them had been sheltered into a cocoon.

"I hid it well until my parents caught me kissing a girlfriend in eleventh grade. We were upstairs in my room, in bed. Her bra was on the floor. They took me to a psychiatrist. He told them he could cure me." Carla laughed. "I was so stupid at sixteen. I ran away from home that night. I tried to get my girlfriend, Reyna, to leave with me. She laughed at me. 'Just practicing my kissing,' she said."

"Not what you expected?"

"Not at all. I was shocked. I had been sure she felt the same way that I did." Carla ran her hand through her hair, brushing it away from her face. "It's not a mistake I would make today. But at sixteen, back then, I was so sure. How could I feel so much and she feel nothing? I never believed her. She was just more scared than I was. Or maybe less gay. I lost track of her." She looked directly into Anna's eyes and said, "I'm a much better judge today."

Anna thought she might be blushing as she signaled to Carla to stay focused on the camera. "Then what happened?"

"The police caught me getting off a bus in Portland. The psychiatrist recommended a lockup for me. My parents just wanted to help. Lots of people did that in those years. The American Psychological Association still thought of homosexuality as pathology."

"Hard to see that as help."

"Yeah." Carla ran her fingers through her hair. "My parents used to visit me every Sunday in the hospital. I would get hysterical, so they kept an attendant in the room. Only under supervision. It went on for months. I wrote them letters constantly, pleading with them to let me out."

"Sounds terrifying."

"It was, until I got smart. I convinced the psychiatrist that I had changed. That I had seen God. 'I'm not a lesbian,' I told him. 'Thanks for helping me.' Self-satisfied egotist believed me. The asshole believed me. So full of himself. That's how I got out."

"Excellent!" Ken interjected uncharacteristically.

"I learned to live underground. After a while, I didn't even know I was underground. By the time I got to college, even though I used to check out women in my classes all the time, I began to think I was normal. Straight. There was this girl in my biology lab who would cross her legs and then swing one of them out. I used to watch her.

"I told myself I was interested in beauty—beautiful things—and I switched my major from biology to art and design. I hung out with men who I thought maybe were gay, but no one talked in those days. One of the men, Raul, and I dated for years. Then we got married. Lots of family pressure. We never really talked about how we felt. Once in a while we'd have sex. Both sets of parents wanted grandchildren. 'Where are the *niños*? Get busy,' they'd say."

Carla motioned to Ken to stop the camera, and she went to the mantle and brought back a framed picture of herself with her children. "First came Orlando. Yes, Orlando. Named after Orlando Cepeda. Big baseball fans. Plus, Raul was a proud Puerto Rican. Roberto, after Clemente, was supposed to be next, but we got Roberta. She's Bobbie today." Bobbie looked liked a younger version of Carla. Orlando was stockier.

When she heard the camera start, Carla faced it and continued, "We were always friends. Sorry, this isn't the stuff you're looking for about the band, is it?"

"Well, yes. That's exactly what this doc is about—why does someone join a gay band to play music? What's wrong with playing music in a straight band? We won't use your whole story; only sentences here and there to help people understand why this band is so special."

Carla nodded.

"We were friends. Weird. We never talked about what was in our hearts. How was that possible? Hey, we grew up in the '50s. Way before Ellen DeGeneres. Way before anyone put the words *gay* and *marriage* in the same sentence. We had kids. We worked. We were busy. Then Raul got HIV. Good-bye, hiding."

Carla stopped and reached for a glass of water behind her chair, out of the shot. She drank, returned the glass, and looked down. They were all silent.

"I think this is enough for today," Carla said as she looked back up at Ken and Anna.

"What happened?" Anna asked quietly.

"He died. In the beginning, everybody died. I've lost my two best friends: Raul and Laura." She sat quietly, her hands folded on her lap.

Anna checked the monitor, the tape still running. She viewed Carla on the screen, but couldn't look directly at her. She wanted to comfort her, touch her cheek, feel the texture of her hair. Hold her.

"So—now I imagine you understand why this particular band is important to me. I want young people to see us marching down the street and feel pride running through their veins, not shame. If I close my eyes, I can still feel the shame I experienced when I was sixteen and got caught kissing my girlfriend." Carla looked from the camera directly at Anna. "I don't want another human being to feel that kind of self-disgust."

After several seconds of heavy silence, Anna motioned Carla back toward the camera and asked, "Why drums?"

Carla took a deep breath. "After Laura died—we had been together for so long—I was mad, crazy mad. I'd played the sax for years, but I essentially lost interest. I just wanted to bang things. Bash my fist through the walls. Bash my head until it cracked. A friend gave me bongo drums. It worked for me. Drums were better than sleeping pills, better than booze, better than crashing my car—all the things I had done when Raul died years before. I'm doing okay now." She grinned.

Anna felt a mirror image grin spread across her own face, catching the contagious joy in Carla's presence. As she unclipped her mic and leaned in to unhook Carla's, Anna said, "You are amazing."

Carla laughed and shook her head.

Anna was aware of Ken in the background breaking down the lights. She took Carla's warm hand in her own and held it for a moment, "Thank you. That was great."

They had planned on taking some B-roll of Carla in her own home, but they were out of time. They'd return later in the week for some background footage.

Carla walked her to the door. Anna didn't have words for all the feelings colliding in her body. Anna reached out toward her, and they hugged tightly. Carla's breasts pressed against her own. She knew she'd hugged other women before, but this hug felt different.

She started her car to drive back to Green Lake, but after a block, she pulled over. Tears came, and then sobs. Parked on Wallingford Avenue, Anna slumped down as low as she could in the car seat and sobbed. She thought about Mort and their lives together, the busyness that had been their lives. She thought about the kids who had both left, gone on to their own lives.

She had a big house full of fancy furniture. She had good health, a good bank balance. She was lucky. Very lucky. She knew it. But she kept crying. She needed to keep perspective. She had a good life. She didn't have to work two jobs or stand on her feet all day.

Carla had passion in her life. Tragedy, too, but life. So Anna had had a dull marriage. Big deal. But Anna cried for the woman who made love with Audrey forty years before and had never mentioned it to a soul. She cried for the woman she had been, shut down, boxed up, disconnected. Maybe she was pushing her way out. She wondered if it were an accident that she was making a video about a gay band—of all the possible subjects in the world.

She thought about Oprah's list and knew she might not have twenty-five things yet, but she did have a few. The heavy plastic shield was cracking, and what was emerging was raw, naked, and alone.

Chapter 12

Anna tossed the mail on the kitchen table when she came home. Mort used to like to take it directly to his office—before Anna had covered it with coffee stains or jelly smears. It was a running irritation with them—that and a dozen other little irritations they largely ignored. Anna had hated the way he straightened his side of the bed each night before he got in, smoothing down the sheets, ridding his resting place of any offending wrinkles. Then he'd lay the top sheet carefully over his side, then the comforter, then he'd plump his pillows, and then, after a sigh, he would lie down. Never in thirty years of marriage did he straighten the entire bed.

Weird that she remembered these silly things now. Thirty years of marriage gathered together in her brain as a list of irritations. Now she could leave the mail all over the table and cover it with chicken fat and no one cared. Their house was paid off. She had Mort's life insurance policy and his investments. Their investments, she thought, but he had managed everything. She knew they owned an apartment building in Madison Park, but she'd never seen it. She got the income. Mort's accountant handled everything. She knew she'd have to get it together enough to at least act as if she were paying attention.

Thirty years and two children later, and here she was, thinking about mail and bed linens and money. Every night, she got into bed with him and often, particularly in the beginning, they had sex. Anna shook her head. Had she shed those thirty years as a snake sheds its skin?

No time to think about Mort now. She was scheduled at the editing lab that morning and then was expected back to Carla's to shoot some B-roll. Ken had to work. He told Anna, "You can handle it alone. The camera will pick up ambient sound. You won't need a mic."

Carla's story had power, and they needed more background footage. She picked up the camera, tripod, and the rest of the equipment at the university and headed to Fremont. As she drove, she noticed the light-green, tiny buds on the maples lining Wallingford. She knew the crocuses would be out soon and then the daffodils, and then all of Seattle would be flashing color.

Anna easily found parking directly in front of Carla's house. She quickly adjusted the rearview mirror to check that her hair was in place and her lipstick fresh before she gathered her equipment and walked to the front door. She breathed the touch of spring deep into her lungs as she rang the bell.

Carla had swept since Anna's last visit, and she wasn't surprised to see two old Adirondack chairs on the wide porch. You could watch the rain from Carla's porch and not get wet, Anna thought. Almost warm enough for morning coffee outside.

Welcomed by that same wide, sunny grin, Anna set up the camera and got to work. She directed Carla in several sequences she thought would be useful in the doc: Carla practicing triple and quadruple stroke patterns on her snare drum and adjusting the cymbals, sipping coffee on her back porch, then glancing through some sheet music.

She asked Carla to look through some old photo albums and managed a close-up of her smiling and then wiping a tear from her eye. As she ran the camera, she had an awareness of Carla beyond the lens, a feeling of rightness being there with her. They didn't talk much, other than to arrange the setting, lights, or camera.

When Anna had enough footage, she connected her camcorder to Carla's TV.

"Wow. You've made me look good."

"It doesn't take any work."

Carla laughed. "More coffee?" she asked.

"I can't resist. It's delicious." Anna disconnected the camcorder and put it in its case. "But I don't want to get in your way."

"Not in my way. I'm not working today." Carla filled Anna's cup and sat down at the kitchen table.

Anna poured milk into her coffee and asked, "What kind of work do you do?"

"Actually, I'm a volunteer now, at the elementary school where my daughter teaches."

"Were you a teacher?"

"I graduated with a degree in art education, but somehow drifted into the field of human resources. I lucked out and ended up at Microsoft in the HR department."

"Was it exciting to work there?" Anna asked. She liked watching Carla think about her words before she spoke, as if she valued the conversation.

"Maybe at first, but after Laura died, I decided I didn't want all the stress in my life. There were so many other things I wanted to do, so I took advantage of the stock I had and retired early." Carla raised her cup and took a long drink of coffee. "Do you have a day job?"

"Not really anymore. I taught at Seattle Community College for years—in the Social and Human Services Department."

"What did you teach?"

"Mostly about hospice." She raised the heavy pottery mug to her lips and sipped.

"No surprise. I noticed that you seemed comfortable with death when you interviewed me—when I talked about Raul and Laura. Some people get a weird look in their eyes when you talk about death. You don't teach anymore?"

"No." Anna smiled and emptied her cup.

"Is there a reason you're taking this video class?"

Anna's stomach tensed. She shook her head. The kitchen felt small. She didn't know how to answer. She had either a trillion words or none. She was a public speaker, not a personal one, not about herself. She didn't feel like doing the usual "blah, blah, blah," but nothing else came. Mort had never required it of her. Neither did Larry and Lily. Not really. They had seemed happy with functions: wife, mother. Anna turned sideways in her chair, facing the backyard. "I see you've got crocus out already."

"Yeah. They always come out early. Looks like spring is here."

"You know," Anna said as she stood, "I have a lot to do today."

She was beginning to feel out of control, as if she were cracking, as if she could lean over and grab at broken pieces of Lucite to try to patch them together over herself. "I need to pack my stuff. Get back to the university. Thanks for the coffee."

Carla helped her break down the lights, and as she zipped up the leather carrying case, she said, "Let's get together sometime when you do have time."

She'd spoken clearly, but Anna still wondered if she'd heard her correctly. "Pardon?"

"Let's get together sometime when you do have time."

Anna nodded, then looked away, and began gathering equipment to carry out to her Subaru.

Carla followed her outside, carrying some of the containers. "I see you drive a Lezbaru."

"What?"

Carla laughed. "That's what we call them. So many dykes drive Subarus, we just call them Lezbarus."

Anna knew her face was red. "Someone should have told my husband."

"I noticed your wedding ring. But for some reason, I didn't think you were married."

"He died last year. I'm a widow."

"I'm sorry."

They were back in the house now. Anna picked up her purse and looked around. "Seems like I've got everything. Thanks again."

They stood on the threshold, Carla in the house, Anna on the porch. Anna's eyes were level with Carla's chin. She must be about five nine, Anna thought, a little shorter than Mort. She'd been scrutinizing Carla's face in the monitor and editing the interview on tape for over a week. Now she could see light hairs on her cheeks. Anna wanted to reach up and feel their softness.

"Do you like Mexican food?" Carla asked.

Anna rarely ate it. Too spicy. "Sure," she said.

"I'll cook my mother's mole for you."

Anna wanted to run off the porch. Actually, she wanted to be beamed off the porch and disappear. Instead, she heard herself say, "I'd like that."

"Sunday?"

Anna nodded. "Perfect. See you then," she said as she turned and walked to her car. She was back at the university in minutes—how was that possible? She got the equipment checked in. Somehow, she got home. She didn't remember putting her key in the ignition.

As usual, Koru went berserk when she walked in. She picked up his leash and a few plastics bags for his walk. No mood for the lake today. Too wired. She chose the alleys around her house. Koru loved to sniff around the garbage cans and the recycling while Anna enjoyed peeking into the yards. Hardly anyone had their lawn furniture out yet. Most of the flowerbeds hadn't even been cleaned. She saw tiny buds on the huge lilac bushes at the McClurys'. A season waiting to happen. So many fences were old and warped. Anna imagined her neighbors had no idea how much was visible to alley walkers.

What should she wear to have dinner at a lesbian's house? Was she going as a recruit? Was Carla recruiting her? She laughed at herself as she remembered the "homosexual agenda" that obsessed the fundamentalists.

Was this a date? She hadn't dated for years. Never dated a woman. Not a date.

When they returned from their walk, Koru followed Anna upstairs, jumped on the bed, circled, settled, and watched her.

She opened her closet door and stared. Suits for teaching. Fancy dresses. Mort loved her in dresses. Dinner parties, fundraisers, art openings. He loved observing his colleagues admire her. She pulled out a black cocktail dress, tiny silver beads along the neckline where the scent of *L'air du Temps* still lingered.

Anna walked out into the bedroom and showed the dress to Koru. "What do you think? Lots of cleavage, Koru. Good for dinner with Carla? What do you think?" Koru closed his eyes. Nap time.

"You're right. Maybe not." Mort had loved it when she wore it, called it her sex kitten dress. She turned and walked back into the closet.

She'd gained weight after Mort died. Half the clothes probably didn't fit. No matter. She hardly went anywhere. No one had been looking at her, anyway.

She needed new clothes. Step-out-into-the-world clothes. Maybe lesbian clothes. Stop, she thought. What were lesbian clothes? No such thing, and she wasn't a lesbian. Someone liked her and had invited her to dinner. Dinner with a new acquaintance. Get a grip.

She sat down on the floor. She pictured herself walking up to Carla's door. Carla would be watching as she approached. She would see…what? Someone sexy? Preppy? Idiot. Wear a nice pair of slacks and a top—any top. She hugged her knees to her chest and wondered what image she should project. She wasn't sure how to be without acting.

Anna had two days to shop to find something new and exciting to wear to dinner with Carla. Did she want to wear something exciting? A voice in her head that she didn't want to hear kept coming at her—what are you doing? Cancel the dinner. You signed up for a class—not a romance.

Who said anything about a romance? I'm merely going to dinner. I am not a lesbian. There is no romance.

Chico's would be her best bet—catering to middle-aged women. Where do lesbians shop? Rich lesbians probably shop at Nordstrom's and poor ones at secondhand stores. Lesbians were like any other women—some liked clothes and some didn't. She liked clothes. Maybe she'd be a lesbian who liked clothes. Maybe she wouldn't be a lesbian at all. Maybe she'd been a lesbian all along.

She studied herself in the large mirror. She'd need to get a sharper haircut, something trendier—or at least get it styled. She looked matronly, sloppy, using barrettes to keep her hair out of her eyes. Maybe it was time for short hair. Mort had liked her hair longer. "More feminine," he'd say. She wondered if she wanted to go back to adding low lights or just let it turn all gray.

Maybe she'd get a new bra. A minimizer. Not only had her boobs fallen, but they'd gotten bigger. She didn't understand—some people gained weight in their butts—but in her case, any cookies she ate went straight to her boobs, so the crumbs landed there as well.

She held her own gaze. Her eyes had always been her best feature, dark, almost black, large and almond shaped. And people told her she had an inviting smile. What had Mort called it? Kind.

In the magnifying mirror in her bathroom, she observed large, dark pores around her narrow nose. Blackheads? She snipped at some white hairs growing on her chin. She needed a facial.

In the brighter light of the bathroom, she studied herself in her red V-neck sweater and black jeans. Lesbian enough? She turned to get an opinion from Koru, but he was snoring on the bed. Maybe Carla liked straight women—she'd invited her to dinner when she wasn't dressed lesbian. Or maybe she had been.

Anna laughed at her own obsessing. She danced around in front of the mirror, a little shuffle ball change. She winked at herself and decided to try on some other outfits after all.

Chapter 13

She heard Carla's voice through the screen door. "Come on in." As Anna entered the kitchen, Carla smiled up at her, leaning over the oven to lift out a casserole dish. "Glad you could make it." Carla was in her usual crisp tailored shirt and jeans. Sexy, Anna found herself thinking.

Anna noticed the worn spots on Carla's jeans, right on her butt. Old jeans, hugging her butt cheeks. Carla placed the casserole dish on top of the stove, and Anna handed her a bottle of wine.

Carla studied the label. "Yum." She pointed to a drawer near the sink for an opener, and then she reached into the cupboard for wineglasses. Anna's eyes were drawn to the material of Carla's shirt as it stretched across her breasts.

What's the matter with me? Anna wondered. This is crazy.

Soft piano music, something jazzy and longing, came from the den.

"I've made a chicken mole for you. I hope you like it. It's one of my favorites. My mother uses Arbol chiles, but I prefer the milder pablano."

Shit, thought Anna. It's probably spicy. She wanted to say, "No, I won't like it. I hate spicy things. They hurt my mouth, upset my stomach. I have a lousy digestive system." Instead she said, "Can't wait to try it. Can I help?"

"Start on the salad if you want. Veggies are next to the sink. Knives in the drawer under the microwave."

Act as if, she thought as she stopped herself from asking if Carla wanted the cucumbers with their skin or without...and the romaine, did she prefer it torn or sliced...and what about the tomatoes? I'm not fifteen, she said to herself, how I cut the tomatoes doesn't matter. I'm an adult. I've been cutting tomatoes for years. If she doesn't like it, tough. We're getting to know each other—that's what this is about.

"How's the film coming? Are you going to make our band famous?"

"Moving along. Editing now. Should be finished after the pride parade."

"Can't wait to see it."

"We'll have a screening for the band."

Carla set the table in the kitchen, an old-fashioned '50s laminate table with chrome legs—a bright yellow. She used red and yellow plates on placemats with a Southwestern motif. When she finished, Carla sat, draped a leg over her opposite knee, leaned back in her chair, and sipped her wine. "Delicious. How did you know that I love a good pinot grigio?"

"Lucky guess."

Carla chatted about the band. "Kelley's a great director. She somehow gets the most out of everybody. Really an inspiration."

Anna watched Carla's tongue lick her lips after each sip. She felt a sudden opening in her own body, a path through her that hadn't been there before—an excavation almost—a discovery of something new. Some warm, new, open place. She tried to stay focused on the actual conversation, not the one in her head or her body.

Anna finished cutting the vegetables. "Is there a salad dressing you want me to use, or do you like dressing it yourself?"

"Whatever you want."

Anna looked through the bottles of salad dressing in the door of the refrigerator. Carla continued to chat about the band while Anna considered French, blue cheese, raspberry vinaigrette, poppy seed, chipotle ranch. Some were low fat, others weren't. Her heart pounded as she took all of them out and placed them on the table. It seemed like too much.

Carla stood and came over to Anna. "Is something the matter? You seem jittery."

"No, I'm not. I just don't know how you like your salad."

Carla reached out and put her hand on Anna's cheek. "It's okay. Whatever you do is just fine with me. Relax." She wanted to lean into Carla, soak up the warmth that came from her hand. Instead, she dropped her eyes and moved away.

"I'm relaxed. The chicken mole smells delicious. Hard to make?"

"No big deal. More wine?" Carla filled Anna's glass, then raised her own. "A toast to new friends," she said softly and touched her glass to Anna's.

Carla smiled as they both sat down, the kind of smile that lit her face, filled her eyes with warmth, invitation. Anna sipped her wine and then concentrated on unfolding her napkin and placing in on her lap.

"Everything looks delicious," she said and wondered if she had just said the same thing moments before. She tried to rally some identity inside of herself who knew how to behave. There was no one to come to her rescue. She sat across the table from a lovely woman, about her own age, to share a dinner prepared with kindness and welcome, and she felt as shy as a young girl at her first dance. Her throat was dry. The wine hadn't lubricated anything.

Carla served the chicken mole, rice, and beans. Anna started with salad and then took a tiny forkful of the mole. The burn of chiles caught her unaware, and she reached for water. Tears filled her eyes. She looked up and tried to smile. "Delicious," she said.

"Too spicy for you?"

"Maybe a little," she admitted. "I'll get used to it," she said, and she ate another small forkful. "I want to like it."

Carla shook her head and chuckled. Anna joined her.

"I've always wanted to like spicy food, and I've really never given it a try." She drank some more water. "Although it might be tougher than I thought."

Carla got up and poured a small glass of milk for Anna. "Try this; it works much better than water."

She sipped the milk and discovered it coated her throat, cooled her. She took another forkful of the mole and then a quick drink of milk. "Much better," she said.

Carla patted Anna's back as she took her seat at the table. "You don't have to finish it. It takes time to develop new tastes."

Anna noticed that the piano music from the den had been replaced by a plaintive sax, and then she heard herself saying, "My husband died last year. We were married for thirty years."

Carla nodded but otherwise didn't respond.

They ate in silence until Anna put her fork down and began to trace the edge of the placemat with her fingernail.

"He had a stroke. Suddenly. We were talking in the kitchen. We noticed it was getting cold, early in September. 'Get in touch with the furnace people,' he said and went to watch the news. I heard a thump. He was on the floor, unconscious, when I found him. He never came to. The doctors told us he was brain dead. We had to decide to disconnect the life supports. My kids and me."

"No time to say good-bye."

Anna shook her head.

"You mentioned your kids..."

"Yeah. Twins. Larry's in Berkeley now. He has two children. Lily's a lawyer at a public justice firm in Arizona. I'm not sure if either of them will ever live in Seattle again—maybe Lily."

"You miss them."

"More lately than ever before. I'd like to see the grandchildren more, too. I talk with Lily often, but she's absorbed in her new job, new people, new challenges."

"You see them constantly, and then they're gone."

"Yeah. They both were in and out of the hospital when Mort, my husband, had the stroke. As much as they could be. Lily was still living here, but she had so many obligations. The doctors said he was brain dead, and that we should let him go. Literally, let them remove life supports."

"I never had to make that decision. Was it awful?"

"I couldn't do it. Even though I taught about hospice at Seattle Community College. I had taught it for years. I knew everything about what the family's supposed to do. Supposed to feel." Anna's chest was tight, her breathing shallow. I need to stop, she thought. I don't need this now. "I couldn't do it."

Anna's attention drifted to a saxophone riff coming from the den. She wanted to tell Carla about the endless hours at Mort's bedside, but didn't have the words for the confusion she'd felt, the fear. She and the twins had been like actors on a set without a script.

She had no script now, either. "You've certainly had your share of death as well," Anna said. "It's always hard." She sat up straighter, adjusted her wristwatch. "Your children are here in Seattle, aren't they?"

Carla started to clear the table. Anna rose to help, but Carla motioned for her to stay seated. "Yes. I'm lucky. Both of my children are here in Seattle."

"Grandchildren?"

"Three." Carla left the dishes in the sink. "Come look at the pictures." Carla took her hand—just took her hand and raised her up from the chair. Carla's fingers, warm and strong, led her back to the den. Photos covered the walls.

"You saw the pictures of Orlando and Bobbie the other day. These are the grandchildren. These two little guys belong to Orlando, and this little tomboy is Bobbie's only one. But I'm hoping for more. Plus," she waved her hand across the wall covered with photos, "I have three sisters and two brothers. All of them have kids. All of them live here in the Seattle area."

"Amazing. I can't imagine..."

"Oh, yeah. Lots of drama."

"I have one sister on the East Coast—a religious nut. Born again, but no better than the first time." Anna had used the same line for years. "She was Jewish and then found Christ. Her kids are double borns, praying for my salvation whenever my name is mentioned. Mort, my husband, was an only child. So there's really not much family."

"Parents?" Carla asked. Anna chest felt heavy. She looked around for a place to sit, but if she sat on the sofa, her back would be to the pictures. Maybe the wine was making her tired.

Carla repeated herself. "Are your parents still alive?"

"Dead. My mother died when I was in college, before I married. My dad, a few years ago."

"I'm sorry."

"It's okay. No need to be sorry. That's just life."

"And it's not over yet."

"I suppose that's true." Anna perched herself on the arm of the sofa, turned toward the wall, and pointed to a photo of a stately woman taken sometime in the 1940s. "Who's that?"

"Ah, Tía Suelo. She's over one hundred now. She lives in Eugene. She had nineteen grandchildren by the time she was forty-five. God knows how many great-grandchildren, and I suppose great-great-grandkids as well. She keeps a saints' calendar with each child's birthday and remembers all of her nephews and nieces as well. She's amazing." Carla pointed to another photograph. "These are my parents on their wedding day."

Anna stood and examined the picture. The woman could have been Carla's twin.

"They were married over fifty years and died within a month

of each other. Here's my nephew Mickey when he graduated from Western. Here's Claudio, another nephew, playing tennis. Ricardo when he joined the Marines. Here's Sylvia and Jim—yes, Jim—on their honeymoon."

Anna listened to the melody of Carla's voice, rising and falling with the lines of the narrative, as she spoke about her family. Anna stopped noting the specific words and instead observed Carla as she talked, her face animated, reflecting a deep interest and sincere caring for the people in her life.

Anna took a seat directly on the sofa. A question that had been hovering along the periphery of her thoughts abruptly emerged. "Do they all accept your lifestyle?"

"Do you mean are they okay with me being a lesbian?" Carla asked as she sat down next to Anna and took her hand in her own. "Now they do. I won't have it any other way. I don't hide anymore. Is that a problem for you?"

"No. I don't know really. It's all so new to me." Anna wanted to pull her hand away and run out of the house, but her hand felt so warm and safe in Carla's, she left it there. She could smell the starch from Carla's shirt and a hint of wine.

She felt a current between them, a solid connection that drew her. She wanted to cuddle into Carla's body, but instead said, "Koru, my dog. He's waiting for me. I've got to get going. Thank you for a delicious dinner."

"I'll have to meet this Koru, the guy who is taking you away so soon."

Anna blushed. "I think he'd like to meet you, too." She moved toward the door.

Carla grinned and said, "Do you want some mole to take home?"

"I'll pass on that."

Anna paused by the door after collecting her things. Carla paused beside her.

"I'm drawn to you," Carla said, and she ran her thumb along Anna's jaw. "I think you feel it, too."

Anna nodded.

Carla leaned into Anna, took her face between her hands, and touched her lips to Anna's. Soft, warm. Supple. Terribly intimate. Anna rested against the door as Carla placed her hands on either side of Anna's face and brought her lips to Anna's again. Oh dear, Anna thought, opening to receive another kiss. Not a light one this time, but a tongue-touching embrace. Oh dear, she thought.

She pulled back and ducked under Carla's arm. "I'm straight, you know," she blurted. She blushed, then raised her palm to Carla's cheek and held it there as she spoke. "I'll call you."

Carla touched Anna's hand with her own and smiled. "I look forward to it."

"Thanks again for dinner," Anna mumbled as she rushed out of the door.

She ran to her car, drove up the block, stopped the car, and giggled. Oh my. Amazing. Oh, God. It had felt so good to kiss Carla. Could she be a lesbian, after thirty years of marriage? No, that would be crazy. Obviously, she was only lonely and attracted to Carla's warmth. It didn't mean anything.

She started the engine again and drove toward her house. This is not a good idea, she thought. I don't want this, don't care if it felt right. It just isn't who I am.

Chapter 14

The glare of the supermarket's fluorescent lighting shocked her after the cozy warmth of Carla's house. Anna wanted to turn around immediately and go home. Almost empty at this time of night, the store loomed large and overwhelming.

At a minimum she needed milk for her morning coffee, and while she was there, she should get some other things. The rattling sound of the shopping cart's wheels broke the silence in the store. At least milk, she thought as she approached the dairy section. Without thinking, she placed a container of cottage cheese in the cart on the way to get her milk.

Mort had loved cottage cheese, the comfort food he cherished—as long as it was served with canned peaches. She'd been buying both for over thirty years. No longer necessary. Anna replaced that cottage cheese container with yogurt.

The cart, one of the impossible ones to maneuver, clattered along between the aisles. No point in going back to the front for one that worked. She stopped and stared at the display of Kraft Mac and Cheese, another one of Mort's favorites.

After his stroke, he never ate again. Only a drip to keep him alive. She'd watched the drip for hours, watched the nurses come in, jiggle the bag a bit, and then exchange it for another. She never figured out the schedule.

All day, every day, Anna sat in a stiff, imitation-leather armchair next to his bedside. A dog walker attended to Koru, as did Becky, their neighbor. Anna returned home only to shower, sleep, and select another fashionable outfit for the day. Jewelry, makeup, clothes Mort had loved—just in case he woke up. She wanted to be beautiful for him.

First he'd been in the intensive care unit, so visitors were limited. She couldn't remember much from the first few days. Larry had flown up immediately, and Lily sat with her when she could take time from her packed work schedule. Larry left after three days. He had believed the doctors when they'd said Mort was brain dead. Anna hadn't believed them.

"His hand moved. And his jaw."

"Very common in coma patients—just the nervous system causing twitching. There is no brain activity."

Machines near his bed droned on, a steady hum interrupted regularly by the hissing sound of the blood pressure machine initiating the next check of his vitals. Other beeps and squeaks of unknown origin surprised her a few times each hour. The scent of flowers from friends and colleagues covered the strong smell of antiseptic.

She remembered Josh Rosen, Mort's internist, standing at the end of the bed with a nurse by his side. "We're going to transfer him out of intensive care, but there will be no change. Mort never completed an end-of-life end-of-life directive, so, Anna, you have to make the decision."

Despite all of Mort's careful planning, including a prepaid funeral, he had somehow neglected to complete an end-of-life preference form. Anna looked to Larry for guidance, since Lily never stopped crying. Larry agreed with the doctors; it was simplest, and he seemed to just want to get back to his work saving the planet. Lily, dazed and bewildered, looked as if she'd been caught in a hurricane. Anyway, the decision belonged to Anna, not to their children.

"I need time," Anna had said. "I need more time."

They moved Mort out of the ICU into a private room. Although there were many messages on her voicemail, visitors stopped coming. Even Jack, his business partner, stopped coming after the first week.

She counted ceiling tiles: eighteen across, twenty down. She raised and lowered the blinds. She let in light because she thought that would help. Then she closed the blinds because too much light might give Mort a headache.

Mostly, she talked to him. She'd heard about cases of people coming out of comas, when patients shocked their doctors. So she kept on talking.

She often took his hand and pressed her thumb into the center of his palm until it sank into the softness—skin with no muscle tone. She rubbed each finger separately. And she talked.

"Your mother was so funny at our wedding. Remember? She kept pulling the photographer everywhere to take pictures. Remember the guy kept telling her to trust him, but she wouldn't? She liked to control everything. Sort of like you." Anna studied him for a reaction, but there was nothing—only the hiss and beep of machines.

Mort's usual ruddy complexion had turned sallow, almost green under the florescent lights. An attendant shaved him every morning, and by the evening he had a shadow. Mort would have hated that. He often shaved twice a day if they had evening plans. She thought about asking them to shave him again in the afternoon, but never got around to it.

She gathered bouquets of memories and arranged them for him. "Remember our honeymoon? Hawaii? I couldn't believe you'd saved that much money. You wanted me to hula dance for you in the bedroom, but I was too embarrassed. Remember? Remember when we walked near the arboretum, yes, before we were married. We rolled around in the leaves piled up and threw them at each other. I wore that red down vest, and you wore that huge, ugly, beige car coat—the one your mother bought for you. You were just out of law school, lots of dreams. You kept trying to pinch my butt. I acted horrified, but you knew I wasn't."

Anna massaged his legs. Used an aromatic cream. She'd heard that sometime scents brought people out of comas. She'd told him she loved him, needed him. She wondered at the time if that had been a lie. Maybe he didn't wake up because he had known she had been lying. Not lying really, but not telling the whole truth, either.

She had needed him. At least she thought she had needed him. The house was so empty now, a big, huge house on Green Lake, great for entertaining his associates.

Each night when she returned to the house, Koru jumped all over her, licked her face, nearly knocked her over. She confessed to Koru in bed about the empty kisses, the faked orgasms, the boredom she had felt listening to Mort's stories about work. Maybe that happened in a lot of marriages after so many years together. She knew Koru would never tell.

The sound of cans being stacked on the shelf next to her brought her from her reverie to the grocery aisle. She looked down at her cart. Milk and bananas. She'd better get focused, she thought. She had no idea what to buy. Maybe TV dinners.

"Mom," Larry had said when Anna was struggling with her decision about Mort's treatment. "Mom. You need to let him go. Dad wouldn't want to live like this. The medical costs alone would drive him up the wall."

"Don't worry. The insurance will pay some, and I'll pay the rest. You're not paying it."

"You're missing the point. The money that's keeping his body going could be used to help people who really need help. Dad is gone."

"You're so cold. I can't believe you. That's your father lying there."

"That's not my father. My father is dead."

She had wanted to kick him. Slap him. Spit in his face. But she had known he was right.

Now she walked toward the freezers at Albertsons to study the selection of entrées. Upkeep here at the supermarket was slipping. Frost was building up on the shelves. She smiled. Frozen. She had been frozen then. She had known Larry and the doctors were right. She was a hospice specialist, for God's sake. She had known better.

Then one morning, Dr. Rosen showed up again. She hadn't seen him for at least a week. He walked into the room wearing a crisp, freshly starched white coat. Very doctorly. Freshly shaven. "Anna. How are you?" He picked up Mort's chart and flipped through the pages.

Anna stood and let him hug her. She'd known him for years. She smelled some kind of fancy aftershave. "The business office called me. They asked me to talk with you."

She moved across the room and looked out at the window. A heavy fog covered the city. The nearby buildings appeared as dark blotches.

"The business office?" They must have asked him to make the pitch.

Rosen walked up and stood next to her. The machines keeping Mort alive droned in the background. "Your insurance gives him another few days here. Then we have to transfer him to a nursing home."

"Can they do more for him there?" She whispered the question, although she knew the answer before she asked.

"No, Anna. There's nothing anyone can do. Every test has been done. His brain is not functioning at all." Dr. Rosen put his hand on her shoulder and held it there. "It's time to let him go."

She looked straight into his eyes. His eyes were compassionate; hers, she knew, were flat and empty.

"Let me know what you decide. We'll make the arrangements." He hugged her again and left the room.

She rubbed her chest. Round and round her hand moved in circles as she continued to stare out the window at nothing in particular. She moved back to the bed and took one of Mort's hands in her own. His nails needed to be trimmed.

She went out to the nurse's station and got a small scissors, trimmed the nails on his hands and then on his feet, and went home early that day.

Koru howled when he heard her drive into the garage. He always knew the moment she arrived. Anna sat down on the floor in the kitchen and held him tightly, rubbed her face against his fur. "It's time, Koru. It's time."

Larry flew up from Berkeley. She and Lily picked him up at the airport. Between Rosh Hashanah and Yom Kippur—the days of awe. They all stood next to the bed when Dr. Rosen signaled the withdrawal of life support. Tears ran down Lily's cheeks. Anna held her hand tightly. Neither she nor Larry cried.

A year had passed, and she'd been in a fog for most of it. Anna loaded several frozen dinners into her cart and headed for the cashier. Maybe soon she'd buy some real food and invite Carla to dinner.

Chapter 15

Koru raced through the dog door when he heard Anna approach the house. He nearly knocked her over before she managed to get the grocery bags on the table. Anna reached into his cookie jar. "Sit, shake." The extent of Koru's education. He took his Milk-Bone into the living room. Anna walked through the house, which was silent except for Koru's crunching. She sat on the floor next to her dog and rubbed his back.

"Koru, I think you'll like Carla. I haven't asked her if she likes dogs, but who wouldn't love you? Maybe you'll meet her soon." Anna sniffed, "Except you stink. It's way past time for a grooming."

Carla's lips had been yielding, delicious. Nothing like Mort's perfunctory kisses. Probably his kisses had once been tender, but Anna only remembered the pursed-lip puckers hard against her mouth. I'm-in-a-hurry kisses. Let's-get-to-the-main-act kind of kisses.

"Bedtime, Koru. Let's go."

She looked around their bedroom. Hers now. She noticed the book Mort had been reading still perched on his nightstand. She picked up *The Path to Power*, the Johnson biography, and put it in a Nordstrom bag she got from her closet. She added a nail clipper, small notepad, a few pens, an extra pair of glasses, a flashlight, and a couple of paperback spy thrillers that were in the drawer. She placed the bag in the hall and then reached for her pajamas, turned down the covers, and stopped when she noticed Mort's closet.

Anna hadn't opened the closet door since she had helped the twins pick some of Mort's things for themselves. Now she opened it. No surprise, there was a sour smell coming from the laundry in the hamper. Shoes sat on their shelves, precisely arranged according to style. The wingtips—brown, black, gray; the Italian loafers; sports shoes—golf, tennis, running. Koru pushed past Anna and sniffed at Mort's dog-walking shoes casually sitting on the floor where he had taken them off an hour before his stroke.

The kids had already taken what they wanted. Lily had wanted the Mariners jerseys, and Larry took a ski sweater and Mort's watch. He had tried on a few suit jackets, but Larry's arms were longer and his shoulders broader than Mort's had been.

Anna leaned against the doorjamb, felt her eyelids heavy after a long day, her legs achy. If she closed her eyes, she could still see Mort standing near the closet in his boxer shorts, the mole on his shoulder visible as he turned and rummaged in his sock drawer. He would sit on the bench at the end of the bed every morning to tie his shoes and often smile at her still lounging in bed as he worked the knot in his tie into the exact correct position.

She stretched and closed the door. Time for a bath, and then sleep. Again she reached under her pillow for pajamas and noticed Mort's gray flannel robe still hanging on a hook on the back of the bedroom door. It had been right there for a year, invisible, and now she scarcely saw anything else in the room.

Koru had been watching her from the bed, but jumped off to follow Anna as she ran down to the basement for a box of large trash bags. She stuffed the robe into a bag, then went back to his closet and added all of his shoes. She would donate it all. His underwear, socks, and T-shirts filled another bag. Dress shirts still in plastic envelopes from the laundry went next.

Her rhythm slowed when she turned to the suits. Flannel, tweed, herringbone, worsted wool. No polyester. Mort had hated polyester. There was the navy flannel he had worn every Rosh Hashanah for years. She smelled the synagogue on his suit—the old books, kiddush. She picked at a long, silken, blue thread she found on the sleeve—likely from his tallis. Where was his tallis? She wondered if Larry wanted it. Had he taken it already?

His size hadn't changed over their years of marriage, unlike her own. His suits had lasted for years…conservative styles, expensive fabrics, three Armanis. He'd been proud that he could afford them and had worn them on court days. She started with the oldest suits and methodically folded them, placing them carefully in separate bags. Her arms became heavy and her fingers clumsy. She sat on the floor. There were more empty hangers now than ones with suits. Mort's smell lingered in the closet—his Old Spice aftershave. All those years he had worn it, never changing to something new. No matter what she bought for him—new, trendy, sexy fragrances—he'd stuck with Old Spice.

She reached for his favorite gray tweed sports jacket and

rubbed the collar against her cheek, remembering the feel of her head resting against his shoulder whenever they danced.

She followed the same routine as she had with the other jackets: checked the outside pockets and then the inside ones. She'd found nothing. He always emptied his pockets. Something crinkled inside this jacket. Anna reached her fingers deep into the inside pocket and pulled out a small scrunched-up piece of paper. A credit card receipt. The Four Seasons Hotel in Seattle. Almost four hundred dollars. One night.

They'd never stayed at the Four Seasons downtown. December 2, 1998. Bizarre. Maybe paying for a client? Why hadn't he submitted it? Maybe he had.

The muscles in her forearms tightened; her shoulders tensed. Impossible. Anna felt like a character in a soap opera. She examined the card number—not their credit card, but it had his signature. Maybe his office account.

Koru didn't budge this time when Anna left the bedroom and went down to Mort's office in the basement. She hadn't been there since Jack, his partner, picked up everything he needed to transfer Mort's current cases. She'd gotten a big check. Jack paid her half of what the practice was worth. Paid in several payments. Was still paying. Jack had taken care of everything. She knew little about their law practice.

Here in Mort's home office, his things essentially remained as they had the last time he had been there. A cleaning crew had dusted, but otherwise it had been untouched. Mort's briefcase stood where she had left it after Jack had taken the files out. She found the calendar for 1999. Where was '98? In the corner of a closet full of Mort's overcoats, raincoats, and jackets, Anna found the large file box of personal belongings Jack had delivered with the first check. Mort's things from his other office. There under some books, she came across the calendar she needed.

She turned to December 2, 1998. Court—the Odegaard case. Embezzlement, she remembered. And there, in his precise printing, next to 6:00 pm, was the letter *H* followed by a dash and then the initials *F. S.* Four Seasons, maybe? But what was *H*? Or who was *H*? Probably a client.

Like a bad movie, she thought. Anna dragged the box across the carpet to the leather sofa where Mort sometimes slept. He would work late and then decide to take a nap. In the morning, she'd come downstairs to look for him, only to find him still fully dressed, his shoes neatly placed under the sofa, sound asleep.

The sofa felt stiff now against her thighs. She'd always hated the slick feel of the leather, ungiving and slippery at the same time. She had rarely spent time in this room. He worked. She ran the house. He had his job and he managed the finances. She also had her work as a lecturer, although not full-time, so that she had plenty of time to care for the children and the dog, maintain their home and garden, and manage their social life.

Especially since the twins left years ago—they had had a clear division of labor. They never fought. Although they didn't have sex as frequently as they had early in their marriage, they still had it sometimes. He thought she was beautiful. He always told her so.

The Four Seasons. Absurd. She started back from December 2 and looked for appointments with *H*. She found them. A lot of them. Not all of them at the Four Seasons, but a lot of *H*s.

She put everything back into the box and dragged it back to the closet. He was dead. What difference did it make? Anna shivered. Too cold in the basement. Despite the fancy remodel, it was still a cellar.

She needed to relax. Needed a hot bath. Needed to think. Needed not to think. She walked through the dark house, the street light on Meridian like a moon hanging through the dining room window. She checked the front door and found it locked, checked the back door and put a chair under the knob so she could hear if someone tried to break in. She set the alarm and then walked around and checked all the windows. No cars were on the street. Such a peaceful, quiet street. Lots of families.

She checked the doors again and went back downstairs to Mort's office. She switched on the thick brass lamp on his desk, sat in his chair, and looked around the room. She saw Larry's tennis awards, Mort's college degree, his framed law degree. Photos of him with political cronies. He had been a big donor. Certificates of acknowledgement from the Jewish Federation. His personal world. Little of that was in the rest of the house. Mementos. She opened the drawers. Neatly lined up pens. Legal pads. Paper clips. Everything neat.

There must be something here about *H*. She thought of all the mysteries she had read, the TV shows she'd seen. Where did people hide things? She pulled each drawer out one by one, searched them, dumped the contents on the floor, and then turned them over to look for envelopes taped to the bottom. Nothing. Law books. The same way. The framed certificates. There had to be something. She rummaged through the file cabinets searching for *H*. She didn't bother putting anything back.

Then she noticed a manila envelope on the credenza in plain sight. In Mort's small printing she read "for Anna." How long had it been there?

She brought it to her nose. An old smell, basement smell, not-touched smell, ignored smell. It was an old envelope, wrinkled. Mort must have used it for something else, or opened and closed this one a lot. Anna knew all the legal papers had been located and processed long ago, so this was something different. Before finding the receipt, she would have been thrilled to find an envelope from Mort for her. Now her trembling fingers could scarcely hold it.

Maybe she should just put the envelope in the shredder,

imagine she'd never found it. Anna had difficulty swallowing, her throat scratchy and dry. She needed to relax, take a long bath, and then she would open the envelope. Taking the envelope, she quietly turned, walked into the small hallway, and climbed the stairs.

The evening had been warm, but Anna shivered as she took off her clothes in her bedroom. She saw herself in the bathroom mirror. A different woman than the one who had spent the evening with Carla. That one was happy, lovely. Big, dark eyes; full lips; thick, luscious hair. This one looked weird, a hyena. Red eyes; thin lips; wrinkled, blotchy skin. She filled the tub with bubbles and hot, hot water.

Anna stretched out in the tub, felt the hot water ease the tension in her body. She slid her hands over her droopy breasts and flabby stomach. Rubbery to her touch now. Slippery. She could barely remember when her skin had been firm, soft, had had a shape. Not the sagging that was her now.

Who would want her? Clearly Mort hadn't. Had she driven him away? Who was *H*? What was in the envelope? If she shredded the envelope now, she'd never know and could go on as before. A new romance, maybe. Maybe Carla would become her lover. Would another woman be kinder to an old body?

She arranged the soapy bubbles over herself and felt tears running along her cheeks. She let them slide down her face and into the tub. She added more hot water and noticed her legs turning red under the bubbles. Too hot in here, she thought. Her heart beat rapidly, and she knew she'd have to get out soon. She added more cold but couldn't get the balance right.

She decided she would open the envelope in the morning. Everything would look better in the morning. Pulling herself up, she stood, stepped out of the tub, and rubbed herself dry with an oversized towel.

Wrapped in the towel, Anna crossed the bedroom and dug

around in her dresser until she found her old navy nightshirt. She remembered Larry's tiny hot body clinging to her chest when he had had pneumonia. As she pulled it from the drawer, she noticed the hem was half out and the lace on the sleeves was raggedy after so many washings. But it was soft, and she needed soft. Remarkably, it still fit.

She lifted the envelope off of her nightstand, got a whiff of his Old Spice. She ran her fingers over its stiff, brittle surface. How long had it been lying in the open in Mort's office? Carefully, she leaned it against his pillow. It would still be there in the morning.

She turned off the lamp and slid between the covers, relishing the soothing feel of the cool sheets against her hot body. The down bed mattress pad she'd bought after Mort died welcomed her, cushioned her. Mort had liked the bed firm.

Anna lay in the darkness. Closed her eyes. Yearned for sleep. She turned away from the envelope but felt its presence like a lighthouse sending out a beacon, a danger signal flashing at her in the darkness.

She dug deeper under her quilt, closed her eyes more tightly. She felt like a frightened child hiding from a bully. Her eyes kept opening. She knew she couldn't stay in the dark any longer.

Chapter 16

Anna shook the standard-sized manila envelope and heard the lopsided sounds of its different-sized contents. The clasp was worn. She turned it over and over. "For Anna" on the outside. No date. No other marks at all.

Koru slept on his usual spot at the foot of the bed. He'd always slept there, even when Mort was alive. He hadn't budged since she got in her bath, although occasionally he'd panted and kicked his leg as if he were in a dream, running.

Anna opened the clasp and peeked inside: some folded documents and a small sandwich-sized baggie. First the baggie, she thought, and spread its contents out before her on the bed. Only two items. A snapshot of a man and a woman leaning against a car and a worn business card with a phone number on the back. Without her glasses, she couldn't make out the faces in the picture, the phone number, or the name on the card. She needed her glasses.

Last chance not to know, she thought. Then she reached for her glasses on the nightstand. She could still shred everything and speculate for the rest of her life. Make up stories about Mort. Would she rather know the truth? Not necessarily, she thought. Mort had wanted her to see this. So? She put her glasses back on the bedside table, closed her eyes, and remembered Mort as he lay in a coma at Swedish Hospital.

Had he been dreaming about someone else? Had *H* known that he had had a stroke and was dying? Did *H* know he was dead? Had this *H*—some woman—thought that Mort had just abandoned her, that she never could reach him. There had been a rather long obituary in the *Intelligencer*. Prominent lawyer, survived by…etc. But did *H* read the obituaries?

She tried to remember if there had ever been phone calls to the house. The suspicious kind: silence and then a hang-up. She couldn't remember. She didn't remember much from that time—only sitting in the hospital and then the fog when he died.

If she wanted a future, she would have to stay awake. See clearly. She put on her glasses.

She examined the photograph first. A four-by-six picture. Mort with a small, thin, blond woman in her mid-thirties. Both smiled brightly at the camera: Mort in his navy polo shirt with beige slacks, his favorite Dockers, and she in a pale pink sundress, tanned and holding a large white hat in her right hand. "February 1990" written on the back—not in Mort's handwriting. Mort would have been forty-eight. They leaned against a car she didn't recognize. Palm trees in the background—certainly not Seattle. Maybe it had been a quick fling in '90, a midlife-crisis fuck. Business trip? Who took the picture? Who else knew about this?

The business card was a fine linen paper, embossed, expensive. Helen Dahlberg, attorney-at-law with a downtown Seattle address. A colleague. Maybe they had worked on some cases together. Why had he left it for Anna? He could have left the business card in his old Rolodex. But not the picture, she thought. Maybe this was a crush? A fantasy on his part. The dream of the blond? A *shiksa*? A younger woman? Was she a real blond? Did it matter?

Then there were the folded papers. She removed her glasses and separated three different documents, one of heavy, note-sized light blue vellum, with writing in what appeared to be a woman's hand. Then some kind of printed document, and then another folded sheet of typing paper.

She'd read them later.

Her chest tight, she realized that she hadn't been breathing. An ache like a huge gas pain. A heart attack? She heard that gas was a symptom in women. She was getting to be that age. Who would find her body, dead, here on the bed, surrounded by these papers? She adjusted the pillows, leaned back against them, and tried to take some very deep breaths. Too much for one night, she thought. First Carla and her chicken mole, and then this. She laughed quietly, and then the tears started again. She swallowed hard and kept trying to breathe deeply, to fill her abdomen and then let the air out slowly. She needed to calm herself. She thought of how she had torn about Mort's office and understood she was in new territory.

Koru looked up when Anna got out of bed but decided to stay cozy himself. He stood then walked in a few circles until he found the perfect spot to settle comfortably again.

Anna found some antacids in the bathroom and took a few with a glass of water. She put on slippers and her robe, picked up all the papers and her eyeglasses, and went to the kitchen. She needed tea.

Her hand held tightly to the railing as she went down to the kitchen, her joints stiff, her walk mechanical. She took each step with precision and caution. The clock on the stove read 2:25 a.m. No noise from the street, no wind tonight, just the whisper of the envelope sliding from her hand onto the table. The clatter of the teacup, the slow bubbling of the water, even that so loud in the silence. She poured a shot of whiskey into her cup, then the water when it was hot enough. She took the tea and went into the den.

Her favorite Billie Holiday collection lay next to the stereo. She pressed play, and Billie's rich voice filled the room. She sat on the love seat, covered herself with the afghan, and sipped her tea. Within minutes she was up and back at the kitchen table. Back at the envelope. She washed her bifocals at the kitchen sink and wiped them on her robe.

Anna ignored the note and folded typewriter paper and unfolded the printed document first. A copy of a birth certificate. A birth certificate? Dated May 11, 1992. Baby girl Rachel Dahlberg. Mort's mother's name had been Rachel. Seven pounds twelve ounces. Mother: Helen Dahlberg, age 37. Father: Mortimer Simon, age 50. Her fingers trembled. She put the paper down.

She could hear Billie Holiday singing from the den—"In My Solitude"—the silky sound of despair. She could feel the whiskey warming her body. So she poured another shot of whiskey into her cup and added more hot water. She didn't know where to put herself. Koru was up now and following her.

Anna walked into the dining room and looked at the china cabinet. Blown glass from Florence. Mort's mother's china. Mort's bar mitzvah kiddush cup. Larry's. Lily's. She glanced at the table; it expanded to seat at least a dozen. Passover. Thanksgiving. Birthday parties. She turned back to the den, could see Mort's leather chair through the doorway, and walked back upstairs to their room. Their bed. His side. Her side. His pillow was memory foam and hers, down feathers. Who had he been?

Anna finally found herself on the floor in a corner of her closet. She scrunched her knees close to her chest and slowly sipped her hot toddy. She noticed the raggedy lace on her nightshirt sleeves. She pulled hard and ripped it all off. She gathered her body in, making herself as small as she could, and sat quietly in the darkness. Koru curled up again and snuggled next to her, hoping for some ear scratches. Slowly the whiskey helped with the pain in her chest—the pain in her heart—and she smiled. She had heartache. It really does ache.

Mort used to drink tea with whiskey when he thought he was coming down with a cold. Anna remembered that Mort's mother swore by tea with whiskey. "Add a little lemon," she'd say, "it'll fix whatever hurts you." Did Helen Dahlberg know that? Did his daughter know anything about the family? Had his daughter known him? Was she alive? Had he ever seen her? Was Helen Dahlberg still in Seattle? Did this child have any legal rights to his estate?

And then for the first time since she'd found the receipt, she thought about the kids. Lily and Larry had a sister, a half sister, but a sister nevertheless. Larry used to ask for a brother. Lily used to want a sister. Now she had one. Anna realized she could still destroy all the papers and try to forget this—move on with her life. Start again, as she had been doing with her video class and maybe even with Carla. But that would never change the facts. The twins had a sister.

The whiskey, the quiet of the closet, and Billie Holiday in the background gradually calmed her. She must have dozed on the floor of her closet. She woke still curled into herself, stiff and tired.

She stretched, stood, walked—tried to work the kinks out of her back, her legs. The clock on her bedside table read 4:00 a.m.

She knew there was more in the envelope. Damn envelope. Damn Mort.

Koru stood, stretched, and then raced downstairs, heading for his dog door. Anna followed him to the kitchen. While she waited for Koru to pee, she glanced back at the unread documents on the kitchen table.

Was there a letter explaining everything? Another birth certificate? An addition to his will? Maybe even a marriage certificate? Maybe Mort had been a bigamist as well as an adulterer.

She rubbed her eyes and stretched again. When Koru returned, Anna gave him a biscuit to eat while she opened a can of wet food and replenished his kibble dish. She replaced all the documents in the envelope. Maybe it looked so used because Mort kept putting things in and then taking them out—trying to decide what she needed to know, what he wanted her to know. The bastard. She had no more room in her brain, let alone her heart, for any more information.

She went back upstairs and crawled into bed. This time she fell asleep and didn't wake until she felt Koru licking her face in the late morning.

Chapter 17

All the cups were dirty. Anna got a stepstool to reach for one of the extra ones stored on an upper shelf of the kitchen cupboard. She'd have to run the dishwasher. Koru had been out already. Independent now with his new dog door.

The envelope lay on the kitchen table where she'd left it. No dream. She reached for the business card in the baggie.

"Washburn, Larson, and Dahlberg," a woman said in a crisp, receptionist voice. "May I help you?"

Anna opened her mouth to speak, but nothing emerged.

"May I help you? Is someone on the line?"

Anna sat on the chair and leaned against the cabinets. "Helen Dahlberg, please."

"I'm sorry, Ms. Dahlberg is in court this morning. May I take a message?"

Questions ran through Anna's mind. Questions about Helen having sex with Mort. Intimate questions about her husband making love with another woman. Questions about Mort and the little girl. But there was really no message. "No, no message. What kind of a law practice is this?"

"Beg your pardon?"

"I wondered what kind of a practice this is. I just got her name from someone, and I wasn't sure."

"Oh, I see. Corporate litigation. And we handle other issues that may come up for our clients. You're sure you don't want me to leave a message for Ms. Dahlberg?"

"No message," Anna said and hung up.

With her coffee in an old Kingdome cup, she walked out to the deck and hoped the chilly spring morning might cut through the thickness in her head. She tried not to rub her eyes, already so red and swollen this morning. She felt their puffiness with her fingers and then ran her fingertips across her dry lips. Anna's thoughts moved slowly, like explorers traveling though sludge.

She still held Helen Dahlberg's business card in her hand. She studied the phone number on the back, the personal number the woman must have written down for Mort. She recognized a Queen Anne neighborhood phone exchange.

Anna walked around the garden, sipping her coffee, studying the buds on the dogwood and the tiny swirling leaves on the Japanese maple. New growth about to emerge. The morning sun warmed her face. She looked back toward the deck. Koru was basking in the sun; behind him, the sliding doors to the kitchen, which now lay in the shadows. Two documents still waited for her there.

She chose the light blue vellum, dated two years before Mort's death and began to read.

My darling Baby Tiger,

Rachel's curled up in her bed sound asleep holding the stuffed walrus you brought her today. She named it Daddy. As you can imagine, that shocked me. What did she mean? Does she understand you are her daddy, or is she missing a daddy? When we talk, she always calls you Mort, and she knows you are Mommy's special friend.

You know, I thought I could do this, but when she hugged that stupid ugly little walrus to her face and said, "I love you, Daddy," I about lost it right there.

I can't do this anymore. We can't do this anymore. The decision is in your court—it always has been.

From the moment we met, your smile, your eyes entered my heart, and they have never left me—not for a moment. There will never be another man for me, and no other daddy for Rachel.

As you know, I am fine. I have a fulfilling career and a full life without you. Rachel and I want you and need you, but I do not want you to make your decision out of fear for our welfare.

There was another page, but Anna needed to breathe before she finished it. Baby Tiger? Baby Tiger? She repeated the phrase and over and over to herself as if it were in another language, an alien tongue. Mort, in his wingtips and suits, couldn't morph in her mind into Baby Tiger.

It was like a direct punch to her gut; she couldn't catch her breath. She stood in a corner of the kitchen, with the letter dangling from her hand, and waited. Koru sat at attention next to her, poised for a biscuit. When she didn't respond, he began one of his chortling howls. Anna realized she stood next to his biscuit jar. She handed him a treat, put on a sweatshirt, and took the letter outside.

She needed to get out of the house. Their house. Her house. She sat on the edge of the deck, Koru now resting at her feet. She started the second page.

We have talked so much about Anna and your relationship with her and the twins. I know that for a man of your integrity, you've made some choices that torture you.

Who knew when we met in Palm Springs so many years ago, that our paths would mingle—that our love would blossom into the beauty of Rachel?

The choice is yours, my darling. I love you and will always love you,

H.

Why on earth had Mort left this letter for her to read? Despite the sun, Anna shivered and went back into the house. What had he been thinking? Anna tried to find a passage through the muck clogging her brain, to find some clarity, but everything was murky. Nothing made sense.

At least now she knew for sure who *H* was. Anna and Mort had never stayed at the Four Seasons. She'd been to receptions, weddings, but it was so expensive to book a room. What about the money? So incredibly expensive. And what about this child? She'd be nine. Had Mort been supporting the child?

Anna knew little about her and Mort's finances. He had done it all. She'd put the money she earned in her own checking account, and Mort never needed or wanted her money. That's what she managed, and their accountant just handled everything for taxes. She used to sign her name at the bottom of the form. Mort knew she never checked anything. And how long had that envelope been in clear sight in his office?

Again, she thought about this path that she'd begun. Did she even want to travel it? She could still burn all these papers. The kids would never know about any of it.

Anna pictured Mort adjusting the covers every night, brushing his teeth. Talking to her. Kissing her good night. But there used to be late meetings, weekend conferences. Maybe afternoon rendezvous. Lying to her. For years. Had they ever had sex after he screwed Helen? She would have smelled another woman. Wouldn't she? Maybe he had showered.

She went back out into the yard, picked up a rock, and threw it against the garage wall. She picked up another and threw that one as hard as she could. She noticed a dent in the siding. Koru howled and ran around her. She picked up a larger one, aimed at the dent, and heard a crack when it landed.

Anna looked around the yard for something larger. She went

to the garage and got Lily's old Little League bat. She scrutinized the garden carefully, looking for a good target. The hyacinths were just starting to appear. The crocuses already blooming.

She clutched the bat and went down to Mort's office. Books and papers covered the floor. She kicked them aside and grabbed Mort's desk chair. One of his prized possessions. An antique, leather-seated, oak captain's chair he'd bought at an auction, said to have come from the office of a rural lawyer in eastern Washington.

Anna took careful aim and bashed the bat down against the arm of the chair. She heard a loud crack. She wrenched the arm off and then adjusted the chair to make the other arm accessible. She raised the bat again and bashed, harder and harder, until the second arm broke off. Then she attacked the back.

Crash, crack, crunch. She cherished the sounds of destruction. She raised the bat high over her head and brought it down on the old wood. Her sobs started somewhere around the tenth bash, just as her momentum built. She rubbed her runny nose with her sleeve and kept pounding the bat until even it cracked.

Koru's barks intensified—he had followed her in. He ran in circles and stumbled over the books and papers. Over and over again until her arms hurt, she bashed the bat into what remained of the chair. Koru was frantic. Anna grabbed his collar, put him in the hall, and closed the door. She leaned back against the door, wrapped her arms around her body, and slowly slid to the floor amidst the debris she had created. Would that she could open his casket and smash up his bones.

One document remained, but she didn't want to handle everything at once. Of course, it didn't make any difference. Since she'd found the receipt, there had been no return, but at least she could control the pace. Give herself time to absorb the blows.

She'd known this man, lived intimately with him: sucked his

dick, had his babies, cut his fucking toenails. Who the hell was he? She often watched *Oprah* and thought to herself, bullshit—they must have known. She herself would certainly know. Apparently not. Some *dybbuk*, some malevolent force, had been living in the house with her all this time, and she'd had no idea. That's the part that made her the sickest.

Anna left the broken bat on the floor with the other debris, opened the door to the hall, and knelt by Koru, still agitated and waiting outside the door for her. She nuzzled her face against his and whispered, "It's okay. I'm okay. We're fine. Just you and me. We're fine."

Slowly she climbed the steps back to the kitchen where she knew the last letter waited. Likely one from Mort. Well, it could wait. Leaning against the kitchen sink, she splashed water on her face, trying to cool her swollen eyes. Anna dampened a paper towel and pressed it against her eyelids and thought about calling someone, discussing it. Who could she tell? She couldn't tell the kids. Not yet. Maybe never.

Friends? Marilyn? Elise? It could be all over town in an hour. Very hot gossip. It would get around. Anyway, since Mort died, she hadn't felt close to any of them. They were all part of her old life. Their life, hers and Mort's, not her life. Carla? Could she call Carla? She hardly knew her.

Anna followed Koru outside and watched as he began his sniff-and-pee routine. Even the full morning sun couldn't warm her. Koru was digging under a peony bush and barking. Maybe a slug. Anna looked more closely and spotted a small turtle trying to escape Koru's nose. She pushed her dog aside and watched the turtle inch toward the shelter of bushes. Anna wondered if Koru had hurt him.

She wondered what the turtle was doing in her yard. She recognized the red stripe along the side of his head and knew he must be one of the turtles she'd often seen sunning on the log on the southwest edge of the lake. A very long walk for a little turtle. Maybe someone had taken him for a pet and then abandoned him. Carefully, she lifted the turtle. He smelled a bit like a rotten egg. Still alive, but barely.

She found an empty shoebox in the garage, placed him inside, and covered it. She grabbed her car keys and quickly drove to the turtle log on the other side of the lake. Anna heard movement from inside the box as she approached the water. No turtles sunning today; not quite warm enough for them. Where were they in the early spring? Not many people around, either.

She parked, got out of the car, tucking the box under her arm. She lifted the lid, pulled open the side of the box, and laid it next to the water's edge. "Go, little turtle, go," Anna said as she sat next to the box and waited. First his head came out slowly, his nose raised high. Then he pulled back into his shell. Maybe he was too weak to move his legs. She slid the box even closer so the edge lay in the water. Again his head came out, and this time his little legs followed, lifting his body as his feet found the ground.

He moved slowly at first, until his front legs reached the water, and then he seemed to melt into the lake. For a moment, Anna could see his limbs stretch and pull as he swam. Soon, she lost him in the darkness of the lake among a cluster of reeds growing near the log.

Anna moved to a bench just up from the shore, hoping for another glimpse of the little turtle. She hoped he would survive. Her eyes drifted from the lake to the path where she noticed an elderly couple engaged in conversation. They looked as if they had been together forever.

Why had Mort stayed with her? Laziness? Cowardice? Had he been lying to this Helen person—just wanted to screw and got stuck with a kid? Had he stayed with Anna out of pity?

She had thought they had ambled along together just fine…but apparently not. No wonder it hadn't made sense to her. Something had been missing. She always believed it was her. She knew it was her. Clearly. But he had been missing as well.

She pictured that damn manila envelope still lying on the kitchen table. She wished for the magical power to disintegrate the envelope from afar, to destroy its contents. Better yet, some drug that would erase the last hours from her memory. Instead, she returned to her home and opened the last letter.

Strange for her to see a whole letter in his handwriting. He had always used a typewriter, then a computer for writing. Accustomed to short notes from him, or lists, she had rarely seen a whole page of his tiny, barely legible writing.

Anna,

You're upstairs now in the kitchen talking with Lily after her graduation party. She's a lawyer now. No question she'll pass the bar.

As I watched our daughter in her cap and gown, I…I don't know where I will find the words to tell you what you need to know. As I watched Lily today with so much pride, I thought about my other daughter, Rachel, and wondered about her education and if I would ever see her graduate.

If you are reading this, you have discovered my secret. I'm sorry that you ever found out and sorrier still that you had to find out this way. I always imagined that I would have this all sorted out before I died, but I must be dead—you would never go through my office. You've always kept your distance from me and from my work and rarely came into my space. I know I can leave this envelope right on top of the desk and you'll never see it.

I wonder how you feel. Are you angry? Feeling betrayed?

You should. I betrayed both you and our vows. I lied about our life together. I am ashamed as I write this and almost didn't write it, but I have to tell you a few things.

I'm not sure what love is or what all the different kinds of love are. In my mind's eye, I always look at you and see the person I saw when we met. The bright-eyed, eager woman—sexy, vibrant, laughing. But somehow, somewhere, you became someone else. I don't know when it happened or how it happened. I wonder if I changed as much. I love the woman I married. And we had the twins, who brought with them so much joy. You were always so busy with them. Then you were busy taking care of my parents until they died.

I don't know why, but you changed. We stopped talking. I think we used to talk, and then we didn't anymore. But you are my wife, and I knew that no matter what, I would never leave you. I knew you would never leave me, either. We both are those kinds of people.

When I met Helen…No need to tell you about that—not too much, anyway. It was a mystery to me how someone, in a tiny space of time, could change my life, transform my insides. As you can imagine, Rachel was an accident. A blessed accident that in truth I cannot even talk about. But I've never abandoned you—I could not and will not. I cannot sever the bonds that I swore to when we married.

I have made all the financial arrangements necessary for Rachel. It doesn't shortchange you, Lily, or Larry in the least. As you know, there will be enough for all of you.

But I do need your help. I want the children to know about their sister, their half sister. I know what it feels like to be an only child, and I want her to know her siblings—should they decide that they want to pursue that relation-

ship. I need you to tell them about this—to let them know that she exists. I am ashamed to say that, although I've wanted to tell them myself, I cannot find the courage.

Will you help me? I know it's asking a lot—but I trust you. I know you trusted me. I know you may want to betray me as I have betrayed you. I hope you do not.

The love I have for you lives in the cells of my body. It is different than what I feel for Helen, but have no doubt that I love you.

Your husband, Mort

Chapter 18

They've passed in a blur, Anna thought—three days since she discovered the receipt and opened the envelope. Three days since her dinner with Carla. Anna wondered how she would remember that night in her own personal history; the two events would likely merge in her mind as if they were related in some way rather than two separate events. As if one caused the other, and maybe it did. Did her lack of passion for Mort force him to find love or sex with someone else?

It had been three days since Koru had a good run in the park; he had been restricted to peeing and pooping in the yard. Other than taking the turtle back to the lake, Anna had left the house only to meet with Ken and attend her video class.

She managed to gird herself to meet the world. Ken agreed on their schedule for the next month, his taciturn personality fit her mood perfectly. She managed to get through the class without anyone noticing she really hadn't been present at all. She wondered if other people didn't show up in their own lives.

Although she needed to move, to get some exercise, she couldn't face the lake or even a dog park yet. She went outside with Koru, leaned against the dogwood, tiny red blossoms just visible, and watched Koru sniff his way across the yard.

Anna heard the phone ring and hurried back into the kitchen. Maybe Lily, maybe Larry.

She recognized Carla's solid voice on the answering machine. Nothing wispy about it, no high-pitched whine. Just full. Melodic. Inviting.

She picked up the receiver. "Hi. Sorry, I was outside—almost missed your call."

"You sound awful," Carla said. "Are you alright?"

"Fine," Anna said as she rinsed her coffee cup.

"Sounds like you have a cold?"

"No, not really. Maybe an allergy. I've been meaning to call and thank you for a lovely dinner." She poured herself a cup of coffee from the pot.

"I had hoped to hear from you, and since I hadn't, I decided to check in with you."

"Sorry. I should have called after your dinner. I had a great time." Her words sounded far short of the joy she had experienced at Carla's. "Not that I didn't want to—I've just been busy."

An avalanche of words started in her throat, and she swallowed them with a gulp. Anna's eyes filled with tears. No surprise—she had been crying for days. She took the cordless out to the deck.

A stunning March day. Anna could see rain clouds off in the west, moving inland, but for the moment, she felt the sun warming her body and breathed in the fragrance of spring.

Koru had curled up on his rug in the sun, already dozing. She wished she could do that. It had been three days since she'd slept more than a couple of hours at a time.

"You sound different," Carla said. "Are you sure you're okay?"

Anna sipped her coffee, left the cup on the deck, and walked toward the rockery along the steps leading out of the yard. Wedging the phone between her ear and shoulder, she sat down on one of the steps and reached under the ferns to pluck old dried-out fronds. "Some stuff came up since I saw you. Nothing much. About my husband."

"After our conversation at dinner?"

"No. Not that at all. I felt wonderful after our dinner. It's not that."

"Do you want to talk?"

Anna hesitated. "Not really. Just a minute." She put down the cordless to pull with both hands on a large dead frond, then wiped her hands together to shake off the dirt. "I'm back."

"Do you want to take a walk around the lake today?"

Anna got up from the steps to find her coffee again. "It's starting to look like rain." Before she could stop herself, she added, "I don't know why you want to see me." Jerk, she thought. I can't believe I said that.

Silence. Anna held her breath, then heard Carla laugh. "I wonder that myself. No. Not because of you. I like you, but generally I don't pursue straight women. Quite out of character." She laughed again.

"Are you pursuing me?" Anna whispered.

"Could be. Rain's not coming until later in the day. Sounds like you could use a friend today. What's your address? I'm on my way."

Anna found some crumpled Kleenex in her pocket and blew her nose. "Sorry. Allergies." She took another sip of coffee, ran her hand across her forehead, and felt the tears return. The silence was lasting too long. She told Carla her address. Koru woke up and nuzzled Anna.

"I've made some more chicken mole. Should I bring some with me?"

Anna laughed. "No—come yourself. Leave the mole home."

"I thought you were ready for some hot stuff."

"Not yet." Anna could hear Carla's laugh as she hung up.

She finished her coffee and thought she should comb her hair, brush her teeth, or at least straighten her clothes. Do something, because Carla was coming over. But she couldn't. She sat in the chair and let the tears fall. Koru kept his face on Anna's knees. She scratched him behind his ears absently as she'd been doing for years. Koru was always the same. He didn't know how to lie.

It didn't take long for Carla to arrive. Anna heard the front door bell. She took the barrette out of her hair, combed through it with her fingers, pushed it away from her face, and reattached the barrette. Koru was already at the door doing his husky howl.

Anna saw Carla through the window before Carla saw her. Anna knew her cheeks were still wet, her eyes puffy and red. Somehow, it didn't matter. She opened the door, letting Carla quickly study her face.

Carla, not intimated by his size or sound, bent to pet Koru.

"He likes you."

Carla gave Koru another pat and then opened her arms and pulled Anna close. "What's the matter?"

Anna smelled soap and sun on Carla's skin. She wanted to crawl into her, hide in a pocket, and stay there. Her body tensed. I hardly know this person, she thought. Carla tightened her arms and led Anna to the sofa in the living room. Anna jerked away and said, "I want to show you something." Carla followed her through the house.

The sound of their shoes reverberated across the Swedish finish oak floors. Anna's eyes glanced off the huge trestle table with its black suede chairs in the dining room. It all seemed so formal compared to the coziness of Carla's house. Even her kitchen, its gleaming stainless appliances, seemed cold and uninviting. The one soft feature, her beloved pine table, was covered in mail, her huge Coach bag, Koru's leash, and so much else Anna couldn't even see the wood finish. Anna could smell the garbage can under the sink. She'd forgotten to empty it.

The basement looked unnaturally bright as they descended from the kitchen. Mort had had dozens of can lights installed to make it look more like the upstairs. They created a glare.

Anna opened the door to what had been Mort's office. Bare bookcases lined the walls, all the books strewn across the floor. The desk drawers lay empty amidst papers, pens, all kinds of office supplies. Amidst the rubbish lay fragments of broken oak furniture. Along the other wall, filing cabinets appeared in total disarray, folders pulled out and thrown in every direction. Picture frames hung loosely from nails, but the pictures—or whatever had been in the frames—were no longer there...now possibly amidst the rubble on the floor.

Carla's eyes widened. "Were you burglarized? What happened? Tornado?"

Anna shook her head, said, "I did it," and swiped the back of her hand across her nose. Her throat felt raw and her chest burned. "I did it."

"You did it?"

"Yes. I did." The story came out, slowly at first, and then in a torrent: the decision to donate Mort's clothing, finding the receipt, the envelope, the letters, Helen and the child.

As she talked, she knew there was another part of the story to tell, one that she did not share. What had she done to make Mort carry on with this woman? Where had she been that she hadn't noticed how preoccupied he must have been? He had had a child, and she hadn't known it. Who was the guilty one here? She knew she could rant and rail against the rotten husband who had done her dirty—and yes, he had. But she had had a role in it. She knew it. She knew the tears were as much about her part in what happened as they were about his betrayal.

She knew she needed time. Somewhere out there was a little girl who maybe looked like Mort. Sister to her twins. And a woman who loved him, held him, caressed him, gave him orgasms, gave him pleasure. How long had it gone on? Who else had known? Who else knew?

"I've got to find out some things. I need to know about his child. About this woman."

"Maybe you don't. You certainly don't need to do anything right now."

Anna slid down to the floor and clutched her knees close to her chest. Carla pushed some files out of the way and sat down next to her.

Debris was everywhere. Koru settled himself on some papers and curled up.

They sat silently until Anna whispered, "I'm okay now. Just fine. I'll be fine. Thank you for coming. You don't have to stay here. I'll be fine."

Carla scooted around on the floor until she faced Anna. "I'm not a fair-weather friend. I don't understand it; somehow you've become important to me. But if you want me to go, I will." Carla waited until Anna shook her head and looked down.

"Then let's get out of here. Let's go upstairs, outside, anywhere away from this mess." She stood and reached for Anna. Koru followed them upstairs.

Anna looked out into the back yard. "It's raining too hard out there now. We'll have to go for a walk another day." She took Carla's hand and led her across the formal dining room and into a small room Carla hadn't noticed.

It was a cozy room, with windows overlooking the garden on the south side of the house, a small, private, fenced garden. "I can't imagine how disturbing this must be for you, how confusing," Carla said as she stared out the window at the rain.

"Right. I can't imagine it, either. Let's leave that mess downstairs and just sit here and watch the rain." Anna took Carla's hand and led her to the love seat with a view out to the garden. "This room is my favorite spot in the house," she said. "Next to the kitchen table and the coffeepot!"

"It's beautiful."

As they settled into the soft cushions their thighs slowly came together. Anna was drained, exhausted, and yet her body hummed. Neither said anything, but the room felt full of words. All the millions of words Anna had never spoken in her life. She wanted to let them out, to let them flow, to speak without editing or controlling. But she said nothing. She felt a gentle kiss on her forehead. Then kisses along her jaw.

"You taste like salt," Carla said as she ran her tongue across her lips. "So many tears." She kissed Anna's eyelids. They heard the rain tap against the windows.

"No tears now," Anna said.

Anna's lips opened to receive Carla's. Her hands, prompted by something deep inside, began to caress Carla, her face, her back, her shoulders, her hands.

They moved naturally together, comfortably. Desire rising. Carla's hands came to Anna's breasts, caressing them through the fabric of her clothes.

Anna savored the soft, wet kisses, craved the feel of Carla's skin. She moved her arm to Carla's white shirt. As she moved, she caught their reflection in the mirror across the room. She saw herself, her blouse twisted, her face flushed, and saw the back of Carla's head.

Anna pulled away. "Oh, dear. Stop. I can't do this. Mort just died." She looked into Carla's deep dark eyes. "I was with a woman once in college. But I'm not a lesbian." She kissed Carla's cheek.

"It's okay," Carla murmured. "You're scared. Honestly, I am, too." The freedom Anna had felt moments before floated away, and her body pulled in on itself and froze.

"I'm sorry. Please just hold me," Anna whispered. "I'm so confused. Maybe I'm not ready for this."

Carla stood instead and walked to the window. She studied the raindrops as they landed on the window and slowly rolled down. With her back to Anna, she said, "I'm not sure if I'm ready, either. I didn't expect this. You've been in my mind since that first rehearsal."

"You think about me?"

"Yeah." She turned back toward Anna. "Some chemistry. Something. You're not even my type."

"Not your type?"

"You were wearing a goddamned red silk scarf. I date women who wear Birkenstocks and jeans."

"What's wrong with silk scarves?"

"Nothing. Honestly. I liked how it moved with you when you walked. Very sexy."

Anna blushed, lowered her eyes, and said, "Do you go out with a lot of women?"

"Not really. I've dated a few times since Laura died. Nothing serious. It's been a long time since I felt this kind of connection." Carla sat down next to Anna on the love seat. She took Anna's hand in her own and wiggled Anna's wedding ring. "And you're straight. You're straight aren't you?"

Anna nodded. "I am. I thought I was. I don't know..." She

yawned and leaned back on the sofa. "I do know that I'm really tired."

Koru snored across the room. Dark clouds now covered the sky, and their attention was drawn to the steady beat of rain against the windows.

"Maybe not the best time to talk about this," Anna said as she curled herself up on the love seat.

"No. Probably not the best time." Carla looked around the room, found an afghan, covered Anna, and tucked her in. She kissed her forehead then turned off the overhead light. "But it's a conversation I want to have soon."

Chapter 19

Koru's barking woke Anna. She looked at her watch. Seven o'clock. Could it be morning? She must have spent the night on the sofa in the den. Carla had been there. She ran her finger across her lips and smiled at the memory of Carla's kisses.

Anna's joints creaked as she stretched and got to her feet. Little crusties had collected in the corners of her swollen eyes, and her head felt heavy with congestion.

Hung over from crying. Anna stopped in the bathroom and blew her nose. She perched on the edge of the tub and placed hot and then cold washcloths across her eyes. It had felt comforting when her mother applied the hot and then cold compresses on her eyes whenever she had been crying as a child.

She found a note on the refrigerator. *Hope you rested well*, it said, then, *C*. Anna felt like a teenager again. She smiled. She'd had the best sleep since she'd found the receipt. Rested well indeed.

An appointment with Ken to tape the band at marching practice late in the afternoon left her most of the day to herself. She made coffee and took the cup outside to the deck, still damp from yesterday's cloudburst. Raindrops on the leaves and flowers shimmered in the early morning sun. Anna picked a few deep-coral peonies, shook off the drops of water, and sniffed their rose-like scent.

Back in the kitchen, she searched through cabinets until she round a delicate Belleek vase that had belonged to her mother. She hadn't used it in years, but somehow today it felt perfect for these flowers. She placed it on the desk in the den and then noticed the framed picture of the whole family taken at her and Mort's twenty-fifth anniversary party.

Perfect family. Attractive. Obviously happy. Had Helen known that there was a twenty-fifth anniversary party? Big celebration. Rachel would have been a toddler. Like mirrors in a fun house, nothing looked as it really was. She took the picture out of its mahogany frame and carried it to the kitchen sink. She lit a match, letting the flame lick one corner, held it until it singed her fingers, then dropped it into the sink.

Anna returned to the den, took their wedding picture from its mahogany frame, ready to repeat the ritual. She looked closely at Mort, remembering the first time she had met him. It had been at some synagogue function, soon after her abortion. She remembered thinking the first time they danced, he'd make a good husband—young lawyer, slim, almost six feet, nice smile, smart, funny. He had flattered her. Treated her with respect.

Anna took the wedding picture to the kitchen sink, lit a match, and watched it burn. She'd been in a maelstrom from the moment she'd found the hotel receipt until the moment Carla walked into her house. This morning, the sun shone, and she didn't want to waste it. A perfect day for a hike in Hamlin Park with Koru. They both needed to get out.

Anna dressed quickly and left a message on Carla's answering machine before she drove up to Shoreline. "Thanks for yesterday. You'll never know how much you helped. I need a few days, maybe weeks, to make sense out of what I've learned." Anna paused and added, "Although it may take years." She laughed. "But I'll call you soon. Don't give up on me."

As Anna drove Koru north on 15th, the impulse to talk to her mother grew, a rare desire, but oddly strong this morning. The parking lots were deserted. Still early. Koru bounded out of the car and raced into the shadows of the forested park. Anna inhaled the scent of the evergreens and the ferns sheltered along the path. She had to stop to catch her breath as she followed Koru up the hill toward the meadow that seemed to radiate sunlight. She wished she had brought her camera to capture the wildflowers.

She thought about capturing wildflowers, ephemeral moments in a lifetime, dazzling in the sunlight. Moments. Moments in her mind. A slideshow of moments. A person's life. Disjointed moments.

Anna remembered a conversation she had had with her mother shortly before she died. She must have been in her junior year at the university. They lay at each end of a scratchy red sofa in their pajamas, watching a TV program about the revolutionary impact of the birth control pill on women's lives.

"Anna, you're not on the pill are you?"

"Mom! No!" Not that she hadn't thought about it, but she was still a virgin, with no boyfriend in sight.

"Good girl. Why would a girl want birth control pills if she wasn't married?"

"You know, Mom, if someone's really attracted to someone, maybe they want to have sex—and not get pregnant."

"I get that part," her mother said.

Anna remembered the furrow between her mother's brows and how her mother went on.

"But Anna, girls should understand that attraction only goes so far. Girls need to be careful."

"Careful?

"Girls need to remember attraction doesn't last. It's easy. Excitement. Big deal. Look for respect, friendship. Love grows over time. Find someone you can count on to take care of you and your children."

Anna sometimes wondered if her life would have been different if her mother hadn't died so early. Would she have gone to that stupid party? Would she ever have had an abortion? Maybe, but she could have told her mother and wouldn't have been so alone.

She'd gone to a party with people she didn't know, somewhere near the Ave. After her years teaching about hospice care, Anna could see how she and her father had ignored their grief after her mother died. He had started dating only two months after, and Anna started to drink.

A guy from her American lit class had told her about a party. Didn't even pick her up. Met her at the party, and then, in a back bedroom, on top of coats, he took her virginity, as if it had been a candy bar at the checkout counter.

For a while, she didn't realize she was pregnant. She'd never been regular, so she hadn't really noticed the missed periods. But given what had happened at the party, she thought maybe it was time for birth control pills. On a windy autumn morning in 1968, Anna swallowed hard, straightened her back, and walked into the student health center at the university. She could barely say the words out loud, but the nurse only nodded and wrote "contraception" on her file.

"Did you realize you're pregnant?" The young doctor had smiled when he asked her the question. "It's a bit late for birth control."

She saw the doctor's cheerful face as he stood between her legs, which were balanced high in stirrups. Her paper gown slid down her thighs toward her belly.

"You're getting pale," he'd said after glancing up at her stunned face. "Sit up. Let's get your head lower than your heart." He helped her and then pushed her head down so it was between her knees and held it. "You'll feel better in a few minutes."

Feel better? She felt numb. Afterwards, she had no memory of getting dressed and leaving the health center. She knew she couldn't go to her father, so she went to the guy from American lit. Years later, she couldn't even remember his name. But she remembered the scene at the Hub, the student union.

Lunchtime. Crowded. Full tables. Laughter. She'd found him sitting with some guys and asked him for a moment. He smiled at his friends, a patronizing smile, she'd thought at the time. Look-at-me kind of smile, all-these-foxy-girls-bothering-me kind of smile. He stood and walked with her to another table. She wondered why she had thought he was cute. He looked dull, thick, stupid as he sat looking at her.

"What's up? We're studying for a test." His eyes shifted back to his table.

"I'm pregnant," she whispered. He stared her without saying anything.

He looked at her face and then down to her breasts. He sneered. Actually sneered. His eyes cold, he asked, "How do I know it's mine?" And then he laughed.

She remembered hearing people talking at the next table, felt a flush creep up her face. Her heart beat rapidly. "I was a virgin, for God's sake. Don't you remember?"

"Yeah, but who's been there since I left? Take care," he said as he stood and walked away, leaving her sitting alone at a table in the Hub.

For years, Anna had blocked the memory of the actual abortion, illegal in the days before *Roe v. Wade*. Now, for some peculiar reason, since Mort died, she'd sometimes wake up thinking of the thin man who smelled like Vicks VapoRub. He'd said he was a doctor. He took her money and gave her a shot to "relax" within a minute of her walking into the motel room in Renton. A scummy, cigarette-infested room with an orange brocade spread and orange shag carpet.

A few hours later, she awoke to the smell of blood in an empty room. He'd put a sanitary pad between her legs, but that was full, and there was blood on her thighs. She cleaned herself the best she could and got back to her father's house. She spent the weekend trembling, crying, and bleeding.

Anna remembered feeling that there was a fetus hanging from her womb—a crazy, insane thought—but wherever she went during those first few days, she felt soiled, wounded, scarred. She thought everyone would know. Fortunately, her father, as usual, was away on business—and her mother was dead.

Anna's legs ached as she followed Koru up and down the hills at Hamlin Park. Totally out of shape. Surrounded by dense growth of Western hemlocks and Douglas firs, where the forest canopy blocked the sun, the strong impulse to talk with her mother increased. Maybe here, in her mother's favorite park, Anna would be able to feel her presence.

"Mom, I'm trying to figure out what happened to me, where I got lost."

Her voice faded as she walked carefully, her eyes along the path, mindful of avoiding exposed roots and dead branches. Would she ever forget the shame of losing her virginity to a stupid stranger, being abandoned by that same jerk, and then arranging for an illegal abortion? Nor could she forget the feeling of fear that had followed her after being with Audrey, the fear that someone would discover she had been attracted to a woman, or worse, that it might happen again.

"I knew I was wild, that I was out of control. I knew a man like Mort, not a stupid little stud waving his penis around, would keep me steady. So I married him."

Anna bumped into a massive fir in her path. The rich smell of evergreen surrounded her as she wrapped her arms around the fir as far as they could reach. The bark was rough against her cheek as she laid her face against the tree. Koru sniffed around the base, trying to discover why Anna had stopped. She didn't know herself. She listened carefully. Could she feel life in the tree? Maybe if she waited a very long time and stayed silent, emptied her mind, she would discover something. Not likely. Not likely her mind would stop, let alone be still long enough to catch something transcendent. Maybe someday. For the moment, she just hoped no one would walk by and see her.

She turned around and leaned against the fir. She heard birds calling to each other, leaves rustling. "So, Mom, I married a safe guy," she said aloud. "A friend. Just like you said. A lot of good it did me."

She listened carefully to her mother's voice in her heart.

"*It did you plenty of good. He was a good husband, a good provider. Don't forget, you did grow to love him. You had a comfortable life. Raised two wonderful children. What's so bad?*"

Anna heard a dog barking, stopped, and looked around. Koru

was sniffing under a pile of dead branches. The barking came from across the park. Her own dog pawed the ground, trying to unearth something. Anna lifted some of the branches and dozens of potato bugs, looking dazed, hesitated a moment and then scurried away to find new hiding places.

Koru moved on to another pile of branches. Anna found a large log and sat down. Her mother continued, "*Mort's gone now. You can just forget everything else. So what if he had an affair, a child? He had the sense to die. You never had to go through a divorce. Be grateful.*"

"No kidding. But I feel like a fool. I arranged my whole life for him, and he lied to me for years."

"*You lied to him, too. Maybe not about how much you spent on clothes, but you never really told him how you felt. Don't forget that. I'm not saying that to make you feel guilty. Just to help you understand; you and Mort had a contract. It's over now. You're still alive. Make yourself a new life.*"

Koru barked. Anna stood and whistled for Koru to come. A pair of black labs came up over the ridge; she put Koru back on leash and had him sit until they ran by. He pulled on the leash, wanting to play, but Anna wanted to get back to her conversation.

"Mom, it's easy for you to say, 'Get a new life.' I don't know what to do about Carla. It's very scary to me. And I need to tell the twins about their father. Their sister. My heart hurts for them and for me."

A loud tapping to her right got Anna's attention, and when she looked, she noticed a little woodpecker that sounded like a dozen tiny hammers pounding in unison. Distracted, she tried to reclaim her thoughts, but something surprising came out. "Mom, I cannot believe how cynical you've become, hard hearted."

"*Death has given me a new perspective. Anna, you're over fifty years old. You've raised your kids. Do what makes you happy. Do you remember your Yiddish? Remember* sturis? *Troubles? You'll have a lot of* sturis. *But you'll get over it. There's a certain advantage in being dead. Not a lot of ups and downs. I guess it's the price you pay for being alive.*"

Chapter 20

On a quick trip to the library for a reverse directory, Anna discovered Helen's address on Queen Anne Hill. She costumed herself in a beige linen pantsuit, pearls, and espadrilles for the upscale neighborhood and took Koru along as a prop.

She bought wraparound sunglasses and then reconsidered wearing them on such a cloudy, overcast morning. Too suspicious. Anyway, she couldn't see well without her bifocals.

Parking a few houses down, she strolled along, stopping at every tree for Koru to relieve himself. Fortunately for Koru, there were a lot of trees. Unfortunately for her, it made for an obstructed view of Helen's house.

As they approached, Anna caught a glimpse of Helen's manicured Craftsman-style home. It sat back from the street, surrounded by rigidly manicured bushes and carefully pruned trees. Likely Helen was compulsive, a better match for Mort. They probably drove each other crazy being perfect.

She tried to get Koru to meander along Helen's walk up to the door, but Koru preferred peeing on the bordering bushes. Anna caught a glimpse of a child's pink bike on the large front porch. Helen wasn't home; Anna had called her office and hung up when she picked up the phone.

Anna couldn't bring herself to peek in the windows. What was she looking for, anyway?

She had no immediate answer to that question, but something drew Anna, compelled her, to learn more about Helen and Rachel. The espadrilles' straps dug into her ankles. She'd tied them too tightly, worried that they might come undone; she'd gone to the other extreme. The day wasn't particularly hot, but sweat ran down her neck. If she had a brain, she knew she'd get in her car, take off the espadrilles, put on the air conditioning, and drive home.

Instead, she hobbled around to the alley to see if there was a fence and if the fence had some holes she could peek through. She needed to pee, but thought maybe the feeling was only anxiety and not the real thing.

Koru loved alleys. He dashed from one side to the other, taking long sniffs around each trash can and recycling bin. A mild scent of garbage permeated the alley. Apparently, their pickup day was close. Anna counted four houses down, just to confirm the location of Helen's. She should have guessed. It was the only house without weeds growing along the edge of the fence. Immaculate. Even her paper recycling was placed with precision next to the cedar fence. Anna glanced into the recycling bag and restrained her hand from reaching into it. Koru was occupied with an overturned bin of bottles.

The espadrilles were killing her. She stepped on Koru's leash with one foot while she bent and readjusted the ties around her ankles. No one else in the alley at this time of day. Anna peeked between the slats of Helen's fence.

A redwood swing set with a little house next to it, a child's playhouse, filled the backyard. She sensed that someone was in the yard, but couldn't see anyone. Then she heard the yapping of a little dog. Koru picked up the scent, barked, and lunged toward the gate in Helen's fence.

Anna yanked hard on his leash and turned to leave the alley when the yapping came closer. Anna stopped and a tiny Yorkie ran up to Koru, who peered down and howled. She held Koru tightly. The little dog, on his miniature legs, yapped louder, and then a child's voice called, "Koru, Koru. Where are you?"

Koru? The Yorkie's name was Koru?

And then small arms reached out and picked up the Yorkie. "Bad boy," she said. Anna's Koru stopped howling and sniffed the slim little girl holding her dog. Obviously, she was not intimated by a husky that was nearly her size. She asked, "Can I pet your dog?"

"Uh huh," Anna murmured. She thought she might throw up. Rachel. Obviously. She looked like Mort: same nose, same smile as she petted Koru, same curly hair. She looked exactly as Larry had at that age, except Rachel had blue eyes. "What's your dog's name?" Anna asked.

The little girl gave the tiny Yorkie a kiss on his face and said, "Koru." She reached out and put her small hand on big Koru's back. "He's really huge. What's his name?"

"Kevin," Anna said. "Kevin. His name is Kevin." She leaned against the fence and tried to catch her breath.

"That's a boy's name, isn't it?" the little girl said as she petted Anna's dog. Often children were terrified of dog's Koru's size, but Rachel—it must be Rachel—seemed to have no fear.

"Well, Kevin is a boy. Your dog has an unusual name," Anna said. "What does it mean?"

"Koru? 'Birth' or something. I don't remember exactly. My mommy gave him to me after my daddy died."

The smell of salami, maybe pepperoni, probably leftover pizza came from one of the garbage cans, added to Anna's queasiness. "Your daddy died?"

"He wasn't my real daddy, just a sort of daddy. He died when I was in third grade, and Mommy gave me Koru." Matter of fact.

There she stood, the little Mort look-alike with blue eyes. No need for a DNA test.

"Oh." Anna moved toward the center of the alley, tried to get some distance from the garbage. "Shouldn't you be in school now?"

"Conferences today."

"So your mommy's at home with you?"

"No. Ashley, my nanny." Rachel looked back at the gate. "Oops, probably looking for me." She gave "Kevin" one last pat, waved at Anna, and ran back through the gate.

Anna stood in the alley, blinking several times. She shook her head. How had Mort pulled it off? How had he spent time with this delightful child and then came home as though nothing had changed? She wanted to scream, to lie down in the alley and pound her feet against the gravel and scream. There was no way at all to make sense of this.

Now the ties on the espadrilles were too loose to walk without wobbling. She took them off completely and walked barefoot back to the car, little pieces of gravel sticking to her feet. She had just put Koru into the back of the wagon when she noticed Rachel on her pink bike leaving her house. A young woman with a long ponytail walked alongside the bike. Anna averted her face and got into the car.

What if Helen had been home? Shit. What had she been thinking? Anna waited until her breathing slowed, and with every intention of driving back on Aurora and stopping at the co-op, she started the car. Instead, she found herself turning the steering wheel quickly and driving into the alley. She slowed as she approached Helen's house and scanned the area for anyone who might be able to see her car. No one she could see. Koru had his nose on the window in the back of the wagon, his tail wagging, probably thinking he had another walk coming.

Anna's hands were sweating, her heart racing again. Swearing under her breath, she stopped the car, got out, and casually walked around her car to open the passenger door. She looked in all directions before she grabbed the bags of paper recycling and threw them on the floor of the car and drove off.

She'd had little sleep during the last few days, but she couldn't seem to slow herself, as if maybe she'd taken speed. She remembered the feeling from college. Racing heart, hyperkinetic thoughts. Compulsive behavior.

Her cell rang as she approached the stop light on 39th. She recognized Carla's number but didn't want to answer. What could she learn from the recycling? Ridiculous. Utterly embarrassing. But she needed information. Didn't she? Not really. Seeing Rachel should have been enough for her. Enough for one day.

She felt the back of her neck, wet with sweat. Ridiculous. How incredibly stupid. She was not a Dumpster diver. A stalker. Someone should tell Rachel not to talk with strangers. She'd listen to Carla's message later. She needed groceries. She needed stamps. She needed to buy mulch for the garden near the garage. She needed to get on with her life. She needed a life.

Anna drove straight back to her house, refreshed Koru's water, and gave him a treat. The recycling bags were clumsy, but not heavy. She took them down to Mort's office; keep all the crap together in one place, she thought. She pushed aside the debris and made room on the desk.

The mess needed to be cleaned up, organized, and thrown away or donated. She imagined St. Vincent's would come and pick up the desk, the filing cabinets, sofa, bookcases. She wanted to eliminate all traces of Mort.

In the meantime, the room smelled stale, airless. A few of the light bulbs had burned out. She must have left the lights on. Anna shivered and wrapped herself in an old afghan still lying on the sofa.

It felt creepy to reach her hand into Helen's recycling. Her hands itched, but one by one, she pulled out the magazines and papers. The Queen Anne local paper. *Time* magazine and *Vanity Fair. Seattle Law and Politics. The Economist.* Anna looked at every flyer: advertisements for tires, roofing, plumbing, and pizza. She examined each piece of paper before she threw it into another paper bag. Nothing. There was nothing that told her anything. The same junk mail that came to her own house.

Another light bulb buzzed and went out. There was just enough light in the room to see the papers. She thought about turning on the desk lamp, but remembered she had already smashed it.

There was a stack of homework assignments. Spelling. Vocabulary. A childish handwriting and Rachel's name at the top of the page. Some stars and "good work" stickers. A 100%. Clearly Helen threw out her daughter's homework, at least some of it. She wondered if Mort had known that detail. He'd always insisted they save all the twins' schoolwork, much of which was still stored in the garage. Anna's stomach was tight, her breathing shallow. She knew she was losing it. Insane. Insane behavior. Certifiable. Where was the Lucite when she needed it?

A bunch of shredded paper remained at the bottom of the bag. She would not, could not try to put together the scraps. Oh, please, she thought. Don't let me do this. Anyway, it looked as if Helen had one of the fancy shredders that made it impossible to piece the tiny bits of paper together. Dammit.

There she sat, a crazed woman in her mid-fifties, wrapped in an old afghan. Her hands dry from rummaging around in two bags of a stranger's paper garbage. A woman with a master's degree. A former college teacher. A mother. A widow. A property owner surrounded by someone else's garbage.

Her hands itched. She walked to the bathroom adjoining

Mort's office. He used to shower there after golf or working in the garden. Sometimes he showered twice a day. Did he ever shower with Helen? She searched through the assorted bottles under the sink and found an old bottle of Eucerin for dry skin. It took an extra push to get the cap off, but the cream came out moist and cool against her dry hands. She sat down and stared at the bottles in the cupboard. Family history. She wondered if it had been cleaned since the remodel at least fifteen years before. Larry's acne medicine was there. Bottles of vitamin C—Mort had been on a vitamin C binge one winter.

In the back, behind some cleaning supplies, she saw a straw basket full of shampoos from hotels. She reached for the basket and pulled it out. Full to overflowing. She had a companion basket upstairs in the master bath. Small bottles from their trips to conferences and from vacations. She hadn't remembered setting one up for Mort's office bathroom. She knew even before she looked closely. Sophisticated miniature bottles of shampoo and conditioner. Four Seasons discretely printed on the label. Why had he saved them? Beautiful memories? Sentimental? Maybe just cheap.

Anna sat frozen on the floor in front of the dusty vanity in a basement bathroom, mildew along the edges of the cabinet. She held one of the small bottles loosely in her hand. Did Helen have a little straw basket in her house as well? Were these little bottles special treats for Rachel? She stared at the bottle as it lay in her hand and tried to make sense of it. In her house. In their house. Had Helen ever been in her house? Had they showered here together?

Anna felt her skin grow clammy and a chill flutter through her body, despite the afghan. Her stomach quivered, and she leaned down over the toilet bowl. She tasted bile for a moment as her head hung over the rim. She gagged, swallowed hard, and then leaned back against the wall. The basket sat on the tile floor, the floor that had been heated in the winter. She remembered the discussions with Mort about putting heating under the tile. He wanted the best. Always the best. Well, it wasn't warm now. Cold. Hard. She looked at the bottles overflowing from the straw basket, got up, walked out, and closed the door.

Chapter 21

For an hour, the clanging of the truck's lift had broken the midafternoon quiet in the neighborhood. Mort's desk was the last of his furniture to be raised into the dim interior of the St. Vincent's truck.

"Here's your tax receipt, Mrs. Simon. Thanks for the donation and the Cokes. Sure helps on a hot day."

"Thank you for taking everything."

"Have a good one. Forecast looks great."

With the donation receipt in her hand, Anna listened to the rattle of the truck's back door as it slid closed. She squinted into the dark interior for a last look at Mort's things: office furniture, boxes of books, trophies, golf clubs. Everything destined for new ownership.

Tipping his baseball cap in Anna's direction, the driver jumped into the cab of the truck and drove off. More clanking from the garbage cans as Anna loaded them on to the dolly and rolled them out of the garage into the street for the next morning's collection. Then she hauled several large trash bags full of the debris from Mort's office out to the street for extra garbage pickup.

Ridding the house of Mort's belonging had direct repercussions on her body: aching lower back, tight shoulders, head stuffed up from all the dust. She could barely lift her arms after filling the bags and lugging them out of the house. She wiped the sweat from her forehead, stretched her hamstrings and her back.

Becky Clayton next door waved the water hose she held in her scrawny arm in greeting. "How's your sister?" Anna asked as she moved toward her back door.

Becky shrugged her shoulders. "So-so."

"Give Dotty my best."

Anna smiled and ducked into the house. No patience to hear more about Dotty's move to the nursing home or about how wonderful Mort had been. Becky Clayton had adored Mort, actually adored all men in suits with fancy cars. She loved telling anyone who would listen about the men she met at the senior center dances. But she had told Anna she'd never marry again. "I nursed Henry until he died. Burying one is enough." She had smiled and added, "But I do love the boys when they dress up. Especially the ones who can dance."

This afternoon, her thoughts drifted to Carla, although she hadn't returned the call yet. She wanted to hear Carla's voice, suck it into her body. Anna imagined saying, "Make love to me. Cover my body with yours. I want to know the feel of you, the smell, the taste." Insane. Calm down. She knew she couldn't go down that trail, a trail full of ripe fruit and extravagant flowers. Fun to have an erotic fantasy for a change, even if it was about a woman.

Maybe she'd call Carla and tell her that since she was no longer an instructor at the college and would likely never be a filmmaker, she was going to explore Dumpster diving. She'd discovered she had a certain flair for it.

Anna took a quick shower and lay naked on her bed, letting the breeze from the open window cool her skin. Carla answered after a few rings. Her voice was close and intimate. "Good to hear from you."

"Got your message. Sorry it's taken me so long to get back to you. I've been busy."

"How are you?" Carla's voice had texture; it felt like a caress across her body.

"I'm fine," she said automatically as she thought about the last time she'd seen Carla, the soft, sinking kisses, her body open and alive. Anna ran her hand over her breasts, her nipples erect in the cooling breeze.

"It doesn't get dark until after eight o'clock tonight. How about a bike ride this evening?"

"Say again?" Anna sat up. Not what she was expecting to hear. Definitely interfered with her reverie. Actually, she'd gotten goose bumps. She needed to put on clothes or close the window.

"A bike ride."

"You've got to be kidding. I haven't ridden a bike for years. I don't even own a bike."

"I've got an extra one. I've filled the tires and oiled all the right places. I think it's all ready for you."

"Think again."

"No, seriously. You'll enjoy it. We can try it out at the lake this evening. The bike trail is flat. No hills to worry about. No cars. Nothing to be afraid of. It's still early in the season. Not a lot of people there."

"Slow down. Let me call you back in a minute." Anna hung up, found her sweats, put them on, and pressed redial.

"How about tomorrow morning?" Anna offered. "Are you free? In the evening, there are tons of people at the lake. I could crash your bike, maybe kill someone." And maybe bump into someone I know, she thought, as the impulse not to be seen with Carla flashed through her mind. "Anyway, I am truly exhausted. I've spent most of the day schlepping the junk out of Mort's office."

"Way to go."

"St. Vincent's came and picked everything up this afternoon."

"Great. I don't go into work until noon tomorrow. How's nine thirty?"

"I'm not sure I'll be able to stay on a bike, but I'll try it. You might be sorry."

Promptly at nine thirty, she heard the doorbell ring, followed by Koru's crazy howling. The moment he saw Carla, he stopped, licked her face, snuggled against her legs, and greeted her as if she was an old friend. Show some propriety, Anna thought, and knew she wanted to jump up and down as well.

Anna helped Carla unload the bikes from the back of the pickup truck. Anna and Mort had parented in the days before Burleys. The twins had bikes when they were old enough, but Mort played racquetball, tennis, golf. She had walked, taken yoga classes.

Carla bent down and rolled up Anna's right pant leg. "It might get caught in the chain. We want to keep you safe," Carla said as she rose.

Anna hadn't seen her for a week. A stormy week. And now the sun lit up the room. "Do you have first aid training?" Anna asked. "I'll probably go crashing into a tree." She knew she should be scared. It had been so many years and her body was stiff, not to mention shaky in the heart of herself. Instead, she felt like a ten-year-old ready for adventure.

They walked the bikes slowly over to the lake a block away. The rhododendrons bloomed in all the yards. Brilliant fuschias, soft pinks, and the amazing, huge coral rhododendrons on the corner. Cherry trees flowered at the lake. Anna and Carla stood next to the bikes and enjoyed a gentle breeze shifting the splashes of pink branches all along the path.

"You ready?" Carla asked.

Anna rolled her eyes and smirked.

Carla lowered the kickstand of her own bike and held the one Anna was to ride.

"Tell me again, you do have first aid training, right?" Anna asked as she tried to sit on the bike seat. Her toes barely reached the ground.

"The last person who road this bike was taller," Carla said as she had Anna slide off so she could adjust the height of the seat. "I'll walk alongside you for a bit until you get going." They started on the almost empty upper path near the street.

Anna had body memory of bike riding. Although she wobbled at the beginning, gradually her confidence grew. "I've got it. Get on your bike. Let's go down to the path near the lake."

Carla ran back for her bike, and they moved down the slope to the wheel path and rode south around the lake. She could see more along the shore from the bike than she could walking. A new perspective. After a few minutes, her legs felt the strain, but she kept on pedaling. With her eyes focused on the path, Anna felt Carla's presence beside her.

She heard a steady stream of encouragement. "That's it, you're doing great. Fabulous. Relax your shoulders. That's it. Great."

As they reached the southern point of the lake, Carla moved ahead and picked up the pace. Anna pushed her tired legs and smiled. She could do this. She appreciated the easy movement of Carla's legs, the shift of her butt on the seat. Smooth, lean, easy. She felt her own clumsiness, but she kept pumping. She wondered if she were too old for this…too old for the exercise. Too old to change her habits.

From the corner of her right eye, Anna saw someone wave to her, heard a voice yell out her name. She turned her head and found her bike moving to the right, into the pedestrian lane. A dog barked. She pressed her brake, and the bike slid sideways. When Anna opened her eyes, she saw Marilyn's sister-in-law, Irene, her face only a few inches from her own. "Are you okay? Anna? Anna? Speak to me."

Of all people to bump into. Anna closed her eyes again. "I'm fine," she mumbled and tried to untangle her legs and arms from the bike. "Give me a hand," she said and looked at Irene. A crowd formed around her, and someone tried to move the bike, pulling on her leg. "Ouch. Stop."

Then Anna heard Carla's voice. "Careful, be gentle." She must have moved people away, because she felt Carla's arm slide between the pavement and her back. Slowly she raised Anna to a sitting position and held her there.

"Thank you for your help," Irene said to Carla as she knelt down next to Anna and started to lift her. "I can take it from here. I know where she lives. I'll help her home."

Anna pulled her arm back and looked at Carla, who tenderly pushed Anna's hair out of her eyes. Anna couldn't see the expression on Carla's face. Whatever it was, it sent Irene back a step. "First we need to make sure she's oriented. What's your name?"

"Anna Simon."

"Did you hit your head?"

"No."

"Who's the president?"

"I wish I could say Gore." Everyone laughed, and the crowd dispersed.

Irene hovered. "Anna, don't you want me to take you home?"

Anna shook her head. "Thank you, but I'll be fine."

Carla helped her to feet. "Can you stand?"

"I'm a little wobbly. My ankle hurts." She wiped dirt off her backside and wiggled her right leg. "My hip, too." She bent over to examine her jeans; they were torn at the knee.

"Take a few steps. Can you make it back to the house, or

should I get my truck?" Carla lifted the bike to see if they could roll it home.

Anna took a few steps. "I'll make it. I think I can get around the lake. I'm not ready to say uncle yet."

Irene was still hovering. "Anna. Don't be stupid. That's a terrible idea. You might have a concussion. I can take you to the emergency room."

"Irene. Back off. I didn't even hit my head."

Carla straddled the front wheel. "Not loose, just twisted," she said as she pulled the handlebars back into alignment. "Let's save the rest of the lake for another day. I'll get the bike fixed."

A light had finally come on in Irene's thick head. She studied Carla, her trim figure, tailored clothing, very short hair, dark skin, and then looked at Anna. "Would you introduce me to your friend?" Irene drew the word out as if it had several syllables.

Anna's mind went blank as she looked back at Irene. Carla stretched out her arm and shook Irene's hand. "I'm Carla Martinez, a friend of Anna's. Who are you?"

Anna regained her wits. "Irene Kaplan. She's the sister-in-law of Mort's law partner, the mother of one of Larry's friends."

"Nice to meet you," Carla said as she handed Anna the handlebars of her bike and led her up the slope toward East Green Lake Way.

Anna looked back to the path. Irene still stood where they had left her, now holding a cell phone to her ear, oblivious of the people around her. She gestured and spoke into the phone. Anna flushed. The news would be all over the city. She wondered exactly what news it would be. Did she care?

By the time they reached her house, Anna's hip ached and the scrape on her knee under the torn jeans burned. And then there was the ankle; it was very sore each time she stepped down.

Anna waited while Carla loaded the bikes into the truck, then they slowly made their way into the house, up to Anna's room.

Anna had only shown Carla the ground level of her home. Now she was in their bedroom. Her and Mort's. Anna cringed at the plaid sofa and heavy dark furniture. Why had she agreed to let Mort design their bedroom? Carla didn't say anything.

Koru had met them at the front door and followed them upstairs. He sniffed at the blood on Anna's leg. As Anna hobbled to the bathroom, she thought about taking off her pants so she could clean the bloody abrasion. Instead, she handed Carla a scissors.

"You want me to cut your pants off while you're wearing them?"

"I can always use a pair of cutoffs."

"Anna, there's nothing that you have that I haven't seen before. Take off your pants and I'll clean that scrape. It looks nasty."

Anna hesitated. She couldn't remember what underpants she had put on that morning. She hadn't shaved her legs, either.

Anna turned on the hot water and handed a washcloth and antibacterial cream to Carla. She closed her eyes, took off her pants, and sat on the edge of the tub.

"This is going to sting," Carla said as knelt on the floor and gingerly placed the washcloth against Anna's leg. Anna's hands clutched the edge of the tub. She stared at the top of Carla's head next to her knee and wanted to feel her hair, its texture, to slide her fingers through the curls, to lean down and kiss the top of Carla's head.

Impulses bashed around in her mind like prisoners clanging on the bars of their cells. Let me out.

Carla rose to her feet, but didn't look at Anna. "I think it's clean now. The ointment will do its thing. There's timing to these things. I'm sure it won't get infected. Just give it air for a while." She opened the medicine cabinet above the sink. "Do you have some

Tiger Balm or something for that ankle?" Her eyes met Anna's in the mirror. Anna shook her head and looked away.

"What about an ice pack?"

"In the freezer."

"Let's get you over to the bed and elevate your leg. Put some ice on your ankle. I've got a tutoring appointment, but you should be okay."

Anna stood on one foot and tried to hop back into the bedroom. Carla stood beside her, wrapped her arm around Anna's waist, and led her to the bed.

Covering herself with a light blanket while Carla went to get the ice, Anna thought about Irene and worried about whom she might have called and what she might have said. Her hip throbbed now. The scrape stung. Koru tried to jump on the bed, but Anna petted his head, scratched between his ears, and motioned to the sofa.

Carla returned and arranged pillows around Anna's ankle to stabilize the ice pack. As she worked, her breast brushed against Anna's body. Desire began to trump the pain of Anna's sore body. She felt an opening between her legs, like the mouth of a river open to the sea. Anna could no longer avert her eyes from Carla or hide her hunger.

Carla leaned over, kissed Anna on her nose, and glanced at the empty side of the bed. "It's good that I need to go to work." She laughed, then kissed the edges of Anna's lips, soft, whisper kisses, prelude kisses. She mumbled, "I wonder if this makes sense for either of us," and started to stand.

Anna reached her arms up around Carla to pull her closer, and as she moved, she felt the ice pack fall to the floor.

Carla pulled away, readjusted the ice, and from the foot of the bed said, "I noticed you weren't eager to introduce me to your friend Irene." Anna started to say something, but Carla raised her hand to indicate she wasn't finished talking. "I spent a lot of time in the closet already. I'm not sure if that's your issue, but I don't want to be anyone's secret."

"Irene's never been a really close friend. She's a loud-mouthed gossip."

"That's not the point, is it?"

"Well, maybe not." She patted the bed, inviting Carla to sit down next to her. "It's nobody's business what I do." Carla got the chair from the nearby vanity instead and sat next to the bed.

Carla's eyes were steady on her, without the glow that Anna usually saw. "I've got a conference in the Bay Area, and then I'm going to visit friends down there. I'll be gone for at least a week. Will you be able to handle this?" She pointed to Anna's leg. "Do you have someone to call if you need help? I know so little about you."

"I'll be okay. Sore for a few days, but no big deal. I do have friends, neighbors." She took Carla's hand. "Everything is upside down, inside out. On top of everything, there's you and this attraction..."

"Is that why you look at me sometimes as if I'm dessert?"

"Does it show?"

"Probably to me, but then, I'm thinking the same thing."

"Really?"

"Really." Carla leaned closer to Anna and ran her fingers along her cheek. "We need to give this some time. I'm a very out lesbian. I'm not up for being anyone's experiment."

"You're not an experiment, not an experiment at all. More like a discovery." Anna adjusted the ice pack on her ankle and reached over to kiss Carla's cheek. "I'm sorry about Irene, about how I acted. I just need some time." She leaned back against the headboard. "I've got to focus on the other things first, got to wade through the mess in front of me before I let myself feel anything else."

"As long as you remember that I'm not into hiding. I won't

do that." Carla adjusted the blanket around Anna. "Are you sure there's someone you can call if you need help?"

Anna nodded. "No problem." She pointed her index finger toward Carla and added, "And I want you to remember that I want to get back on that bike one of these days. Will you go with me?"

"Absolutely. I'll call you when I get back to Seattle." With a sweet kiss on Anna's cheek, Carla left the room. Anna heard muffled footsteps as Carla left and then heard her run back up the steps and poke her head in the door. "I almost forgot; will you come with me to a birthday party when I get back? Maybe a little different than other birthday parties that you've been to—only women invited."

"A lesbian party?" Anna tipped her head and looked over the top of her glasses. "A date?"

Carla nodded, "Yes, a lesbian party, and yes, a date."

"Okay," Anna said. "Thank you. I'll look forward to it."

"It'll be fun," she said as she blew Anna a kiss. "I'll call you with the details." Carla called back as she ran down the steps and out the front door.

Chapter 22

No long walk for Koru for three days. None today, either, Anna thought as she stood in the kitchen and watched Koru in the yard, intensely engaged in his sniffing circuit. She shaded her eyes against the sun coming through the window as it rose over the dogwood tree. Another clear day. Still in her pajamas, she limped over to the coffeepot and poured herself a second cup.

The dog door flapped opened, and she laughed when she

saw Koru stick his head in, look around, and then back out again. Looking for what? She had no idea. She wished Koru could talk. She'd discuss Mort with him. "Koru, what did you notice? He must have been gone often, don't you think? Where was I?" Maybe even then, Koru would have little to offer on the subject.

Discussing sex with Koru also seemed pointless. She wished she could talk with someone about how it had been with Mort. He had his routine, a little neck action, a breast or two, some finger, and then the main act. Sometimes she used her mouth and that seemed to help him. As the years passed, she started using lubricant. Her own wetness didn't come naturally very much anymore. But when Carla had touched her breast, she felt a flow she hadn't felt in years. Hot. Hungry.

Did that mean she was a lesbian? Had been one all along? Maybe her feelings had little to do with lesbianism and more to do with simple attraction. Or something new. When you are attracted, you get aroused, and when you're not, you don't. Or you pretend.

She knew a lack of estrogen made a woman dry; there was some truth to dried-up old lady. Now that she was on replacement therapy, maybe she would stay wet. And hot. She blushed.

Koru came through the dog door just as the phone rang.

"Lily. Good morning." Anna took out two slices of fresh whole wheat bread and put them in the toaster.

"Is this a good time to catch up?"

"Not really. I'm not even dressed, and I've got to meet Ken for an editing session. But I've got a few minutes. How are you?"

"Good. Busy. I love it here. You?"

"Well...I promised to tell you how I was, so...I fell riding a bike." She reached for a clean plate among the already clean dishes in the dishwater.

"Riding a bike? Are you kidding?"

"No, Lily. I'm not kidding."

"Are you hurt? What were you doing riding a bike? Where did you get a bike? I didn't know you even knew how to ride."

"Whoa. One question at a time. I scraped my leg and bruised my hip. It happened a couple of days ago, and I'm getting around just fine."

"Why bike riding?"

"A friend, from my video class, had an extra bike. No big deal."

"Did you go to the doctor?"

"Lily, don't make me sorry I told you. I'm fine." Anna buttered the toast and sat down at the table.

"I'm just surprised, that's all. You could have really gotten hurt. Do you have a helmet?"

"Yes. I had a helmet."

"Can I believe you?"

"Lily. I thought you wanted me to tell you the truth. That's the truth. Be nice, or next time you won't hear anything." Anna finished one slice of toast and started on the second.

"Sorry, Mom. I'm glad you're okay. So you're making friends in the class?"

Anna pictured Carla's lips. "Yes. I'm enjoying it. Our documentary is taking shape. Wait until you see it."

"I can't wait."

"Maybe you'll come to the premiere in June."

"Maybe."

"I've got to get going, Cookie. Thanks for calling. I'll talk with you soon. Love you."

Anna put the phone down, gathered up her dirty dishes, and placed them in the sink. She washed the coffeepot, filled Koru's dishes, and made a quick grocery list. She didn't expect a long meeting with Ken and knew there would be time afterwards to go to REI and shop for something to wear to a lesbian party. She'd ruined her one decent pair of jeans and could get another pair there as well.

The new REI was already a few years old, but for Seattleites, it would always be the new one—opposed to the old one on Capitol Hill, the one with rolling wooden floors and a labyrinth of rooms. Not that she'd shopped there that often, but it had been an institution.

Upstairs in women's clothing, Anna looked for a salesperson to help her, someone butchy, she thought, who could subtly direct her to appropriate clothes. How ridiculous. What she thought looked like a butchy woman could easily be a married woman with five children. Of course, even then the woman could still be a lesbian. So much for stereotypes. It was all rather confusing.

And what was she? Maybe she could call herself a lesbian. Probably not. But she was sure she could never say "dyke" clothes, call herself a dyke. Maybe she could say she was a straight and just happened to fall for a woman. Was she in love? Why did she have to say anything at all?

She picked out a few pairs of jeans to try and then studied the racks of clothes for something lesbian to wear to the party.

"Hi. My name is Brook. Can I take those from you and start you in a dressing room?" Anna looked at the young woman, maybe twenty or twenty-one, without makeup and with a ponytail and a sleeveless shirt that showed her muscles. Did having muscles equate with being a lesbian? Anna laughed at herself.

"Can I help you find anything?"

Anna looked at the racks of heather-toned clothing, muted colors, khakis and browns. So not her. She was a winter and needed jewel tones, but she needed to try. "Maybe some cargo pants, not too casual. Maybe trousers?"

"Are you looking for moisture wicking? Sun protection? Convertible?"

"Convertible?"

Brook pointed to a rack of assorted beige pants with zippers near the knees. "They convert to shorts, so they're very versatile."

She tried on a number of beige cargo pants in a synthetic material, some with two pockets on each leg, some with only one. Brook brought her a navy shirt, moisture wicking, whatever that meant, with pockets over the boobs.

She stepped out to look in the three-sided mirror. She looked at the woman in the mirror and didn't recognize herself. Maybe a lesbian look, whatever that was. But definitely not her look. She needed clothes that flowed, clung, something more sophisticated, not big pockets stuck on her legs.

Mostly young people walked between the racks of clothing. She saw few other gray-haired people. But they were there. Maybe it wasn't an age thing or a gender thing or a sexuality thing. It was more about growing comfortable with who she was, inside and out. No fancy cocktail dresses, no cargo pants. She'd have to figure it all out. Lesbian or not.

Anna folded the pants she'd tried on and hung them on their hangers again. The active shop at Nordstrom's would be a better fit. She knew that. "Brook, I'll take these two pairs of jeans, but that's it for me today."

God, she thought as she walked to the checkout counter. Obsessing about Carla, about lesbians, was a distraction. She and Ken had set a tight schedule, and she needed to focus on editing. Mostly she needed to concentrate on what to do about Helen and Rachel. Rachel who had a little dog named Koru. What would she do about Mort's letter? Would she tell Larry and Lily they had a sister?

Yet as she stood in the checkout line, she contemplated the bodies in front of her. The line of a woman's back, the light hair on a young man's arm. Tendrils of curls along a tall woman's neck. It had been so long since she'd felt desire. She thought about the list of twenty-five things that would make her happy, the list Oprah's expert had suggested. She probably could think of twenty-five sexual things she wanted to do. Is this what Mort felt when he met Helen Dahlberg? The smile left her face as she paid for the jeans, found her car in the lot, and drove home. Along the way she listened to *All Things Considered*, but by the time she pulled into the driveway, she couldn't remember a word she had heard.

Chapter 23

Carla called to check on Anna's bruises and then again to make arrangements to attend Carla's friend's birthday party, but she hadn't seen her since her bike crash. Anna studied herself in the floor-length mirror for the thirtieth time. She'd changed slacks twice, blouses several more, and experimented with pendants, beads, earrings, and then no jewelry at all.

At the last minute, she noticed she still wore Mort's diamond and took it off, placing it in the wall safe. No longer married. And not just a widow. She would have divorced him had she known about Helen; at least she liked to think she would have. She was brave in her imagination.

She heard the bell ring. Koru barked, and she took one last look at herself in flat shoes, black slacks, and a blue silk blouse. She had no idea what was appropriate for a lesbian party, but she pleased herself. That was her new criterion.

Carla wore her usual very crisp white blouse with slacks, her dark eyes laughing as she pulled Anna into a long hug. Koru jumped around them. Anna felt stiff, too nervous to relax. Carla released her and kissed her cheek. "Nervous?"

"A little."

"Miss me?" Carla asked, as she petted Koru.

"A little." Anna got a biscuit to distract Koru as they left the house. Were any neighbors watching? Could they tell she was going on a date?

She felt awkward climbing into Carla's pickup; she'd never ridden in one before. Carla probably needed it for her drums. The height gave a great perspective as they drove over Lake Union and headed south. She could see some of the houseboats along Eastlake.

Pristine inside. No wrappers, straw covers, receipts. No mud on the mats. A miracle in Seattle. Had Carla cleaned it for the date, or was she compulsive? She noticed Carla's strong fingers glide along the steering wheel as she hummed to a CD Anna didn't know.

"'Sweet Woman,' Cris Williamson."

"Lovely voice. I've never heard her before."

"This is a very old song," Carla said as she turned up the volume. "It's a classic. Women's music. Actually lesbian music. Maybe Olivia Records' first album. I don't remember exactly."

Anna looked out at Capitol Hill as they drove through on I-5. She'd heard a lot of gay people lived there. "Lesbian music?"

Carla nodded as she moved into the HOV lane. Sure. "Holly Near? Meg Christian? Tret Fure?"

Anna shook her head.

"This album's as old as dirt. It's full of memories for me, good ones. It felt right to play it today."

Anna studied the CD case, *The Changer and the Changed*. "Wild Things," "Sweet Woman," "Tender Lady," "Dream Child." She'd never heard of any of them. "What a lovely voice," Anna said.

"Came out in the mid-seventies. They were all very political.

Very out. When few people were. It was the most amazing experience to go to a concert—an auditorium full of women, most of them lesbian."

They sped along I-5 listening to the haunting voice. Carla sang along to "Waterfall," her voice rich, vibrant, melodic, "*Sometimes it takes a rainy day...*"

Carla's voice drifted lower until she stopped singing and said, "Laura and I used to go to hear anyone we could when they came to Seattle, felt pride to belong to something so amazing. An auditorium full of lesbians listening to this incredible music. They were our heroes at a time when gay heroes were scarce. Gave me a lot of strength when I needed it."

Anna listened carefully, trying to catch the lyrics, floating along the freeway in a capsule with Carla. Private. Intimate. No longer nervous as she discovered a whole world that had been previously invisible to her: music, history, heroes, battles, successes. A world of its own. It is a whole lot more than whom you might be sleeping with, Anna thought. Or maybe would sleep with sometime soon. Could she do that?

"Yeah, this music gave me a lot of strength when I needed it. That's when I was coming out. When my husband and I came out. Seems like a hundred years ago, but there was so much pain. Memories of being in the psych ward so many years before. The music was liberating, and after twenty-five years, it still feels good to listen."

They were driving to Gig Harbor, an hour southwest of the city, for the birthday party. Surely she wouldn't know any of the other guests. She didn't have to worry.

When they arrived, Angela, the host, the birthday girl, more like a birthday grandmother, met them at the door of the three-story contemporary home facing Puget Sound. She grabbed Carla and squeezed tightly.

"Let go. I need to breathe," Carla yelled.

"I'm so glad you decided to come. It's been so long. You hermit, you." Angela kept her arm around Carla and looked at Anna. "Who's this?"

"My friend, Anna Simon. Anna, meet Angela Ortega. We've known each other since high school." Angela pushed Carla away and put her arm around Anna's shoulders. "Come, let me introduce you."

Carla pulled Angela's arm away. "I'll take care of that."

Angela laughed as they all walked out to the deck, where twenty to thirty women sat around small cocktail tables facing Puget Sound. No one she knew. Not even anyone from the band. "Drinks are in the kitchen. Appetizers in there," Angela said, pointing to a long table in an adjoining room.

Anna felt like an item on *Antiques Roadshow*—not because she was that old or even potentially valuable, but rather because she was the object of intense scrutiny.

"Carla, come here and introduce us to your friend," someone said, the word *friend* attenuated, full of innuendo, *friend* as *paramour*. Or did she just imagine it? Some of the women looked like old jocks: muscular, short hair, solid like Carla. Were they butches? She wondered. Carla was probably a butch. They hadn't talked about any of that. She figured she must be a femme, but did it matter? Did those things matter anymore?

Carla had hold of Anna's elbow as she guided her around the deck, introducing her to old friends.

"Meet Sandy. Sandy, Anna. Sandy and I played fast-pitch together for years. She was the best pitcher in the league. She took us to nationals." Anna had no idea what that meant. Was that another name for baseball?

A white-haired woman with clear blue eyes and a huge smile grabbed Carla from behind, turned her around, and hugged her tightly. "*Querida*, so happy to see you." They held each other for a moment. Anna stood to the side and tried to look comfortable.

Actually, she wasn't that uncomfortable. No one seemed to be posturing, angling for position. Carla wasn't working the room, and she certainly didn't have to. The atmosphere was relaxed, comfortable, warm.

"Anna, meet Louisa. She was Laura's first girlfriend, and they always stayed close, almost like sisters. I couldn't have gotten through those last months of Laura's cancer without Louisa." Carla kept her arm around the older woman. Louisa leaned her head against Carla, who continued, "This angel organized a support team for us—meals, rides. Whatever we needed." They hugged again, and Anna saw Carla's eyes tear up.

"I wish you only happiness," Louisa said as she looked first at Anna, then at Carla. "It's about time."

Anna heard music coming from someplace in the house. Carla obviously heard it as well. "Dance?"

Anna looked around, then nodded. Carla took her hand and led her toward the sound of the music.

An actual disco ball twirled in the huge room on the lower level. Several women danced to "Stayin' Alive." The Bee Gees. Time warp. She loved it. They stood on the sidelines and watched the dancers. Carla waved to a few and then went to get drinks.

Some amazing dancers, Anna thought as she tried not to stare. One tall woman, in a tank top, very tight jeans, and stiletto heels moved alone to some internal beat. A gray-haired couple doing a swing gyrated together as if they'd been practicing for years. A beautiful Latina woman with amazing cleavage in a sundress danced with her back to a woman who looked like a *Vogue* model in sweats. Anna looked for some common denominator: haircuts, clothing, anything. But each woman seemed unique. Her own self. The only common denominator seemed to be the laughter.

The song ended, and a new one began. Anna didn't recognize it at first. Slow. Carla placed the drinks on a table and took her into her arms. She put her hands where Mort usually did. She obviously was going to lead.

Very weird, this feeling of breasts so close. Carla's face only inches away. Something unknown. Not uncomfortable. Just very new.

"*I always dreamed I'd find the perfect lover....*" Streisand sang to Donna Summer. Anna looked up at Carla and felt a rush of something hot in her body. Carla smiled and pulled her closer. Her head rested on Carla's chest. The moved together slowly around the room. Carla kissed her temple, and Anna wanted all the other women to disappear. She wanted Carla's hands all over her, along her back, caressing her breasts.

And then suddenly the tempo turned upbeat. Carla spun Anna out over the dance floor, and they separated. Anna stood dazed for a moment, full of the feel of Carla's body. Then the rhythm took over. She could feel it vibrating through her veins. The beat whirled her around the room. Without hesitation, she twirled and stomped and laughed. Each time her eyes caught Carla's, she saw the heat in Carla's eyes and knew it matched her own.

"*Enough is enough,*" the singers' voices reverberated around the room. "*I can't go on... I want him out.*"

In Anna's brain, the refrain changed to *enough of Mort*. Enough of disappointment. Enough of anger. She wanted him gone. Him and his deceit. That life was over. She wanted to move on.

Carla reached out and pulled her close. They twirled around the room. "*Enough is enough. Is enough.*" Then the music stopped, and Carla kissed her. A hot, wet, messy, delicious kiss. Anna forgot where she was and who might be looking. This was her life now, that moment.

Carla laughed as she twirled Anna in circles surrounded by strangers. Strangers? Not really. A bunch of middle-aged women who looked natural and comfortable with who they were. Fat ones. Skinny ones. Well dressed and not.

She knew each one probably had her own issues, but they all seemed truly present on that dance floor. She wanted to be one of them. To be real. To be Anna. Just Anna.

Chapter 24

An overnight marine push left a deep fog in its wake. Little visibility that morning, but Anna knew the sun would burn it off soon. The murkiness appealed to her as she and Koru headed out for a loop around the lake.

Blurry shadows emerged to become people as Anna and Koru walked. Body memory led her along the path. Koru remained indifferent to the ambience and peed, as usual, near the edge of the lake. Anna recognized what must be the shore from bright yellow Japanese irises rising like little flags from the reeds.

Faces became clear only at a distance of a few feet. As she looked forward along the path, a body would slowly materialize out of the fog. Gradually edges would form, then colors, and suddenly a face would loom up and pass her quickly. An old man wearing a fishing hat. A runner in shorts and a tank top. Koru barked at a young girl walking a corgi. Revelations out of the fog. Surprises. Too many lately.

Gilda Radner used to say, "It's always something—if it ain't one thing, it's another." Did Roseanne Roseannadanna or another character say that? Anna couldn't remember, but she had loved Gilda with a passion. Loved her irreverence, her energy. Her fuck-you attitude. An attitude to which she planned to aspire.

Hormone replacement therapy, the stimulation of her video project, Carla—everything combined to reduce the Lucite that had encased her. Revelations about Mort and her meeting with Rachel had added a new layer of confusion and doubt, but it was more like cordite. Wasn't that the stuff that makes things explode? She wondered.

This morning would be dedicated to going through the photo albums—part of the steady elimination of Mort from the house. She'd put off dealing with their life in pictures. Today was the day.

The albums stood neatly shelved in the den. Dated. Easily accessible. When the twins had been young, she'd often taken out albums, not so many then, and talk to the children about each picture. Study them carefully. They loved to name everyone in the wedding album. Ask questions about their parents' honeymoon in Hawaii. Pictures of them as infants threw them into fits of laughter.

She didn't print hard copies any more. Everything was now digital. Mort had uploaded them on the computer, and she'd lost interest in the albums. Lily set up the screen saver to flash these more current pictures. As she sat in the den watching TV or reading, she'd see Mort's smiling face pop on and off the screen. She had deleted all of them. Each picture of Mort. Delete. Delete. Delete.

Pictures in the albums were trickier. Mostly she'd been the photographer. She had a Nikon 35mm with numerous lenses. She'd wait for the pictures to be developed in the old days. She always had them developed by professionals. No messing around with drugstore prints. She wanted high quality.

She'd open each envelope before she left the photography center, study the photos, make sure nothing needed to be reprinted. Once at home, she'd select the ones for the albums and put the others, along with the negatives, in special storage boxes. Every picture had dates and occasions. All carefully recorded. Their life documented.

Now she knew someone else had taken photos of Mort. Anna had one of those photos now in a little baggie in her purse. How many others were there? Was there one of Mort with Helen and Rachel? Probably many.

Could she rip him out of the albums—out of a time when they had been closer? When they shared a life? When they raised a family? She knew she should save some pictures for the kids. Maybe she would just give them the albums. Did she want to give the record of so much of her own history away? Even to her children? What would they do with these albums after she died? Keep them or throw them away? Why had she bothered?

When they were first married, the albums had come from Woolworth's. They were cardboard, coated in cloth. Mostly blue. They were lined up on the bottom shelves of the wall of bookcases in the den. Some of the backs were now taped together. Later, Mort decided they should come from Aspinal of London. Leather bound. Rich mahogany colors. There were seventeen altogether. A record of their life together.

Although it was mid-May, it was still so foggy outside and chilly that she decided to start the gas insert fireplace in the living room. Anna prepared a cup of Egyptian licorice tea. Mort had hated the smell of it. Couldn't tolerate herbal teas. Only black teas. He'd started importing them as well.

She decided to start with the early albums, the wedding album. The first page opened to Anna and Mort standing with her father and sister. Page two with his parents. She closed the album and put it back on the shelf for another time. Too many memories. That generation dead, long gone.

Her stomach hurt already. Maybe she didn't have to make any decisions today. Maybe she could just look and think.

The twins' first album. It always stood out—thicker than the rest. The babies at the hospital wearing the sweet knit hats Mort's mother had crocheted. Then the four of them in the hospital, Mort leaning over her while a twin rested on either side of her chest. So tiny.

Anna closed her eyes and sniffed, trying to find that special smell, the baby smell she often could bring up at will. Their baby breath. The baby oil mixed with the ineffable scent of infant. She lay back against the sofa and stared into the flames shooting from the artificial log.

In her mind, Anna gathered the smell to her, and then the memories came. She'd run her index finger carefully along each of their noses. Tiny eyelashes fluttered against their cheeks as they slept. She often wondered if babies dreamed. When she held them, she'd be kicked by a leg or hit with an arm flaying. Little fists would clutch and then open.

Koru now lay cuddled up next to her by the sofa, kicking and twitching as well. Was he dreaming? Do our bodies act out our dreams in real time?

Each time Anna would nurse the babies, her concentration narrowed. She knew other women tried to read or watch TV; they found nursing boring. She never had. But Larry had had difficulty latching on, so she held him while she gave him pumped milk. She breast-fed Lily for several more months. She studied their every movement. Every tiny gesture. The house silent around her. After feeding, they would fall asleep, and Anna would drift off as well.

Anna wondered if her own mother had felt the same heart-stopping emotion she had felt when the twins had been born. Did twins intensify the experience? Her mother had not lived to see them. Mort's mother had taken her place; only she was Bubbeh to Anna's children. Mort was in a lot of the pictures.

She couldn't destroy them. Maybe just the ones after he'd taken up with the girlfriend. The for-sure-liar pictures. She put the childhood albums back and pulled out 1990—apparently it had been an eventful year. A whole album devoted to that year.

The fog outside had lifted. The sun shone through the living room window, and Anna turned off the gas jet. She went upstairs to her secret stash and chose a Fran's GoldBite. She resealed the bag and realized there was no need to hide candy anymore. No one was watching; actually, no one had ever watched. She took the bag of candy and put it front and center in the kitchen pantry.

She unwrapped the gold foil and sucked in the rich blend of dark chocolate and caramel. Never again would she worry about what someone else thought about her weight. Her figure. She had always wanted to stay attractive, sexy for Mort. Desirable. She had a feeling that the size of her tummy wouldn't matter to Carla one way or another.

The 1990 album started in the month of May, when the twins graduated from Roosevelt High School. She and Mort standing next to Lily and Larry in their caps and gowns. Lily and her friends. Larry with his. The graduation party on the deck. So many people. Catered by Canlis. Anna studied each picture, carefully trying to remember. There had been no clues. The picture she had found of Mort with Helen Dahlberg had been dated February 1990. He had been seeing her by the time of the graduation party.

She couldn't remember some of the people in the pictures. Maybe the round bald guy had been Lily's chemistry teacher. Larry's track coach was there, and the blond with him must be his wife. Pictures of all their childhood friends. Were any of them still in touch? Lots of candid shots of people at the party. Why had she put them all in the album? Some of the group pictures didn't have names of the people. Now, ten years later, she couldn't remember many of the people. Mort had always invited clients, cronies. He loved playing host.

She scanned the pictures, and one taken next to the buffet table caught her attention. In the background was a blond standing next to Jack, Mort's law partner. It couldn't be. Absolutely not. Carefully, she raised the plastic covering the page. She tried to lift the picture to get a closer look, but it was stuck.

Anna got a knife from the kitchen and slowly pried it loose. She raised it to her eyes. Even with her bifocals, she couldn't see the face clearly. She returned to the kitchen and dug around the junk drawer, looking for the magnifying glass she knew was there. Yes. There it was.

She took it back to the living room, into the best afternoon light. She adjusted the magnifying glass over the picture. There she was. Clear as day. Helen Dahlberg on the deck. It must be. At the graduation party. Unbelievable. She looked closer. That son-of-a-bitch. Had Jack known? Maybe she'd been Jack's date? Is that when Mort met her? But he had known her in Palm Springs in February. Was she Jack's girlfriend then? Or had Mort invited his mistress to their home?

Her hands shook as she started to rip the picture in half. This was a picture easy to eliminate. Maybe she'd burn it instead of tearing it. Have a little ceremony. She went to the kitchen to look for matches. Anna rubbed her right forearm with her left hand. The tension she carried was literally painful. Her jaw clenched. She stopped herself before lighting the match and had a better idea. Anna wanted to see the look on Jack's face when she showed the picture to him. She would confront him. Had everyone known except her?

Carefully, Anna placed the picture of Jack and the blond in an envelope and replaced the album on the shelf. She closed the French doors to the den and walked upstairs for a long soak in the tub.

Chapter 25

Colorful paper shades covered tiny bulbs strung above the booths that lined the cozy restaurant. Anna hadn't been there since Mort died. The manager greeted them at the door. "Haven't seen you for so long. Welcome, welcome. Your favorite booth is empty," he said as he led them to a corner booth near the window.

Anna's body tensed as she walked along the booths and glanced into each, hoping she knew no one; no old friends, neighbors, or anyone who might know her, Mort, or the twins. She relaxed as they were seated. Only strangers this evening. The citrusy, sweet smell of lemongrass came from the neighboring table.

"Yum. I'm starving," Carla said as she studied the menu. "Any recommendations?"

"Mort and I usually ordered the pad thai and the orange beef."

"Two or three stars?"

Anna laughed. "Nope, maybe one star."

"Willing to take a risk, eh?"

"Maybe. Maybe. Give me some time." She read each item on the menu, looking for something different, something new. Each time the door opened, she tensed, looked up over the top of the menu to make sure it was no one she knew. Anna hadn't seen Carla since the party in Gig Harbor where she had been perfectly comfortable. Here, in a popular restaurant in her neighborhood, she felt her back stiffen and pressure on her chest. Edgy.

She'd had dinner with friends before, other women over the years. No big deal. But this was a date. A romance blooming. With a woman. Very different. She was comfortable with the easy flow of conversation, but there was something humming beneath the surface.

Carla ordered swimming angels with a few stars. One of her favorites. Anna agreed to shrimp pad thai with one star and added an order of lemon chicken. They sipped wine while they waited, and Anna kept her eyes on Carla, trying not to look up each time the door opened.

The huge, steaming platters of food arrived quickly. Anna sniffed the pungent smell of peanut sauce. She dipped her finger into the swimming angels and tasted it with the tip of her tongue. "Too much for me," she said and grabbed her water.

Carla reached her chopsticks into the pad thai and wrapped several noodles tightly, then sucked them into her mouth. She licked her lips and looked at Anna. "Did you miss me?"

Anna raised her brows, tilted her head, and said, "Maybe." She pierced some chicken with her chopstick and slowly drew it into her mouth, chewed slowly. Then she reached out her tongue out and licked a drop of sauce that had remained on her lip.

Carla brought an orange slice to her mouth and began sucking its moisture.

"Stop. Uncle." She slipped off her shoe and ran her foot over Carla's leg under the table.

Carla made little noises as she ate. Smacked her lips, hummed. "Fabulous food." Anna reached across the table and wiped some sauce away from Carla's chin with her index finger.

"Anna Simon? Anna. That is you." Anna looked up into Marilyn's smiling face at the edge of their booth.

"Marilyn. Hi."

"I just came over to pick up some food for dinner. I looked up, and there you were. Here you are." Anna imagined Marilyn's eyes popped out of her head, bobbing back and forth on springs as she studied Carla but pretended not to. "Are you the woman that took Anna biking? Carla?"

Anna answered for her. "Yes. This is Carla." No doubt now that Irene had called Marilyn after the bike crash at the lake.

"You don't mind if I just sit down here while I wait for my food? Don't let me stop you from eating." She didn't wait for an answer, but slid into the booth next to Anna.

Silence. Carla sipped her wine and looked at Marilyn. Marilyn stared back. Carla picked up her chopsticks, dug into the swimming angels.

Anna found her voice. "So I guess Irene told you about my fall."

Marilyn nodded but didn't take her eyes off of Carla. She studied her as if she were a rare specimen in a laboratory, as if she had never seen someone use chopsticks before. "Are you hurt?" She glanced quickly at Anna but continued to look across the table.

The food felt thick in Anna's stomach. She wanted to push her elbow into Marilyn and shove her off the seat. She could barely breathe. "I'm fine. It was nothing. How are you? Jack?" As soon as Anna said Jack's name, she saw the image in her mind, the picture of Jack standing next to Helen Dahlberg at the graduation party. Then a sickening thought. Had Marilyn known about Mort's affair?

She turned to Anna. "We're fine," she said, then looked back to Carla. "It looks like Anna's not going to introduce us." She extended her hand across the table. "I'm Marilyn, an old friend of hers. I've known Anna for over thirty years. Our husbands were law partners. Have you known her long?"

Carla shook her hand. "For a while."

Anna interjected. "I met Carla through my class at the university. Don't you think you should check on your food? It's probably ready."

"Right. It's probably ready. Nice meeting you, Carla. Call me, Anna. I'd love to hear what you've been up to lately." A huge weight lifted off the seat when Marilyn rose to leave. Air flowed around the booth again.

Carla didn't say anything, just continued to eat, slowly finishing her food.

"Dessert?" the waitress asked when she saw they were finishing. "We have lemon sorbet, green tea sorbet, and mango today." Anna looked at Carla, who shook her head.

"Just bring us the check, please."

"My treat," Anna said as she took the bill. "Remember. I invited you. I don't cook much lately, and I owe you a dinner." Anna left a few bills on the small, black tray, and they left the restaurant.

Red and orange slashed across the sky as they walked west toward Anna's house near the lake. The days were longer and longer as they approached the summer solstice.

"That brought back awful memories for me," Carla said. "I told you before, I won't be anyone's secret."

"She's the biggest gossip in the city. Worse than her sister-in-law. She doesn't have to know my business."

"That's not the point, is it?"

"No. I'm sorry. You're right. I just didn't know what to say to her."

"Actually, it's very simple. How about, 'Marilyn, this is my friend Carla. Carla, this is my old friend Marilyn.' The fact that you were so obviously uncomfortable makes it an issue."

"I didn't want to lie."

"And you didn't want to tell the truth, either."

"What was I suppose to say? 'I'm hot for this woman . . .'?"

"Anna, I know this is hard for you, that you've gone through a lot. You never expected to fall for a woman, but you're going to have to figure it out. I'll hang in for a little while longer, but you need to decide whose life you want to live."

"What do you mean?"

"Do you want to lead your life, or some made-up life, whatever you think everyone"—Carla waved her hands out across the horizon—"expects of you. Dance to some tune out there that you can barely hear."

Anna stopped and picked a delphinium growing at the edge of a rockery they passed. She handed it to Carla. "I just wasn't ready. You're right. I'm sorry."

"Okay."

Carla stopped in front of a retaining wall, and they studied the succulents lining its top. "I used to steal plants like these on walks Laura and I took in our neighborhood. We started sections of our yard in Fremont with slips from all our neighbors' gardens: hens- and-chickens, sedums, aloe, jade plants. You just stick them in the ground, and by the next year, they're all over. We bought the house when we first got together, maybe thirty years ago."

"Have you been in another relationship since she died?"

"No," Carla said and wiped a residue of dirt from her hand.

"Why?"

"I don't know. I wasn't ready. Haven't found the right one. I don't know."

"Did you ever think about being with men again?"

Carla shook her head. "No."

"No doubt there?"

"None. I was always a lesbian. My marriage was . . . an aberration."

"Some people think being a lesbian is an aberration."

Carla stopped on the street and turned to face Anna. "Yes, they do. Do you?"

"I don't think I do. But I don't know. I mean, it's fine, no problem with anyone being gay. Not about other people. But I don't understand it for myself." Anna turned away and pretended to look at a Japanese maple on the parking strip. Carla came up beside her. Anna felt her arm drift back to Carla, felt a yearning in her hand to reach for Carla's hand. She didn't act on it. But she certainly felt it.

Mort had always taken her elbow, guided her about. They hadn't held hands for years. Maybe never. She reached out and took Carla's hand firmly in her own as they walked slowly back to her house. No, Marilyn wasn't the issue. Marilyn would likely get a kick out of hearing about Carla. She'd probably be happy for Anna.

Anna's squeezed Carla's hand. "I don't want to lose you, lose this amazing feeling I have when we're together. Will you give me a little more time?"

Carla nodded as they reached her truck parked in front of Anna's house. "We'll see how it goes. But I'm not into pretending," she said, leaving a soft kiss on Anna's cheek.

Chapter 26

Loud barks from outside woke Anna, and then a long loud howl interrupted by the phone ringing. Bark. Howl. Ring. She pulled the pillow over her head. More rings. Anna reached for her glasses to check the caller ID. The rings stopped. So tired. Anna closed her eyes trying to recapture the dream. Nothing. It had taken her a long time to fall asleep. She hadn't slept well. Images of Carla and Marilyn staring at each other in the restaurant…awkward and embarrassing.

Koru had stopped his barking. Whatever had been was resolved. The squirrel had disappeared, the bird had flown off, the mail carrier had moved on. The dog door gave Koru freedom to explore his world. Autonomy. She needed her own dog door.

The phone rang again. This time she answered. Maybe Lily or Larry. Why would they call so early?

"Anna?"

"Marilyn?" Anna yawned and cuddled deeper under the covers.

"Yes. Marilyn. I've been calling you for the last half hour. Did you just get home?"

Anna sat up and leaned back against the headboard. "What are you talking about?"

"Sounds like you're just waking up."

"I am."

"Is someone there with you?"

Anna pulled off the covers and walked to the window. Morning sun filled the room when she pulled back the heavy drapes. "What? What are you talking about?"

"I was just wondering if someone was with you."

She opened the window and looked out. Koru was sunning himself on the deck. "Why would you think someone's here. Mort's dead, remember? "

"Dammit, Anna. Why do you have to be so bitchy?"

Anna took a deep breath. "Wait, Marilyn. Let's start this again. Good morning, Marilyn. How are you?"

"Fine, thank you. And you?"

"I'm fine, too. Thank you."

"Glad to hear it."

Silence. Anna leaned against the wall and heard nothing but Marilyn's breathing for a few seconds. Then in a rush Marilyn said, "You treated me like shit last night, like a stranger. Like you hardly knew me. How long have we been friends? Thirty, thirty-five years? Dammit. I deserve an explanation."

"Wait a minute, Marilyn. I just woke up."

"You can't keep putting me off. Who is this Carla?"

"Marilyn. I will talk to you, but really, I just woke up. Can I call you back? I need to pee," Anna said as she walked into the bathroom.

"I need to see you in person. Not on the telephone. I don't have any appointments until this afternoon. Meet me at the lake in an hour?"

"At the lake?"

"Yeah. The turtle log. Remember? We used to meet there all the time. Or have you forgotten?"

"Okay, okay. I'll meet you there."

"Good. I'll see you then." Anna heard the receiver slam.

She put the phone on the vanity and sat on the toilet. Koru ran up the stairs and nuzzled his wet nose in her face. "Good boy. You smell like spring," she said, kissing his face. "Want to go to the lake this morning?"

Anna threw on a pair of sweats and arrived before Marilyn. She crouched among the reeds at the shore where she could watch the turtles on their log. At least a dozen perched in a line, their heads swaying as they sniffed the air. One still in the water began a slow climb on to the log, which then began to tilt. She noticed the other turtles manuever to retain their balance.

She wondered if her little turtle was among them. No red markings were visible from a distance without binoculars. She decided he was indeed there; she trusted her little guy had survived and now sat with his buddies on the log.

Anna turned and saw Marilyn sitting on the bench with her hands folded on her lap clutching her purse. As usual, she was spiffy and coordinated. She wore black capris, a black-and-white sailor top, and black sandals with small heels. Always well turned out. Her sunglasses hid her eyes, but her back was rigid against the bench. She's nervous, Anna realized. Two of us then. Anna was glad she had decided at the last minute not to bring Koru.

She took a deep breath, walked toward the bench, raised her hand toward her shoulder, and waved slowly. Her heart raced.

Marilyn lowered her purse to the bench and waved back.

"Thanks for meeting me," Marilyn said as Anna joined her

"Actually, I'm glad you called. Last night felt awful to me, too. Stupid."

"Really?" Marilyn took off her sunglasses. Her blue eyes blinked as they adjusted to the sun. She looked soft this morning, vulnerable.

"Yeah. We have been friends for a long time. I was rude. You're right. I'm sorry."

"Don't apologize so quickly," Marilyn said and laughed. "I've been practicing, calling you names. Being pissed off."

Anna shook her head. "You should be pissed off. Last night was awful. I should have introduced you to Carla."

"Okay. So, who's Carla?" Marilyn turned toward Anna, who continued to stare out at the water.

"Carla's a woman in the band. I didn't mean to be rude. You just surprised me."

"What band?"

Anna turned to face Marilyn. "You know, the class I'm taking—making documentaries. I'm working on one about a marching band."

"You never told me about a class, but then we haven't talked for a long time." Marilyn's fingers lifted toward her mouth and touched her lips, then shook her head. She looked back toward the lake. "We haven't really talked since Mort died."

"No, we haven't." Anna's jaw tightened. "I'm sorry."

Marilyn reached out and briefly touched Anna's arm. "It's not all your fault. Not really." She pulled her hand back. "I thought about it after we talked this morning. After I heard your voice.

Your morning voice, so familiar to me." Marilyn looked down. "Actually, I really didn't want to be around you that much."

Anna raised her eyebrows.

Marilyn nodded. "I remember Jack and I came up to the hospital that first night after Mort's stroke. Before we knew what was going to happen. Except we knew. We saw all those machines. They would only let one of us in at a time. Remember?"

"I don't remember much." Anna tried to focus on that first night. All foggy in her mind now as it was then.

"You were trying to be polite. Thanking people for coming. But your face. You didn't really know who I was. You just looked through me. I hugged you, but you weren't in there. Blank. Just as gone as Mort. Creepy. I kept wondering what I'd look like if Jack was lying there."

"I don't remember."

"I do. What a night. Jack and I came straight home from the hospital and had crazy sex. Like we were twenty again. Amazing. The stuff of fantasies."

Anna smiled. "At least something good came out of that awful night."

"Didn't last long," Marilyn said and chuckled.

Anna felt her shoulders loosen and her stomach soften. So familiar for her to be talking with Marilyn. "I know I hardly returned your phone calls. I just couldn't."

"No, you didn't." Marilyn reached down for her purse and pulled out a package of cigarettes.

"You haven't stopped yet?"

"Barely a couple a day. Don't you dare tell Jack." Marilyn lit a cigarette and took a deep drag. "Anna, if we're going to be honest here, I need to tell you that I didn't try that often to reach you. Not really. I called at times when I thought you might not be home.

You were too sad to be around. I looked at you and thought about Jack dying. It depressed me."

"Stop with the confessions. You don't have to apologize." Anna reached for Marilyn's cigarette and took a puff. "I thought it was all my fault. I disappeared. Honestly, for so long my life was all about Mort. Wrapped up in Mort and our lives together. He was gone, and then I was gone..."

"There's life in your eyes again, a gleam I haven't seen for years."

"I feel like I'm back in my body, back in my life."

Marilyn took another deep drag and watched the smoke as she exhaled. "Is it that woman, Carla?"

The muscles in Anna's thighs tightened. She felt the rough wood of the bench through her sweats. "Maybe. Maybe just time. Maybe hormone replacement. I'm not sure." She stood and stretched her hamstrings against the wooden bench seat. "Something shifted inside of me." She sat again, raised her knees to her chest and held them tightly to her. "I wanted my life back. I lost it for a while, gave it away. I thought I wouldn't make it, wouldn't find my way back. That maybe I was already dead."

Marilyn leaned in and in a quiet voice said, "When you love someone as much as you loved Mort..."

Anna nodded, released her knees, and stood again. Not the time to think about that. Loved Mort or didn't love him. A thirty-year marriage was very different than happily ever after. Then she wondered, for a moment, if she had misunderstood Marilyn's tone. Was she actually poking around about Mort's other life? Had Marilyn known? Jack had. Maybe someday she would have a real conversation with Marilyn about Mort. Not yet.

Marilyn stubbed her cigarette out on the concrete and put the butt in a nearby trash can. They resumed their seats and quietly observed people walking along the path between their bench and the lake. A middle-aged man with a big belly led a honey-colored cocker spaniel. A skinny old man wearing a tank top and plaid Bermuda shorts whizzed by on rollerblades. A little girl passed riding a small yellow bike with training wheels followed by a gray-haired woman who likely was her grandmother.

"Do you get to see your grandchildren often?" Marilyn asked.

"Not much."

"That's too bad. I always envied you having grandchildren. I wish we did."

"You probably will. Or you won't. Just another thing we can't control!"

Marilyn grinned and said, "You know I like controlling things, knowing everything." She poked Anna in the shoulder. "You know that about me."

"I do. Nosy. Pushy. Controlling. The perfect realtor."

"Don't kid yourself. It helps. Okay, so here's pushy. Carla. Tell me all about Carla."

No surprise to Anna. But she realized she did want to talk about Carla. Wanted to tell someone. Wanted not to be uncomfortable. Embarrassed. "Okay. But I have to get going soon. I'll walk you to the boathouse and head home from there."

"Alright. But you have to tell me something about her. I could tell when I sat down at your table last night that something was going on."

"Okay," Anna said as they walked south along the path. "Carla's the drummer in a lesbian and gay marching band, the band I'm making a documentary about."

"I thought so." Marilyn nodded her head and stopped walking.

"What do you mean?" Anna stopped and faced Marilyn.

"She had that look."

"What look?"

"She didn't look like she belonged to Hadassah. I mean, she looked what I imagine a lesbian would look like."

"You think there are no lesbians in Hadassah?" Anna began walking again.

Silence. Then Marilyn asked, "Do you think there are?"

"Of course. I think the saying is, 'They're everywhere'."

"I suppose. I don't think I know any." Marilyn stopped again. "Do you think you might be one? A lesbian?"

Anna paused, and they both stood still. "I don't know. Maybe," she said and continued walking.

Marilyn caught up to her. "You're serious, aren't you?"

"I'm very attracted to Carla. You'd like her. She's smart. Funny. Warm." Anna pictured the wall of family photos in Carla's house. "She's got kids and grandkids. And she sees them all the time."

"No kidding?"

"No kidding." Anna stopped to pet a black-and-white springer spaniel wearing a yellow bow, pulling her owner toward Anna and Marilyn. Likely just out of the groomers. The owner apologized and jerked her dog back.

Marilyn studied Anna as she petted the dog. When the dog and her owner left she said, "You looked so happy when I saw you at Krittika's last night. Laughing, smiling, your eyes twinkling. When I came over, you barely said hello." They continued on the path. "If you're going to be with her, does that mean we can't be friends anymore?"

"Don't be stupid. That's not it at all. Maybe there's a part of me that's embarrassed. Not the right word. I don't know the right word. Uncomfortable. I never thought about being involved with a woman."

"She's attractive."

"Yes. She is. This is hard to talk about."

Marilyn grabbed Anna's arm and stopped walking again. "Anna," she announced, "I don't really care about who you sleep with. Don't be uncomfortable with me." Marilyn didn't say anything for a moment. Anna started to walk, but Marilyn held her back. "As long as it's not Jack. Don't sleep with Jack." She chuckled. "Or me, for that matter." She paused and pulled at her lower lip. "Were you attracted to me all these years?" Marilyn placed her hand over her heart. "I'm sorry. Is that a stupid question?"

"No. This is weird. I don't think it's a stupid question. It happened the first time I saw her. Just very drawn to her." They were nearing the boathouse.

"Anna, I'm dying. What's it like?"

"What?"

"Sex with a woman."

"I don't know. I haven't done it yet."

"You haven't. Are you going to?"

"I hope so."

Marilyn's voice got louder. "When?"

"Maybe soon. I don't know. When the time is right."

There were a lot of people congregated near the bathrooms at the boathouse. Anna and Marilyn moved away into the shade and stood under a large oak.

"I always wondered if it's really different—better or maybe worse," Marilyn said.

"What?"

"Sleeping with a woman."

"I don't know. But making love with any person might be different. I've only had sex with two men in my whole life. I don't know. But you know, actually even with Mort it was different over the years."

"I'll second that one," Marilyn chuckled. "My friend, Anna, the lesbian. Amazing."

Anna felt lightheaded and leaned back against the tree. "If I have sex with a woman, am I a lesbian? Even if I was married for thirty years? How many times do I have to do it to make me a lesbian? If I end up with Carla, I suppose then I am. If we don't, then what am I? Would I have to get involved with another woman to be one? Otherwise I'm not? I hate that we have to pick a box and live in it."

"I suppose, if the box fits? Maybe you're bisexual?"

"I have no idea what to call myself. I don't really care. I just know what I feel. I want to trust that. Just see what happens." She pulled away from the tree. "Marilyn, I have to get going. I've got a meeting at the university about the documentary."

"Okay. One more question. What about the kids?"

"What about them?"

"Are you going to tell them?"

"Tell them what? That I'm attracted to a woman?"

"At least Lily. She'll be supportive."

"I suppose. But not yet. If they lived here. Or if there's some occasion when they'd meet her. But for now—they've got their own lives to deal with." She thought about Mort's secret child. The kids did not need more surprises now.

"Are you afraid to tell them?"

"I don't think so. It's more about having my own life. I am attracted to her. I feel alive when I'm with her. Happy. Is this a passing thing, maybe—or a forever thing? It's about letting myself discover what's happening before I send out a press release. Which reminds me..."

"What?"

"Marilyn, I'm hoping you'll keep this to yourself. Not tell Jack. Not Irene. Just between you and me now. I don't want anyone else to know at this point. Certainly not before I talk to the kids. Can you promise me not to send out a press release?"

"Anna, you know I have a big mouth. This is true. But if you find out that I spread this stuff, you'll never talk to me again. Not worth it. I've missed you." Marilyn leaned over and kissed Anna on the cheek and gave her a big hug. "Thanks for trusting me."

Anna watched Marilyn cross the street and walk toward her home in Wallingford. Odd—when Marilyn had hugged her, kissed her cheek, she had felt nothing in particular. No racing heart or throbbing in her body. A warm, nice, cozy feeling, but nothing like the rush she felt with Carla. Would Marilyn keep her mouth shut? Maybe. Hopefully. She had missed their friendship, missed hanging out with someone who had known her for so many years.

Jack and Marilyn, Mort and Anna—friends for thirty years. Were there other secrets hidden in those friendships? She stopped at the fountain for a long drink of water and headed home. She needed to talk with Jack, needed to know what he knew about Mort and Helen.

Chapter 27

Anna hunched over the editing machine, the shades drawn in the classroom that was their editing lab. She'd spent the previous two hours with Ken, studying the transcriptions of each interview, looking for the quotations that would further the story, illustrate the themes, the quotations essential to their documentary. They had a rough draft now of the script, everything they needed until they got the footage from the pride parade at the end of June.

Anna's task was to search hours of footage for the perfect shots to sequence into their ten-minute documentary. She started by identifying the opening sequence using the interview with Kelley, the band director. A close-up of Kelley talking about the band's history and then B-roll of the band as they practiced marching.

Time disappeared for her as she studied the quotations and

looked for the perfect shots to illustrate them. Other students sat hunched over their own machines, the room silent except for papers shuffling and keyboards clicking from time to time. Anna concentrated as she selected shots that lasted two seconds and strung them with others lasting five seconds, three seconds, quickly creating a story. She laid the audio track carefully, building confidence with each new sequence.

She knew Carla's interview was crucial, not only her words, but the strength of character manifested in her face. Anna paused on a shot of Carla, beautiful even at sixty, with high cheekbones and luminous, dark eyes. As she released the hold, Carla's brow furrowed, her head tilted slightly, and she looked directly at the camera.

"I found that, for me, the only way out of shame is straight ahead—forward. I had to face my own fear and tackle it, beat it out of myself by letting it hit the light. You have to do that, no matter how overpowering the fear. That's what I've learned."

Great quotation. Could be a voice-over of a key shot, maybe images of Carla during the interview, maybe Carla playing the drums, maybe the band marching forward, maybe a collage of faces, maybe a Seattle sunset shot...something. Anna wasn't sure what yet as she lay down the audio track.

She focused on timing Carla's statement, how many seconds it took, and scarcely heard the words. Then she played it back and listened. What had been just sounds a moment before, words without content, now suddenly blew into her brain, opening doors, full of meaning for her. It was exactly what she needed to hear.

"Yes. Yes. Of course, I'll see her," Anna heard Mort's partner say loudly behind the closed door to his office. The receptionist was new. They came and went. Probably didn't pay them enough. Or maybe Mort had leched after them. Anna had been rethinking everything she thought she had known about Mort. She could make a list of lies, half truths, and distortions over the years. So much guesswork. Maybe Jack could help her. Then again, maybe he would lie, or had been lying. Maybe even about how much the partnership was worth. The idea of opening that door overwhelmed her. Maybe she would just threaten. Maybe later.

Jack met Anna at the door. She got a whiff of the garlic he must have had for lunch when he hugged her and gestured toward the seating area. Her feet sank into a thick Persian carpet that defined the informal conference area. Large leather wing chairs, brass lamps, and mahogany end tables communicated prestige and comfort, while his massive, more contemporary desk spoke of efficiency.

"What brings your beautiful self to the office?"

"No need for flattery."

"What do you mean, flattery? It's a simple truth. You've always been a beautiful woman. Mort was a lucky man."

Anna turned slightly and looked directly at Jack. "Then why did he have a mistress for so many years?"

Anna observed Jack's face carefully. She noted his eyes turn down, then open wider. Then he smiled. "Why on earth would you say such a thing?"

She knew he was lying. She'd let him for a while. "Well, I just started having this funny feeling."

"Please sit down. Sit down." He gestured toward one of the wing chairs. "Let's talk. What kind of a feeling? I've neglected you. It's barely been a year. How are you? Grief. Grief can take over, makes you think crazy thoughts. Water? Can I get you some water? Some coffee? I remember you love coffee."

Jack walked to his desk, pressed an intercom. "Millie, get us some coffee." Jack opened and closed some files on his desk. "Let me just put this brief away."

Anna adjusted her suit jacket. She saw his eyes flit back and forth across the room, glance at her for a nanosecond and then dart away.

"I should have called you more often, checked in on you," Jack said as he sat across from her. "You must have been lonely. Have you been? You seem so independent. Marilyn was going to call you. Maybe she did. Did she? She said you're always busy. I thought you were fine. I mean, as fine as a person could be when her husband dies. You looked fine at Eva and Joe's anniversary party."

The receptionist arrived and served coffee. Anna kept her eyes on Jack's face. She didn't remember him having saggy jowls.

"So, tell me how you are?"

"Jack. Relax." Anna sipped her coffee. "You don't have to cover for him anymore."

"You have more than a feeling, don't you?"

"Yes. Mort left me a letter."

"Left you a letter? What kind of a letter?" Jack looked directly at Anna and leaned forward in his chair.

"An envelope, actually, with a copy of Rachel's birth certificate, a picture of Helen, and some instructions as well…and then there's this…" She reached into her purse and pulled out the picture of Helen standing next to Jack at the twins' graduation party.

He glanced at the picture and shook his head slowly. "Tell me you're kidding. He left you a picture? What a jerk." Jack folded his arms across his chest. "I told him he was a jerk. May he rest in peace. What kind of instructions?"

"He wants me to introduce his children, to make sure the twins meet Rachel."

"What a schmuck. I never knew he was such a schmuck." Again he shook his head.

"What did you know?"

"We met her at a conference in Palm Springs. There were a lot of lawyers from Seattle. I don't remember exactly. You and Marilyn were busy, I think. We decided to go without the wives."

"You know, Jack, I don't want to hear much about it."

"Okay. So why are you asking?"

"I want a legal opinion."

"A legal opinion?"

"Yes. I want to know if they have any claim on the estate."

"For sure Helen doesn't. You're the legal wife."

"You call her Helen. Did you spend time with her, too?"

"What do you mean? Did I *shtoop* her, too?" He made a loose fist with one hand and stuck the index finger of his other hand in and out of the hole. "Of course not."

Anna felt sick to her stomach. The crudeness of his gesture somehow disgusted her in a way nothing else had. For a moment, she actually felt sorry for the woman. Some men were such pigs.

"What about the daughter?"

"I'll have to check," he said. Jack looked down, shifted his eyes toward the clock. "I've got a meeting soon. I'll call you."

"Jack, what aren't you telling me?"

"Anna, why don't you just go home and try to forget about this?"

"Jack."

"Okay. Okay." Jack rose, walked to a window, and looked out at the clouds deepening across Elliott Bay. He spoke with his back to Anna. "He asked me to set up a trust for the kid. It clearly states that the trust is her inheritance from him and she is legally bound by its guidelines. Meaning, she could forfeit it and go after more. But I doubt that will happen. It's enough. From what I know, the woman didn't even want that." Jack turned to look at Anna. "I don't think she's greedy."

"Is she a slut?"

"No."

"Did he love her?"

"Yes. I think so."

Anna knew that would be the answer, thought she was prepared, but instead, it felt as if a heavyweight boxer had punched her gut. She pressed her stomach with her hand and tried to regain her composure.

"She's actually a decent person."

"So now you know her?" Anna asked. She lost whatever composure she thought she had. "Does a decent woman fuck someone else's husband? How many times? Once? Twice? So if it's an ongoing thing, a relationship—then it's okay? Even though there's a wife, children. Not a slut. Decent."

"I'm sorry, Anna. I can't believe he left you a letter. The *putz*." Jack walked toward Anna. "What's next? You're not going to do anything, are you?"

"I don't know, Jack." Anna stood, tossed the picture back into her purse, and walked to the door. "I don't know. I don't know what's best for the kids. That's what I'm going to do—when I figure that out."

Chapter 28

What was best for the kids? It had been a much easier question to answer when they were toddlers and she had to make nutritional decisions about Cocoa Puffs. Damn Mort for dying. Coward. Maybe she could leave a letter for the twins in her will, a confession about Mort's confession. Or just leave his envelope lying around, as if she had never found it.

That would be complicated, now that she had emptied his

office. Where could she leave it? Would that make her a coward as well? Or a loving, protective mother? Or maybe a jealous, controlling bitch? Damn him.

A list might help. Pros and cons. To tell or not to tell. She'd add another column for the consequences of each choice. Known and unknown. She shuffled through the mail on the kitchen table, looking for an empty envelope for her list. Just as she wrote number one, Koru came through the dog door. Before she could get a towel over him, he shook himself, spattering rainwater all over the kitchen.

Before he managed another shake, she got him into the bathroom and covered him with a huge old towel. He backed himself away from her, but she grabbed his collar and held it while she wiped the mud off each paw. The downside of a dog door, she thought, limited control of the inevitable mud in Seattle.

The doorbell. Koru barked and moved toward the now-closed bathroom door. His paws clean, she opened the door, and he ran to the front of the house. Becky Clayton stood huddled under a poncho waiting for her to open the door.

"Oh, Anna. Golly, Anna. You're home. I was afraid I'd miss you."

"Come in." She motioned Koru away as Becky dripped her way into the living room.

"Let me have your poncho?"

"Not going to stay." Becky shook her head. "Can't stay, but I need a favor…"

As Becky talked, Anna realized she'd rarely seen her neighbor without makeup, at least without her eyebrows penciled in and lipstick. This morning, water dripped from her wrinkled, barely visible brows.

"Don't want to bother you." She paced across the living room. "It's so early. I didn't want to wake you. Afraid I'd miss you. I'm sorry." She was back at the front door. "Dotty's maybe on her way out, and I'm beside myself. She's all I got left now."

"Slow down. How can I help?"

"I hate to ask..." She swallowed hard and held on to the doorknob. "But I remember how good you were with your husband's parents when they were dying. Then you went and did whatever you did with hospice. Dotty has hospice, but they're all strangers. She don't know them. Real nice, but all strangers. She knows you."

"She sure does." Although Anna hadn't seen her for years, she remembered Dotty well.

"Will you come with me to the Hearthstone? You know, up by Albertsons? Sit with us some? I've got no one else. I don't know what to do."

"Sure, I'll come. This morning?"

She nodded her head. "Please. I'm going there now. She's on the second floor, intensive nursing. Dotty Walters."

Anna watched Becky clutch the railing with one hand and slowly move down the front steps, a small stooped figure in the rain.

As Anna drove quickly in the rain, she realized that walking would have been faster, wetter, but faster. She circled the surrounding streets, finally finding a parking space two blocks away. What had been a cozy working-class neighborhood when she and Mort bought at Green Lake twenty-five years earlier had now become a trendy, upscale, dense, condo-infested place short on parking.

Anna rushed through the still-falling rain to the retirement home. A blast of warm air steamed up her glasses as she entered the lobby of the Hearthstone. She said hello to two women who sat hunched in wheel chairs, dressed for rain, likely waiting for rides. The lobby itself resembled any upscale hotel in the area, except for the sign-in and sign-out clipboard. Anna removed her raincoat, shook it out as much as possible, took a comfortable seat in an armchair near a window overlooking the lake, and wiped her glasses dry. The rain had slowed. A mist hung over the water, blurring Phinney Ridge off to the west.

Anna rested her hands on the arms of the chair, closed her eyes, and tried to calm the rapid beating of her heart, tried to find the spot of stillness. Focus on breathing. She hadn't been able to do it with Mort on his deathbed, but in the years when she had served as a hospice volunteer, she had been able to do it—briefly, in the situation, but she had done it.

No need to hurry. She knew she would be useless to Becky and her sister if she didn't enter the room grounded and at peace. She breathed into the tension in her back and let go of the tightness in her forearms. An image formed in her mind of what to expect in Dotty's room—not carefully drawn, but enough to ease away any fear at the sight of a dying woman.

Anna sat for another minute before making her way up to the second floor and to Dotty's room. Dotty lay on her back, covered by a light blanket. Her eyes were tightly closed, almost sunken under her now prominent cheekbones. Flushed color in her face and erratic breathing suggested that pneumonia had further compromised any chance of recovery.

Directly next to the bed, Becky sat and held her sister's hand. Anna stood by the door for a moment, observing Dotty's almost lifeless hand clutched tightly by Becky's liver-spotted, clawlike fingers.

Anna pulled another chair next to the bed and leaned in to hear her neighbor's words as she whispered to her sister.

"Dotty. Can you hear me? Dotty. You're going to get better. You can come and live with me again. We'll have such a good time." Becky leaned over and kissed Dotty's hand. "I made some strudel that you love, Momma's recipe. Remember? I've got it in the freezer, and I can warm it up quick."

Tapping Becky's shoulder, Anna motioned her out of the room, leading her to the family lounge down the hall. The faint smell of air freshener seemed to cling to the furniture. She took her neighbor's fragile hands in her own. Although Anna had several age spots already, her hands looked like that of a young woman, resilient and soft, next to Becky's mottled, parchment skin.

"What have the doctors told you about her condition?"

"They say she's dying, that there's nothing they can do. No hope, they said." Becky looked back along the hall toward her sister's room. She pulled her hands away and folded them in her lap.

"Is she in pain?"

"No. They're giving her morphine."

"What have the hospice people told you?"

"They told me she's dying. That it might help her if I told her I was okay and that I loved her."

Anna watched Becky's eyes fill with tears.

"But I won't be okay. She's all I have." The tears overflowed and ran down the furrows in her cheeks. She didn't seem to notice.

Anna leaned forward. "How else did the hospice people suggest you might help Dotty?"

"I don't want her to die." Becky brushed the tears from her cheeks, then covered her mouth with her hand and shook her head.

"Of course you don't, but from what you tell me, she is dying."

Becky nodded her head, her eyes wide and her mouth tight.

Anna's impulse was to remain silent. The sage green walls, comfortable furnishing, the lamps instead of overhead lights, sharply contrasted the conversations that were likely conducted in this family sitting room every day, like now. Dotty had come to her for help, so she leaned forward and took a deep breath. "Do you know what you sister might need from you now?"

Becky shook her head and then looked down.

Anna took Becky's hands again, rubbed them, trying to warm her cold skin. "She needs you to let her go. To really tell her you'll be okay. That you love her. I don't know what your religious beliefs are, or Dotty's, but you might want to tell her that your parents are waiting for her, that people who love her are waiting for her."

Becky began rocking in the chair, forward and back, forward and back. Anna noticed the tears drip down, but there was no sound. Only the rocking back and forth. She smelled the stale odor of sweat as Becky continued to sob silently.

Gradually, her rocking stopped, and Becky leaned back in the chair, her eyes red rimmed, her skin pale. She reached into a pocket and pulled out a crumbled handkerchief and blew her nose. She looked each and every day of her eighty-six years.

"Let's go back. I hate to leave her alone."

Anna put her arm around Becky's thin shoulders, and they returned to Dotty's room.

Shortly after they sat down next to the bed, a nurse entered, a large man in light green scrubs. Anna wondered if she'd ever get used to men as nurses.

"It's time for her bath. Would you like to leave the room, or stay and help me bathe her?"

Anna noticed a light smell of urine that she hadn't noticed before. Dotty's eyes were still tightly shut, her cheeks hollow, her breathing erratic.

"I'll help you," Becky said, and the nurse pointed to the sink and the disinfectant soap. Anna stood against the wall and gazed at the slow ritual of bathing a dying person. This nurse worked with a delicate touch, respectful in every gesture. Anna had seen caregivers handling living souls as if they were hunks of meat, and she was grateful her neighbor did not have to witness any callousness in the face of death.

Becky squeezed the water out of a washcloth and gently patted her sister's face, then laid it against Dotty's warm forehead and held it there. In a hoarse voice, Becky whispered to her sister. "I'll be okay. Don't worry about me. I'll eat that strudel myself. It's okay for you to go now. I love you. It's really okay."

They spent the next half hour sitting side by side, Anna holding Becky's hand, Becky holding her sister's loosely in her own and breathing, setting the slow rhythm that brought a measure of peace to Dotty's struggling body.

"I'm okay now," Becky said and squeezed Anna's hand. "Thank you for coming."

Anna stood, stretched, and gently rubbed Becky's back. "I'll check in with you later," Anna said, but Becky had already turned back to her sister. She scarcely noticed when Anna left the room.

Still chilly and overcast, Anna thought as she walked out of the Hearthstone and onto the street. Through the huge display window of a dance studio across the street, Anna saw dozens of women in leotards dancing to a soundless beat. She made her way to the car, and on the way home, stopped at Albertsons, bought a pack of cigarettes and matches, and drove to the parking lot near the boathouse. She put the car in park, lit a cigarette. Her first deep drag led to a coughing fit. It had been a long, long time since she had been a smoker.

Thoughts of Mort's funeral filled her mind as she looked out at the gray lake. The cemetery. A prepurchased plot in the Gan Shalom sections of Abbey View Memorial on Alaska. She had a reservation there for herself—next to Mort and near his family. Everything had been arranged: casket, headstones. Mort felt they couldn't count on the kids to get things done correctly, so he did it.

She pictured Mort's decomposed body in the traditional casket he had ordered and wondered how the casket fared a year later. Mort had insisted they be prepared. Always be prepared. She wondered if he had been prepared for his stroke. He had cajoled her into looking at caskets and meeting with the *chevrah kadisha*. Not the old-fashioned groups whose members actually used to come and prepare the body. But the newer version of Jewish burial societies who now came with laptops and development plans for the future of Jewish interments in Washington.

She'd sat in the synagogue surrounded by Mort's colleagues and their friends, Lily on one side, Larry on the other. Lily had barely stopped crying since Mort's stroke. With a yarmulke precariously planted on his curly hair, Larry had sat stoically, his jaw tight as he prepared to read the eulogy that the twins had written together.

Anna remembered Larry's eyes tearing when he talked about his father's vision for a better world. "Dad was committed to *tikkun olam*. Lily and I hope to follow the path he created for us."

Then Jack spoke, then Marsh Edelman, president of the synagogue. His old high school friend Murray Schwartz made everyone laugh with stories about their days at Roosevelt High. Her sister, Rose, sent a card, a condolence card from some evangelical church. They rarely talked. No communication since that card. It seemed like a century ago.

Her mind crowded with images of Mort and the twins. Her past. Empty now. As if there had been a house full of furniture and suddenly one day, all that remained was a shell of a building, maybe just the two-by-fours to indicate where rooms had been. Gone now.

She took a much shorter drag on her cigarette, not inhaling; it didn't taste as good as it used to. Opening the window, she touched the lit cigarette to the rain still gathered on her car, heard the sizzling sound of water as it extinguished the embers.

She pictured Becky holding Dotty's hand, and Anna wondered who would sit with her. Certainly not her own sister. Maybe her children. Maybe. She had the present and whatever life she could carve for herself in the future. No guarantees of anything really. None.

Over the weeks, she'd imagined dozens of ways she might tell Larry and Lily about their father. "Oh, by the way," she could say casually, "you have a sister." Or maybe she would say, "Your fucking father had a mistress and a bastard." Or "Children, I have some difficult news for you." Or maybe she would say, "I have some exciting news for you. Our family has grown. No, I'm not pregnant, but you do have a sister."

She'd kept the car running, and the windows had steamed up. She turned on the wipers and cleared the condensation off the inside of the windshield with her hand. She needed to make a path for her children, needed to know more about Helen before she decided anything. Was the woman rapacious, a greedy, scheming slut, or was she like most people, muddling through life, trying her best?

Rachel had nothing to do with her own life, but eventually she needed to talk to her children and let them decide whether they wanted Rachel to be a part of their lives. She put the car in drive, tossed the pack of cigarettes into a trash can at the edge of the parking lot, and drove home.

Chapter 29

What kind of a woman sleeps with another woman's husband? Lots of women. All kinds of women. Anna knew it happened. Things happen.

Anna did not want to meet Helen. The pictures were enough.

Younger. Willowy. Blond. Blond wasn't the issue. She, too, could be blond. But Helen was younger. She probably still had perky breasts.

The situation gnawed at Anna. She needed to focus and resolve the mess Mort had left before she could go on with her own life. So what if Helen was younger, maybe prettier, and God knows what else? Anna had been the wife, the legal wife. She had the house, the money, the respect.

She had to stop making it a contest about who was somehow better. There was a mess on the floor, and she needed to clean it up, one way or another. She needed to be an adult. To stay calm. Gather the information she needed and then decide about telling her children. Or not.

She left a message for Helen with the receptionist at Washburn, Larson, and Dahlberg. Anna had cleared her throat, coughed. She sounded as if she had laryngitis. "Ask her to call Anna Simon." She left her cell phone number. She did not want to walk into her own kitchen and hear Helen's voice on her answering machine. "No. No message. Just tell her to call Anna Simon." The telephone receiver was wet as she unclenched her sweaty fingers.

"Come on, Koru. It's a perfect day for a long walk."

Halfway around the lake with Koru, she heard her cell and recognized Helen's office number.

"Hello, Anna Simon here." She walked off the path toward a bench along the shore. At that moment, Koru chose to squat and poop. "Oh great," Anna said to herself, "a little more shit in my life."

"This is Helen Dahlberg." Her voice reminded Anna of a robocall. No emotion.

"Hold for a minute." Anna put the phone on a nearby bench and picked up Koru's deposit with one of the bags she always carried and then dropped it into a nearby trash can. Her hands shook as she held the phone to her ear.

"I think we have some things to discuss." No sense in small talk.

"You found the letter?" Emotionless. Robotic.

Still standing, Anna felt nauseous, a jittery feeling in her stomach. Mort had told Helen about the letter. Of course. What else did this woman know about her? Anna gripped the back of the bench—the wooden slats rough against her hands. "What other reason would I have to call you?" She didn't wait for a reply. "Starbucks at Green Lake? Monday at four?"

After a short silence, in a quiet voice, Helen said, "I'll be there."

A family of ducks waddled out of the lake. Koru spotted them. He pulled sharply on his leash. Anna held him back. Koru continued to pull at the leash. She wondered if she had breathed during the conversation.

Anna eased herself down on the bench, leaned back, and took several deep breaths. Someone whizzed by on roller skates. A few children squealed as they ran along the shore frightening the ducks who flapped their wings and waddled back into the lake. Koru relaxed and lay down at Anna's feet.

Maybe she'd stiff her. Leave her sitting and waiting at Starbucks. But then she might show up at the house. Anna wondered if Helen had ever been there. The bitch had been there at Lily's graduation party. Had they ever had sex in her bed?

She decided to wear as many diamonds as she could tastefully wear. Her earrings, a pendant, then she added a slim bracelet her father had given her and added her wedding ring as a final touch, very prominent on her hand. Red was her best color—and an aggressive one—so she wore a new red blouse. A chic haircut, very stylized now, enhanced the contrast between her olive complexion and rich gray hair. A distinguished image. A woman of stature. At least she looked it.

No doubt, Anna was attractive, not the thin, blond, fortyish type, but the mid-fifties, voluptuous type, sexy in an earthy way. Hormone replacement therapy had put juice back into her body, and she planned to flaunt it. She wanted Helen to remember she was the wife Mort always chose, regardless of what he had told Helen.

Anna maneuvered between the crowds sitting outside on the spectacular sunny afternoon. She came early to establish herself before Helen's arrival. Busier than usual: mothers with strollers and dogs tied to the tables, toddlers underfoot, pigeons pecking at muffin crumbs. Not conducive to intense conversation. She had hoped for space around her, a zone of quiet. Bad choice of coffee shops. As she moved between the tables, she happened to look inside and noticed a blond woman sitting alone at a table near the back. The woman in the photo, but older now.

She wore a beige linen suit and beige pumps. Taller than Anna had thought. WASPy. Every Jewish man's fantasy *shiksa*. The woman glanced at her watch, sipped a coffee. Looked around the room. Waited. It had to be Helen. She looked thicker, more substantial than in the earlier picture. Childbirth would do that.

Anna's heart raced. Damn him. Let her wait. Anna stood outside, the sun hot on her face. She moved into the shade, wiped the sweat from her forehead. She'd worn underarm pads to ensure there would be no perspiration stains. A Yorkie, held by an elderly man, barked at a standard poodle tied to a nearby table. The poodle barked back, pulling at her leash, pulling the table. An Australian shepherd joined, pulling at his leash. As the commotion increased, she noticed Helen look toward the windows.

Anna slipped behind a column where she couldn't be seen and refreshed her lipstick. She took a deep breath and walked inside. The air conditioning hit her immediately. She shivered and wished for a jacket. Freezing inside. Then the heady smell of good coffee. Helen had seen her. Let her wait, Anna thought as she approached the counter to order a mocha. Jazz played in the background.

Anna slipped into the vacant seat across from Helen and put the mocha down quickly. She didn't want Helen to notice her hand shaking. "Thank you for coming." She placed her sunglasses carefully next to her coffee.

"You found the letter." Helen smiled. She had a pointy nose, exaggerated by her smile. "This is a bit awkward."

In person, Helen's voice was richer, stronger. Was she a trial attorney? She wasn't the honey-skinned blond type, but rather the translucent, pale-skinned one.

"Yes, I found the letter." Anna adjusted her watchband and put her left hand on the table. She had cleaned her diamond ring. It flashed when she pulled it toward her knuckle and then pushed it back again. "I have one question for you. Do you plan to make any claims on my husband's estate?" She shocked herself with that question, asked in a harsh voice.

Helen's pale blue eyes widened. "No. Not at all." Rachel's eyes were a darker blue.

Anna surprised herself again when she started to stand. "That's all I wanted to know."

"Wait a minute," Helen said, putting her hand out and touching Anna's arm. "Please wait. We need to talk."

Anna sat again, picked up her mocha, and then put it down without drinking, her lips tightly closed.

Helen looked down for a moment then put her hands on the table and leaned forward. "Mort always wanted Rachel to meet the twins."

Anna leaned back in her chair. "There's no need for that to happen now. Mort is dead."

Helen lowered her head. Gray roots showed along her part

line. Not so young after all. Anna observed Helen's body as it sagged from the shoulders. She's in pain, Anna thought. Good. Then Helen lifted her head, her pointy nose aimed at Anna. She looked like a robin pulling a worm from the ground. "It's something Mort always wanted," she repeated, her blue eyes intense. "And I want her to have some part of Mort in her life."

"She's walking around with his genes. That should be enough." Anna leaned forward. "Look. Mort chose not to do anything about this. Why should I? Keep my children out of it. Larry respected his father. Lily idolized him. Let's keep it that way."

"I don't think there's a roadmap for this type of situation. I think we both want to keep this as quiet as possible…I want to avoid dragging Rachel into some kind of nastiness."

"Nastiness." Anna slammed her mocha on the table. She ignored the coffee that spilled. "You should have thought of that before you had an affair with a married man. I have no idea what our children would think. I won't burden them with this. I want you to promise not to contact them."

Helen turned from a robin into a raptor. Her mouth flat, narrow, her eyes darker, focused on Anna, she said, "I won't promise you anything." Her voice crisp, she continued, "I know what Mort wanted. This may be difficult for you. I get that. But it's what Mort wanted. I hoped we could work this out."

She heard a chair slide across the floor, a laugh, the clicking of a laptop. She looked around her and noticed the nearby tables. People were listening, watching.

Anna took a long drink of her mocha and lowered her voice, "Okay. You've talked with me. Don't contact them. Don't do any more damage than you've already done." She opened her purse, dug around for lipstick, and reapplied it as Helen talked.

"When you called, I thought you had decided to honor Mort's request, no matter how painful it might be for you." Helen paused, smiled at Anna, and added, "Mort had a feeling it would be difficult for you to understand."

Anna stood, leaned on the table, her face close to Helen's. "Don't you dare talk to me about what Mort thought. How dare you talk about honor? You fucked a married man and got knocked up. Get over it." Anna bent, picked up her purse, put on her sunglasses, and walked out of the coffee shop.

If rage could be converted to jet fuel, she'd be circling the goddamn planet, Anna thought. Blast off and out of here. She tried walking to her car, but had to stop and lean against a telephone pole. Anna felt as if she could explode and splatter all over the street. Blow up. She had never been so enraged. She wished she had a dagger—she'd walk back in there and stab that bitch in the chest. Cut off her breasts. Attack her face. Write *whore* on her forehead.

She got back to her car in the parking lot, her body trembling, and got in. The sun still shone. People still sat at tables. Still talked. Laughed. Soaked up the sun. Anna clasped the steering wheel with both hands to steady herself. Apparently she hadn't been ready to meet Helen. No plan to lose control. Calm and reasonable had been her goal. Was Helen a decent person, one her children could meet? That's what she had wanted to know. Instead she had morphed into Nurse Ratched—and Lady Macbeth was now in the wings.

Chapter 30

Anna wanted a drink. She rarely drank. Sugar was her drug of choice. Not alcohol. But liquor seemed more appropriate to the occasion than pinwheel cookies. She knew there was a pub on

Latona, a neighborhood bar not far from her house, and she found herself driving there. Arriving and parking out front, she wondered what it was like inside. No time like the present. Anna got out of the car, walked up to the large, dark door, and swung it open.

Nearly empty at the beginning of happy hour. She crossed to the bar, climbed up on a stool, and ordered a drink she remembered from the movies, a black Russian.

She tossed the first one back quickly and then ordered another. Anna loved the smell of Kahlua. She felt the sweetness and the cold rush through her body. She calmed a bit and looked around the room. A few groups of twos and threes. She bummed a cigarette from the bartender, puffed without inhaling.

Mostly a young crowd, wearing shorts, tennis shoes, sweats. One older guy at the end of the bar, about Mort's age, wore a designer tracksuit. She knew she was overdressed. These were the people who ran around the lake every day. Or maybe these were the ones who never ran the lake, just drank around the lake.

She ordered a third. She heard a steady buzz around the room. Conversation? Music? She couldn't distinguish. An old man in a wrinkled suit, whose belly hung over his belt, hiked himself onto the seat beside her. Then again, maybe he wasn't that old. Probably her age. His speech was slurred. She wondered if hers was.

"Whaja drinkin? Can I buy you another?"

Anna looked closely at him. Probably sixty. If she decided to date, he might qualify. Disgusting. And then she thought, why not? "Sure."

The man gestured to the bartender and pointed to Anna's drink.

"That's quite a rock you've got. Married, eh? Stepping out on your old man, eh?"

She laughed. After the fourth black Russian, he looked younger.

They leaned on the bar and talked about the Mariners. Early

season results were bad…at least so far. He bought her another drink. They talked about dot com's…he hated computers but liked the stocks.

As they talked, she began to notice the hairs that grew from his ears and then she saw he didn't trim the ones in his nose. Mort had always trimmed his. She moved her head closer and adjusted her bifocals so she could really see the hairs in his nose.

"Wow," she said. "My husband used to clip his nose hairs. You should do that."

He pulled his face back. "Lady, nose hairs are private business. Keep your nose out of my nose." He slapped his knee and laughed, thought he was very funny.

"I was just saying…" Then she started to laugh. "You don't have to get so defensive. They have these little scissors just for that. I'd do it for you if I had a scissors."

He shook his head. "Thanks, but no thanks." Then under his breath, he muttered, "Not putting a scissors near my nose." He shifted his big belly, got off the bar stool, and moved away. Anna looked around. People were looking at her. She ordered another black Russian.

She knew she'd blown the whole conversation with Helen Dahlberg. The mistress. The mother of Mort's child. Almost related to me, but not quite, she thought as she sipped her fresh black Russian.

The bar stool seemed to be getting smaller. She wiggled around, trying to find the shallow part for a person's butt. She got off the stool and stared at the seat. She climbed up again. It seemed higher than when she first sat down. Wasn't it? How high had it been? She got off again and wondered how she could measure it.

She squinted at the stool. The stupid thing can be whatever height it wants to be. Bar stools get to decide for themselves. Anna climbed up onto the stool and picked up her glass for another sip, but found it empty.

She banged the glass on the bar. "I need another drink," she yelled, and then she started to laugh. These black Russians are stronger than they used to be. Russia is weaker, but the vodka is stronger. She cracked herself up. Had she said that out loud?

The bartender walked over to her. "Am I laughing too loud? Or is there a no-laugh zone in this bar?" He looked very serious, and she wondered if she had bad bar behavior. BBB.

"I'm sorry," she said, but knew she was giggling. She could hear herself. She sounded like a hyena, whatever a hyena sounded like. The bar was full of young people, and she felt everyone was looking at her. She kept laughing.

She tilted her head to the right and then to the left. People were staring. She directed her face to the bartender. "Time to leave," he said.

She got off the bar stool and had to grab the edge of the bar so she wouldn't fall. Anna reached around for her wallet, found it, and discovered it wouldn't open. She handed it to the bartender. "Take out what I owe you."

He took some money, put it in the register, and then walked around the bar. After replacing her wallet, he poked around in her purse until he found her car keys and put them in his pocket.

"Come get them tomorrow," he said. "I'll call you a cab."

"I don't need a cab. Can you take my keys? Can you really do that?"

"Absolutely. It's against the law for me to let you drive. Lady, you're drunk. Do you live around here? Let me get you a cab. "

Anna shook her head, straightened her shoulders, and made her way to the exit. Very bright light outside. She closed her eyes, trying to adjust after the dim bar. "I'm fine," she mumbled to no one in particular. "Leave me alone."

She leaned against the wall for a while but started to feel paranoid. Someone might attack her. She tried to orient herself. Wasn't sure which way to walk.

She asked a young man as he approached the door. "Which way is it to the lake?"

He pointed to his right. "Are you okay, lady?"

"I'm fine. No problem." The street moved from side to side. She heard her high heels click against the cement and a car horn blare as she crossed the street. Her stomach felt queasy. She tasted bile. Swallowed hard. Kept walking down the hill toward the lake. She could see the roof of her house above the trees. Maybe just another couple of blocks. She tasted bile again, swallowed, but she could feel spasms going through her stomach and then coming up through some other part of her. She didn't know what.

She tried to run, but couldn't in high heels. Anna knew she couldn't make it. She stopped and looked frantically around. She knew a few people who lived on the block, but couldn't knock on their doors drunk. Even not drunk. She just didn't do that. Not that kind of a person.

She spotted a boxwood hedge one house down, managed to hide her face between the bushes in the hedge and vomit. She gagged and then it came pulsing out in a steady stream. Tears started at about the same time. The taste was vile. It went on for a long time, and by the time she had stopped, her sobs were loud. A woman came to the door and leaned out. She didn't see the vomit and apparently didn't smell it, either. Anna stood and wiped her mouth with the sleeve of her silk blouse.

"Are you okay?"

"I'm fine. Just got some bad news," Anna said. Her chest was heaving, and she sobbed again. "A death," she said to the woman. "A tragic death." She hiccupped, wiped her mouth again, and tasted the black Russian. Sour coming up. She made it to her back gate and then remembered she didn't have the keys anymore. She'd forgotten to take her house key.

Where was a spare key? Mort always kept a spare key outside. Her head felt so heavy. She lifted all the flowerpots around the back deck. Nothing. She heard Koru howl inside, and then she remembered the new dog door. Maybe she could squeeze in that way.

She felt spasms start in her stomach again. Oh, my God. I can't do this again. I need to get into the house. Anna got down on her hands and knees in front of the dog door. She could make it through. She heard Koru's frantic leaping against the back door, and then he shifted and ran through the dog door knocking Anna over. "Damn dog," she said as she slapped at him, "get away from me." She tried to push him away and found herself crawling toward the edge of the deck where she vomited again. Koru sniffed and started licking.

The back door opened. "Mom? *Mom*. Is that you? Are you all right? What's the matter?" Lily stood in the in the doorway.

Anna looked up from the floor of the deck. "Lily. What are you doing here?"

"I thought I'd surprise you. I've got a meeting here in Seattle." Lily knelt next to Anna. "Mom, are you sick? Mom! You look terrible. What happened?"

Lily put the back of her hand against Anna's forehead. "Are you sick?" And then the stench hit her. "Mom. Have you been drinking? You stink. Did you throw up? Mom, what's going on?" Lily didn't stop asking questions and muttering "Mom" as she helped Anna up from the floor and onto a chair in the kitchen.

Anna's stomach flipped again, and she managed to make it to the bathroom before she felt the spasms overtake her. Anna looked up from the floor where she sat next to the toilet. "Just a bad dinner—the food must have been bad."

Lily handed her a glass of water. "Where did you eat? Who

did you have dinner with? Do you think they're sick, too?" Lily chewed on her lower lip.

"There's no class action suit here, Lily," Anna giggled.

"Mom. You're drunk. You don't have to lie to me." Lily looked closely at her mother's face. "Why are your eyes so red? Have you been crying?"

"I felt so sick, I just started to cry." Anna leaned against the bathtub and let Lily put a cold compress on her forehead.

"Who did you have dinner with?"

"No one you know. Ken, the guy from the video class. He drinks a lot, and I thought I'd have a few." Anna's eyes shifted down, then side to side.

"Let's get you upstairs. Take a shower, lie down. I'll make you some tea." She tried to help Anna off the floor, but she had curled up. Lily could hear her mother whimpering, starting to cry.

"Should I call the doctor? Does anything hurt? I've never seen you like this."

"Nothing, honey. I'll be just fine." But she kept crying. Anna tried to pull herself together. Tried to control her emotion, but whatever had been holding things together was totally gone. She'd never hit Koru before. Ever. Never hit a dog ever. Now Koru lay by the door of the bathroom with his eyes on Anna.

Lily waited until her mother exhausted herself and then got her upstairs to the master bath. She peeled off her mother's clothes, her shirtsleeve stained with vomit where she must have wiped her mouth. She threw all the clothes down the laundry chute. She knew her mother preferred a bath, but a shower was quicker. She adjusted the water temperature.

"Can you stand in the shower alone? Should I stay in here with you?"

"No, I'm fine."

"Hold on to the bar."

"Okay, okay. Leave me alone. I'm fine."

Anna stood under the shower and felt the hot water hit her body. She had removed the flow restrictor thing Mort had placed in all the showers. If she was going to shower, she wanted it hard and fast on her body. She leaned against the tile and let the water warm her. She clutched the bar and swayed as she turned to let her back feel the pressure of the water. Anna thought about washing her hair, tried to reach for the shampoo, but couldn't make it.

She liked baths. Why had Lily insisted on making her take a shower? She hated getting her hair wet and not washing it. It would look stringy and nasty. Again she reached for the shampoo, but couldn't get to it without letting go of the bar. Anna thought about calling for Lily to help, but she couldn't do that. Maybe just for a second she could let go, but she swayed as she reached and felt her legs buckle beneath her. She clutched the shower curtain to stop her fall, but instead it came down with her. A huge crash and then the slapping sound of her butt as it landed hard on the bottom of the tub.

From a distance Anna heard Lily yell, "Mom. Mom. Are you okay? Mom, answer me." The voice got closer, but she couldn't answer. She had no breath. Her head hurt, and the water kept raining down on her. Lily turned off the shower. She struggled to lift her mother out of the tub. Anna seemed dazed.

"Why did he do it? Why? Why did he do it?" She looked at Lily, her eyes unfocused. "Why did he do it?"

"What, Mom? Why did who do what?"

Anna shook her head trying to focus. She saw Lily, her blouse wet, standing at the edge of the tub. Her eyes wide and frightened.

"Help me out of here. Please."

"You'll have to work with me, Mom. Try to get onto your knees. Okay. Can you raise yourself up with the bar? Okay, great. Step out carefully. I've got you. That's it."

Lily wrapped her mother up in a bath sheet, and Anna's mind drifted to a scene in some old Italian movie. She thought maybe it was Marcello Mastroianni being lifted out of a tub as if he were an infant. Now she understood it.

Anna clung to her daughter as they made their way to the bed. Somehow Anna got up on it, and Lily covered her with a blanket. She placed a towel under her mother's wet hair and tucked her in carefully. Anna's breath still stank of alcohol and vomit. She had not brushed her teeth.

Chapter 31

A huge turtle lumbers toward her. On the horizon, only turtle. Scaly skin, head sways right and left. There is no give in the ropes that stake her to the ground. Can move her eyes only. Nothing can spare her from the coming of the turtle. Do turtles eat people, she wonders? The stale, wet smell comes toward her. Disgusting stink, like old milk. Maybe this turtle will walk on by. "Walk on by," she sings to herself in her mounting fear.

Why is she tied up like a pagan sacrifice? What brings her to this parched ground along the edge of the sea? She drifts between sleep and panic. The fetid smell of the turtle comes closer.

Bile rises in her throat. She fears she will suffocate in her own vomit.

She feels wet near her leg. Hears a sucking, chewing, grinding sound. Is he eating her alive? Wet ankle. Right leg loose now. The smell is closer. She looks into a flat black thing that may be an eye. She sees nothing but her own reflection.

He lowers his head, chews the cords that tie her right arm. His teeth grind the rope. Her arm is free, as is her leg. She is afraid to move. She holds her breath as long as she can. Does he think her already dead?

She sees his scaly leg covered in sand. What might be called toes are coated in a layer of tiny pebbles he gathers as he walks. She hears a sliding sound each time his legs move.

Will he eat her next? Will her captors return before he frees her? Where will she go if he frees her? Is she dreaming now? Lying here in the sun for two days, unable to move. Is this St. Peter in his incarnation, coming to take her to Jesus on his back?

Infinitesimal slowness as he moves around her body releasing her bonds. She wants to move, to stretch, to work her stiff muscles. She does not want to distract him from his task, for she knows it is a task. Go out, old turtle, and free the woman who lies dying in the heat. He was sent. By whom?

She must move. Slowly, she moves her right arm, flexing it at the elbow, trying to make the blood flow again. The pain is excruciating. She tries to lift her body off the ground, at least raise her head, but she is too weak.

The turtle lowers himself to the ground. She can no longer see a head. Only the hard shell, which looks as old as time. Slowly she stretches, moves each limb, falls back, and catches her breath before the next exertion. She should rise and flee. Too weak. Where would she go?

She needs water. She sucks hard at the edges of her mouth, trying to release moisture.

Scratchy throat. Anna coughed and her eyes opened. She closed them quickly, hoping to recapture her dream—turtle, sand, water—but couldn't find the thread again. Gone. Her mouth was dry, her head heavy as she turned to see the clock. Foggy numbers. She patted around the nightstand, searching for her glasses. She moved slowly, each slight move creating a banging above her right eye. Terrible taste in her mouth. Vomit? Koru wasn't at the foot of the bed. Was Lily home? Where were her eyeglasses?

Slowly, Anna raised herself to a sitting position. The walls shifted as she adjusted her body. Oh dear. Anna remembered the bartender taking her car keys. Everything after that was hazy.

Someone had filled her brain with lead during the night. She reached again toward the nightstand, feeling for her glasses. She knocked the phone off the edge. The sound of its crash on the floor like an explosion. Anna groaned and lay back on the bed.

"You're up?" Lily asked as she came into the room and pulled the drapes open. Light swept into the room. Anna pulled the covers over her head.

"Close those drapes. The light hurts my head."

"If you want them closed, you'll have to get up and do it yourself. I've been waiting for you to wake up. I'll get you coffee. Don't move."

Don't move, Anna thought. If I don't move, I'll wet the bed. Gingerly, she moved her legs over the side of the bed, raising her head slowly as if it were a large bowl full of eggs, and turned away from the light. She needed to pee and brush her teeth.

The evening came back to her in snapshots as she struggled to get to the bathroom. At the table with Helen. The man with the hairy nose. Vomiting in the bushes.

Anna reached the sink and hung on to it as she stared into the mirror. Her hair tangled in clumps around her head. Eyelids swollen, drooping over red eyes, livid against her sallow complexion. Anna tried to think of a story, something believable, that would mollify her daughter, but she couldn't focus, couldn't herd her thoughts along a coherent path. One thing at a time, she thought. She brushed her teeth and listened to the buzz of the electric brush reverberate through her head.

Lily waited on the bed. She had propped up the pillows all

along the headboard as she used to do as a teenager. They used to watch *Hill Street Blues* and *Cheers* on Thursday nights together. Mort had always played racquetball on Thursdays then worked out at the gym. Now Anna wondered what he had really done.

Her coffee waited on the nightstand, alongside two aspirins and a glass of water.

"Your cell phone rang a few times last night. Someone named Carla," Lily said as Anna sat on the bed, took the aspirins.

"Did you answer?" Anna's voice sounded rusty.

"No. Who's Carla?"

"Someone in the band." She prayed her voice sounded casual. Slowly she leaned back, swung her legs up, and settled on the bed.

"She really wanted to reach you last night." Lily chewed on her lower lip.

"I'll call her later." Anna picked up the cup of hot coffee, sipped, grateful for the distraction. "Thanks for the coffee. You make great coffee."

"It's delicious, isn't it?" Lily asked as she savored her own cup. "You dropped your purse on the floor when you came in last night. Stuff fell out all over the floor."

Anna nodded carefully, trying not to move her head too much. "Will you close the drapes, please? I forgot." Anna noticed that Lily's shoulders were rigid as she walked across the room and closed out the glaring morning light.

"There was a picture of Dad and a blond. It was in a baggie." This must be her litigator's voice, Anna thought.

"Uh huh."

"Do you know who she is?" Hard voice. Determined. Persistent. It made her a good lawyer. She'd never let go of this.

"I do. I didn't, but I do now." She needed to proceed carefully, but in which direction? She swallowed the aspirins and positioned her head strategically against the headboard.

"Who is she?"

"Her name is Helen Dahlberg. She's an attorney in town. "

"A friend of Dad's?"

Anna put her coffee cup back on the nightstand. She reached her hands behind her neck and rubbed, pushing hard against the tight muscles. Lily stood at the end of the bed, brushing her hair away from her face with a sharp motion of her hand.

"Mom, what's going on? Who is she? Not just her name. Who is she?"

"A friend of your father's."

"Mom, I can do this like a cross examination, keep at you all day, or you can tell me what's going on and get it over with. You were drunk last night. You stank of vomit. Dad's office is empty, no sign of him anywhere in the house. His closet is empty, and there's a picture of Dad with a strange woman in a baggie in your purse."

"You opened Dad's closet? I didn't hear you in here."

"Why would you? You passed out. Drunk."

"I packed a few boxes of things you might want."

"Thanks. What did you do with everything else?"

"I donated everything. No sense not to give his things to people who could use them."

"Bullshit. Mom."

"I did donate everything."

"That's not what I'm talking about." Lily folded her arms across her chest, her brow furrowed. "I'm not a child anymore. Talk to me."

Anna got up off the bed very slowly and moved to the chaise. The aspirins weren't working yet. Was she protecting Mort? Protecting the kids? Protecting herself?

She had known she'd have to talk with Lily, but she thought she'd have a lot more time to plan it. She wanted to manage—control—Lily's response. To tell her in such a way that…what? That

Lily wouldn't hate her father? Wouldn't hate her? Wouldn't hate her sister? Wouldn't want to meet her sister?

She thought about all her experience with hospice care. She knew how to talk with families in the face of imminent death. And this was a death. She needed to be clear, direct, and unflinchingly honest. Lily's reaction would be Lily's. She was a separate person, an adult now. Twenty-eight years old. Old enough.

"It's not pretty. Are you sure you want to know?"

Lily got off the bed. "Absolutely." She slid her mother's legs to one side and sat on the end of the chaise. "I've never seen you like this. You're scaring me."

"I had planned to tell you about Helen, that's her name. Oh, I told you that. I'm sorry, my head is killing me." Anna pressed her fingers to her temples. "I'm sick."

"Don't drink so much next time. Go ahead."

"Okay. Okay. I met her yesterday. I planned to be calm. I never imagined you would find out this way." Anna cleared her throat. "Can you get me another glass of water? I can't even swallow."

Lily got her mother a glass of water from the bathroom. Anna moved her legs slightly to make room for Koru, who jumped up on the chaise. Lily sat on the floor facing her mother. She drew her knees up and held them to her chest. "Start at the beginning."

Anna reached out and ran her hand through Koru's thick fur. "A few months ago, I decided to pack up your father's clothes. I thought it was time to start letting go. I did donate everything. I can't remember where. They came to pick up the stuff. Where was I?"

"Packing Dad's clothes."

"I checked all the pockets. You know, like when you're doing laundry. I found a receipt from the Four Seasons Hotel. In his pocket. In that old gray tweed jacket. Remember it?"

Lily nodded, scarcely moving her head, her jaw tight.

"We'd never stayed there. It was from the December before he died. I went down to his office to look for his calendar. Jack had left a bunch of your father's things from the downtown office in the closet down there. I found an envelope addressed to me from your father. The picture you found in the baggie was in the envelope, along with a letter from him and some other things."

Lily sat with her head cocked at an angle, stuck in an alert position, unable to relax. Her eyes wide and unblinking.

"It was obvious to me that there was another woman, had been for some time."

Lily was shaking her head.

"There's more. It's actually much more than that. There was also a copy of a birth certificate." Anna spoke very quickly. "Your father has another child. A little girl. Now nine years old. Her name is Rachel. Helen Dahlberg is the mother."

"A child? Rachel," Lily whispered. "Wasn't that Bubbeh's name?"

"Uh huh. Your father had wanted to name you after her, but it's against Jewish tradition to name a child after a living person, and Bubbeh was alive when you were born..."

"But he named her Rachel?"

Anna slid Koru off the chair and managed to get down next to Lily. The aspirins had started to work. She took her daughter's hand into her own. She stroked it lightly. "Lily, never forget that your father adored you. You and Larry. He loved you both completely. Absolutely. He was prouder of you than of anything in his life. Never forget that."

Lily shook her head slowly. "I can't believe this. There's more to this. There must be. You're not talking about my father. It's impossible. Impossible." She pulled her hand away.

"Your father wanted me to let you and Larry know about your sister."

"Sister?"

"You don't have to believe me. You can see the birth certificate and the letters if you want."

Lily stood up and walked across the bedroom to Mort's closet. She opened the door and stared in at the empty closet. Anna leaned back against the chaise.

"I don't even want to see any documents. There's got to be another explanation. It's just not true." Lily slammed the closet door. Opened it and then slammed it again.

"I'm sorry." Anna wondered why she was apologizing. She wished her head didn't hurt. She wished she hadn't come home drunk. She wished Lily hadn't surprised her. She might have been able to make this easier for her daughter.

Lily leaned against the closet door. "Does Larry know any of this?"

"Not yet."

"He won't believe it, either."

Anna knew she couldn't control Lily's reaction. Actually, there was very little she could control in this situation. "I'm going to get dressed now. The envelope your father left is in the drawer of the nightstand on his side of the bed."

Anna got some sweats out of her closet and went into the bathroom. She saw Lily walk toward the nightstand out of the corner of her eye.

Chapter 32

A soak in the tub, more aspirin, and several glasses of water later, Anna could move her head without shuddering. She found her bedroom empty, the nightstand drawer open, and the door to

Lily's room closed. No answer to her knock. No response. Then she knocked louder.

"Later, Mom. Not now." Lily's voice harsh, thick. She'd been crying. Listening at the door, Anna couldn't really guess Lily's state of mind. She waited a few minutes, hoping Lily would appear. Nothing.

She turned and put one foot carefully in front of the other as she started down the steps. She looked around at their lovely home, but saw only cymbals crashing. Thunder. Confusion and debris. The image of the Kingdome imploding came to her mind. Gone. Everything they knew as family, as home, had been changed forever.

When only Anna held the secret, the structure had stood. Maybe not for her, but as long as the twins knew only what they had known growing up, the image of their family remained intact, whole.

Anna went out to the deck where Koru lay basking in the morning sun, stretched out, relaxed. Calm. Lily was upstairs sobbing in her childhood bedroom, where Mort had read her stories. Had he read Rachel stories? Adorable Rachel. Entirely innocent in this mess. But then, so were the twins. Older, but still innocent.

Anna lowered herself next to Koru, ran her hands through his thick fur. He raised his head and then put it down again. She reached behind her, placed her palms on the deck, and raised her face to the sun, felt the warmth seep into her pores. She could see spots and colors through her closed eyelids. She remembered doing that as a child, squinting and trying to glimpse the excitement of color in motion, endless hours and hours of carefree exploration. That time was long gone.

"It's not a dream, is it?" Lily sat down next to her on the deck, pulling her knees up to her chest.

Anna shook her head. "Not a dream."

"Just a nightmare." Lily's voice was nasal, congested. "What are you going to do?"

Anna listened to the song sparrows perched on the bushes along Becky Clayton's fence, not offering a melodic song, but rather a sputtering. "Nothing." Anna lay back on the deck, closed her eyes, and absorbed the sun. She should have sunscreen, she thought, and then let it go. "I'm not going to do anything."

Lily pulled her knees tighter against her chest. Anna squinted up at her daughter. Lily's eyes were flat, blank, hollow.

"I said I wasn't going to do anything, Cookie, not that I didn't feel anything." She sat up, moved closer to Lily, and put her arms around her daughter. Lily's body remained stiff, unyielding. Anna held on until she heard Lily sigh, loosen her arms from around her knees, and wrap them around her mother.

"How could he have done it?" She buried her face on her mother's shoulder and cried tired tears without energy.

Anna leaned back, brushed the hair away from Lily's face. "Why don't we go for a walk? Koru could use one. So could I."

"How can you be so calm?"

"Calm? Believe me, I wasn't so calm when I first found out. And I certainly wasn't calm yesterday when I met Helen. But I've known about it for a few months."

Lily pulled away. "I can't walk now. I need to think. I need the details, but not now." She pressed her hands against her temples. "I've got to get rid of this headache. I had meetings scheduled today, meetings with immigration attorneys." She massaged the back of her neck. "That's why I came to Seattle."

Lily stood, stretched her arms above her head, took in a deep breath, and let out a slow exhale. "You were so drunk and sick last night that I postponed everything until I knew how you were. And now...I can't go for a walk. I can't even think. I need to pull myself together. I need to call Larry."

Anna's headache had resurfaced, and she needed to get out of the sun. She wiped off one of the deck chairs with her hand and moved it toward Lily. "Let's sit in the shade here for just a few minutes. Can you wait to call Larry until we've talked more?"

"Why?"

"Sit down for a minute." She dusted off another chair and moved it close to Lily's chair under the awning. "Stay here while I get us some water." Koru stood, circled, and stretched out again in the sun.

Anna added ice to two glasses and observed Lily through the sliding glass doors. She had left the chair and was pacing across the deck, her hands in the pockets of her jeans. She looked very different than the young woman who had flown up for her birthday only a few months before. Her shoulders were scrunched together, her gait jerky, no longer the lithe Audrey Hepburn image.

Anna filled the glasses and slid a door open, then closed, with her elbow. Motioning Lily to the empty chair, Anna sat. "It's like hot potato. Remember that game? You touch it, it's hot, and you pass it around, and everyone gets crazier and crazier, tossing it around. I had no one to toss it to. It burned for a while, but now I'm okay." Anna leaned forward and put her hand on Lily's thigh. "Let things settle inside of you. Find a place in your mind for this craziness before you hand it to Larry. He won't help you. He'll make it worse; at least I think he will."

"Mom, I can't not call Larry. Somebody needs to do something. I don't know what." She stood and paced across the deck. The sparrows quieted. The only sound, that of a lawnmower from somewhere down the street. "Did you have any idea this was going on? The man who wrote that letter can't be my father. Mom, we've got to do something. I can't believe you're so passive." Lily's voice was loud, shrill.

They heard a noise from behind the fence. Was Becky Clayton listening? Maybe. Then the neighborhood would know. Who else knew? She raised a finger to her lips. "Shhh..."

Lily glanced at the fence and then back at her mother. She slapped her hand against her head. "I'm an idiot, Mom. A total idiot."

She knelt beside Anna's chair. "I'm truly sorry," she whispered and looked again at the Clayton fence. "Not about Becky hearing me. Who cares if she knows? I can't believe how selfish I've been. Here I am going off... You must have been crushed. I'm only thinking about myself. Are you okay? Is that why you stopped teaching? You seemed a little down when I came for my birthday. Did you know then?"

"No. Not until February, I think. I can't remember exactly. I've had a lot more time to think about everything." Koru stirred, barked at a squirrel running along the fence, then walked to the shady area and settled next to Anna's chair. "I was trying to decide if I needed to tell you and Larry. Could I protect you? Should I? I was trying to figure that out."

She leaned down and scratched between Koru's ears. "Helen Dahlberg and her daughter have nothing to do with my life, not really. If I had found out while your father was alive, it would have been different. It's awful, but your father bequeathed them to you. You get to choose. I can't protect you. Do you want Rachel in your life? How much? How little? Those are your decisions, yours and Larry's, not mine."

"Why did you go to meet her?" Anna heard movement behind the Clayton fence and motioned for Lily to come into the kitchen. She opened the door for the two of them, then slid the door closed.

"I wanted to find out what kind of a woman she was, to get a feel for her. I needed to know before I told you and Larry. If she were a truly scummy person, I would have kept it from you completely. It was my decision to tell you or not to tell you. I never expected you to find out this way."

"What's she like?"

"Your father had good taste." Anna laughed. "I think she loved your father, and she loves her daughter. Actually, your half sister."

"Don't say that. I'll never want to meet her."

"That's your decision." Anna refilled her water glass and sat down. Never another black Russian, not as long as she lived. Never.

"You're right about Larry." Lily now paced around the kitchen. "He'll go crazy. Is there money involved?"

Again Anna thought about her hospice training. Truth. Straight up. "He left Rachel a trust. I don't know how much. He mentioned that in his letter, and I talked with Jack about it. The mother has her own money."

"Jack? He knows? Oh God," Lily said. She sank into a chair facing her mother, and they sat in silence until Koru came through the dog door. He headed straight for his water bowl, slurping as he lapped up all the water.

"Koru needs his walk. Me, too. Need to move, clear my head. Come around the lake with us. The grebes have little baby grebes, grebbettes. I have no idea what they're called, but they're very cute."

"Not today. I can't. I have to figure out how I can reschedule my meetings."

"Would it be better for you if I told Larry?" Anna asked.

"No. We're going to have to deal with it. I want to tell him myself."

Anna stacked some mail that was strewn across the table as she watched her daughter brood. "I wanted to protect you and Larry from having to deal with this, but it's in your hands now. Whatever happens, you and Larry need to remember that your father loved you completely and unconditionally. I am not excusing his behavior, but whatever happened to him, whatever crazy choices he made, he loved you. He was proud of you. He adored you."

Lily lowered her face into her hands. Anna could barely hear her when she said, "He had another daughter."

"Yes, he did." No need to tell Lily that she'd met Rachel or that Rachel looked exactly as Larry had at that age. She wouldn't tell her about stealing the recycling, either.

"And he named her after his mother."

"Yes. Look at me, Cookie," Anna said as she pulled her chair next to her daughter and put her hand on Lily's shoulder.

Lily raised her head, her eyes bleary and red.

"There's just one more thing to hold tight, no matter what choices you make. Don't ever forget I'm in your corner always. I love you. Don't ever, ever forget that."

"Thanks, Mom."

"Do you want me to stay with you this morning?"

Lily sat up, shook her head, and rubbed her eyes. "I've got work to do."

Anna kissed her daughter's cheek. "Come on, Koru; let's see if one hung-over old lady and an old dog can make it all around the lake today."

Chapter 33

Lily kept herself busy during her remaining time in Seattle, and Anna didn't force any conversations. Over and over she told herself that her task was completed. Lily would tell Larry in her own time. But there was no real closure for her. Not for some time, anyway, if ever.

Anna, one of a handful of people, attended a small memorial service for Becky Clayton's sister who had passed away. The next day, Becky delivered a box of strudel with a thank-you note.

Larry called one evening after she'd returned from a class on post-production issues. She took the phone out to the front porch and watched the sun beginning to set over Phinney Ridge. The smell of barbeque floated along the street. Someone was grilling.

"Mom, Lily called me today. I guess you know why she called."

"About your father?"

"Yeah. I don't know what to say to you. I talked with Naeema, and we can't believe it."

The stoop felt warm on her bottom as she sat on the front steps. Lights came on across the street. Becky Clayton's house was dark; she was probably already asleep. A woman she didn't recognize walked by, leading an Italian greyhound.

"Lily said Jack knew. Who else?"

"I don't know." She heard Koru scratching to come outside. She got up, let him out, and sat back down. He lay next to her, pressing against her side.

"I don't care if the whole damn city knows."

"You might in the future," Anna said. "You might want to take some time and think about this for a while." Slowly she scratched between Koru's ears and massaged his back. "I've had a long time to absorb it all."

"What the hell are we going to do about this kid?"

"That's up to you and Lily. A gift from your father."

"Who knew he was such a hypocrite?"

"Larry, I don't really want to talk to you about this now, maybe later."

"He was chickenshit, a coward. He should have told you. He shortchanged everybody."

"Larry, I know it makes you feel better to vent, but I can't do this now."

"He was so full of shit."

"Larry, I know you're angry about this. We all are, but I can't do this now."

"Sorry, Mom. Lily said you were busted up about it, but I'm glad he's dead. The asshole. Always so righteous."

"Larry, I can't have this conversation with you now. Calm down or call your sister."

"Okay. I get it. Are you sure you're all right?"

"I'm fine."

"Okay then. Naeema and I were talking—we should figure out a time for you to see the kids this summer."

"I'd love that."

"I'll talk with Naeema. Mom," Larry paused and added, "I just don't get it. It's too crazy to believe."

"Believe it, Larry. Give my love to Naeema and the kids. Send me some new pictures." Anna realized he had probably hung up before she asked for the pictures. Perhaps she would see them soon and take her own pictures.

An orange glow still covered Phinney Ridge, the sky dark above and below, the streetlights glimmering against the darkness of the hill. She and Koru stayed outside and watched the sun as it disappeared into the horizon.

Koru sniffed his way around a cluster of maples at the lake. Anna stood on the path and watched his tail wag back and forth. She felt a tap on her shoulder and turned to face a gray-haired man wearing running shorts and tank top. He ran his hand across his forehead, brushing away sweat.

"This lake gets bigger and bigger," he panted.

"Do I know you?"

"Probably don't remember me. But I remember you. You're the

lady I saw at the Latona Pub a few weeks ago. Anna? Is your name Anna?"

She nodded, trying to remember, the evening hazy in her mind. She remembered walking out on Helen, going to the pub, talking to someone. Maybe that's why this guy looked familiar. "You're right. I'm afraid I don't remember much about that night."

"That's what I figured. You didn't seem the kind that made a habit of getting wasted in a neighborhood bar—or any bar, for that matter."

"That's the truth."

Koru pulled on his leash, dragging Anna along.

"Mind if I walk along with you for a few minutes? My car is parked down this way."

She nodded her head and pulled Koru closer. A woman walking three Pekingese came toward them, and Anna knew Koru would go after them, which he did. Barked. Growled. Pulled at his leash. Anna yanked on Koru's collar the way she hated to, but it always worked, got Koru back in line, and they walked past the noisy, little yapping dogs.

"By the way, I'm Matt McCarthy. Nice to run into you."

Anna nodded again, trying to remember that night. She remembered an old guy hitting on her, a guy with hairs in his nose. She looked up at the man on her right, surreptitiously looked to see if he had overgrown hairs in his nose. No. A different guy altogether. Not as fat. A runner, apparently.

"You may not remember. I was sitting down at the end of the bar. No, not the guy with the nose hairs." He laughed. "You were bombed. Flat-out bombed. When I saw you just now, it took me a moment, but then I remembered where I'd seen you, remembered your name. You have an easy face to remember."

Anna wondered if that was a compliment.

"Feeling better?"

Anna smiled. "Much. Thanks. As I said, I don't remember much about that night. Definitely not at my best."

Koru moved toward the reeds lining the lake. He's going to poop, Anna thought. One of his favorite spots. Two grown people, strangers, watching a dog poop. So bizarre.

"I was going to stop at Starbucks. Want to join me? We're almost there."

He seemed nice enough. Broad daylight. Nothing else to do. Why not? She nodded.

"I heard you talking to that guy. You told him your husband had died."

"Last year. Actually, a year and a half ago now."

They waited at the crosswalk for a break in traffic and then chose one of the tables outside under an umbrella. June sunshine. Late afternoon. Matt went in to order drinks, and Anna waited outside with Koru. Very pleasant to sit and observe people walk by. For most of her adult life, she would have felt self-conscious sitting at a table alone, even with Koru by her side. Now she found she actually enjoyed it.

Matt retuned with the coffees. Anna learned that Matt's wife had died of breast cancer six months earlier. She had been ill for several years before she died. He talked about her as if she were just around the corner. Claudia this and Claudia that. Anna found her mind drifting.

He was attractive. Attractive for a guy about her age. She didn't know how old exactly. He was in decent shape. Lonely, obviously. Needed someone. Men always needed someone. Don't we all, she thought. He seemed nice. Loved his wife. Had grown kids. Two of them still lived in Seattle.

"Maybe you'd like to go to dinner sometime?" He waited, smiling, eyes wide.

Anna took a long sip of her mocha. Maybe she could fill his

emptiness. It felt that random to her. She pictured him sitting at his kitchen table surrounded by the week's mail, dirty dishes in the sink. It depressed her. "Thanks, Matt. I don't think so, but thank you. Really."

She felt nothing. Not an extra beat of her heart. He was eligible. She had found out that he worked for Microsoft. Probably lived a comfortable life. Maybe she could grow to care for him. Relationships grew out of less.

"Thank you for the invitation," she said, standing and getting Koru ready to go. Anna took Matt's number—he insisted—and Anna said that maybe she'd call sometime when she felt ready. As she walked back to her house, she imagined being with Carla, thought about how she felt in her presence. Alive. Hungry. Engaged. Present.

Matt was perfectly suitable, a good potential if she had any interest in getting married again. Not Jewish, but definitely a family man. She noticed her brain looking around for ways to make it work. If not with Matt, maybe with another man. Maybe she should get online with JDate, the Jewish online dating service. Her brain looked for resolution, looked for a way out of thinking about Carla, a way out of being attracted to her. A way out of wanting her.

Chapter 34

Anna schlepped a camera, along with her tripod, through the crowds, looking for a vantage point. She was grateful to have a function, something to do at the gay pride parade. Ken would focus on close-ups of the band as it moved through the parade route. He could stand motionless, hold the camera perfectly steady between the rows as band members marched past him in formation. Amazing shots.

Anna needed a tripod. Maybe because she was older, a bit less steady, or maybe her basic personality needed some sort of ballast to keep her level. Regardless of the reason, she needed a tripod.

Waves of noise came at her from all directions. Laughter, babies crying, people yelling across the street to friends, clown horns squeaking, dogs barking, music, people clapping, singing. Celebration filled the air, even though the parade hadn't started yet. Rainbow flags, all sizes and fabrics, waved from windows, balconies, street lamps.

She kept her eyes down as she walked, trying to stay balanced amidst the swirling images, but it didn't help. Birkenstocks, Reeboks, three-inch patent-leather high heels walked next to railroad boots decorated with chains. Bare hairy legs in shorts, bare shaven legs in tutus and black fishnet stockings, a train of peacock feathers attached to a harness around someone's butt. A miniature poodle with its fur dyed the colors of the rainbow walked alongside a young man dressed in a gold lamé Speedo. As she looked up, she walked into another man with the colors of the rainbow painted on his otherwise bare chest.

Her stomach churned. She needed to stay focused. She had never considered attending a pride parade before. It was something that happened up on Capitol Hill. Something that other people did. Nothing to do with her life. But now…If she liked making out with a lesbian, did that make her one? Were these her people?

Anna pulled her mind back to the task. She and Ken would select the best shots from the parade footage and add it to what they had already edited. Ken would do the music track. He had a fabulous ear and a great sense of pacing. Then they would be finished. Deadline was July 15. Nineteen days after the parade to complete the doc. She knew it would be tight, but their documentary would culminate with footage from the parade. They could do it.

Crowds of people lined up behind the curbs, blocking her view. She had no idea how to get close. Everything was there. From the outlandish to the boring. She stopped to catch her breath, leaned against the window of Fred Meyer on Broadway, and took a huge gulp from her water bottle.

Stay focused, Anna thought. She needed to select a location quickly before the actual parade started. As she looked north and south along Broadway, she happened to look up and see a balcony across the street. At least a dozen drag queens in silks and satin gowns, tiaras, and feather boas waved fans to the people below. Could she get up there? Was that a private home? She made her way across the street toward the building with the balcony and discovered a narrow staircase leading to a restaurant on the second floor. A waiter met her at the door.

"Sorry. We'll open up after the parade. A private party, ma'am. It's reserved until after the parade." Off-key strains of "Everything's Coming Up Roses" drifted in from the balcony.

On his—or was it her?—way from the bathroom, a very tall person—weighing, Anna figured, somewhere around 250 pounds—sashayed toward the door, wearing stiletto heels and a shimmering emerald gown. The person stopped where Anna stood talking with the waiter. She or he? Anna wondered again. She wasn't sure how to think about the person, but decided "she" might be the appropriate form, considering the garb. The gown was a very large size of a style Rita Hayworth might have worn in the '40s. A diamond tiara sat comfortably on a Veronica Lake wig.

"What's this, Ramon? Who do we have here?" She patted Anna on the head.

"Oh, Chi Chi. This woman wants to get out to the balcony. I told her we were closed."

Chi Chi leaned over and looked directly into Anna's face. "Oh, sister woman, has Ramon been nasty to you?"

Anna's heart beat quickly at the possible opening. She knew she could get superb film from the balcony, but she had no idea what would influence Chi Chi. She had been good at maneuvering her way through Mort's associates, but this was an entirely different situation. She decided to stick to the truth.

"I'm in a class at the university, and we're making a movie about the marching band. I want a shot of the band from above as they march through the crowd."

"How sweet, Ramon." Again she patted Anna on the head. Over six feet five, for sure. "Let this sister woman through." Chi Chi turned toward the balcony then looked back over her shoulder and said, "But there is one condition."

"What's that?"

"We must be included. Me and the girls, even that beastie bitch draped in the ugly blue rag." Chi Chi pointed in the direction of the balcony, where the queens were now singing "Diamonds Are a Girl's Best Friend." Chi Chi went on. "Record us for posterity. Document our beauty." She gestured toward the balcony. "Come forward and meet your destiny." Anna picked up her tripod and followed Chi Chi outside.

The queens were all big men. Chi Chi introduced Anna to Coco, Margo, Dame Edna, Victoria, and Miss Aurora, along with several others. Anna complimented them on their couture, admired the queens as they posed and paraded for her. They loved the audience, Anna noted, even one as small and as insignificant to them as a gray-haired straight woman. Then she wondered if they thought she was gay. Maybe that's why they were generous to her. Or maybe they knew she was straight and that's why.

She stopped her mind. Anxiety lurked behind every thought. She tried to be present to exactly what was happening. She had no idea about how she fit or didn't fit, or what any of it meant.

The queens modeled their dresses for her, primped a bit, but soon grew bored. They turned their attention back to the street. Anna kept her focus on her work behind the camera.

Chi Chi had ordered a mimosa for Anna and now insisted she drink it. "Get with the program, girlfriend. Let loose. Don't you have pride? Celebrate!" Then Chi Chi was off, calling and gesturing to the people below.

Anna knew there was still some time before the parade started, so she shot footage of the crowd below her, zooming in on families, two men or two women with strollers, toddlers, young children in their arms. She shot men in leather, women in leather. Clowns ran through the streets throwing candies at the children.

Dame Edna tapped Anna on the shoulder. "We need you now." Before Anna could object, Chi Chi picked up her tripod with the camera attached and set it up inside the restaurant, facing the balcony.

The girls gathered together some distance from Anna as she adjusted the camera for height and focus. Light coming from the east shone perfectly on their faces. The queens argued about what song to sing until Chi Chi, who must have been paying for the party said, "'Somewhere Over the Rainbow.' It's rainbows today, girls."

"Will one of you hold this mic? There's a lot of background noise," Anna said. "This will help."

Could she fit them into her documentary? This was definitely not in the script. She would give the queens copies of them singing, and maybe she and Ken could use some of the footage as well. Maybe or maybe not. She asked them for verbal releases on camera just in case. They were happy to oblige.

Loud cheers came from the distance, and she knew the parade would pass soon. The girls went back to their drinks, gestured to the crowds below, and ignored Anna, who had moved the camera back onto the balcony and skillfully focused it on the path of the parade.

First came the Dykes on Bikes. Forty or fifty large motorcycles ridden by women roared and growled. The sound of their bikes was drowned out by the huge cheer coming up from the crowd. The riders revved their engines and rode in circles in the street below. Through the lens of her camera, Anna noticed the muscular women, some wearing sports bras, grab the handlebars. With her telephoto, she could see their muscles tense, ripple under the skin. They grinned, laughed, and waved at the crowds.

Beautiful women, some like fashion models. Scary-looking women she wouldn't want to meet on a dark night. Women with tattoos. One wearing a pink baby-doll blouse and short shorts. All kinds of women. Feminine women. Masculine women. Nothing in Anna's experience had prepared her for the spectacle. Some had women riding along behind them, hugging their backs and smiling.

Anna's throat was dry, her heart raced. This is crazy, she thought. Shivers ran through her body despite the hot day. Only the power of suggestion. Yet, she couldn't deny the fascination or the attraction. She certainly didn't understand it, but she felt a hot wind move through her body, blow open every pore, every cell. She imagined someone focusing a lens on her, filming her from above. What would they see?

A middle-aged woman deftly focusing her lens. Nothing more. No one could see the riot in her body, the aliveness the drag queens acted out. She had it, too. Not now, she thought. Again she shut her mind and directed herself to the task.

After the Dykes on Bikes came the Sisters of Perpetual Indulgence, men wearing nuns' outfits—the old-fashioned habits tied around the waist with leather ropes, scapulars with wimples and veils attached. Many had huge crosses dangling across their necks. They wore white makeup with big eyelashes painted in black, some with the image of a tear rolling down their faces. Grotesque and beautiful.

They must be dying of the heat, Anna thought. Again the crowd went wild. Some of the "nuns" raised their crosses toward the crowd in blessing.

Politicians on the back of convertibles, all kinds of floats, firefighters, police, nurses, men in leather snapping whips. Contingents of Catholic GLBT people, followed by a Mormon group. And then Tikvah Chadasha, apparently a synagogue. A synagogue she'd never heard of in all of her years in Seattle. People, men and women just like those who belonged to her synagogue, carried a huge banner with a Jewish star. Behind them came scores of people following a banner reading "J-Pride."

Anna looked for people she knew, but the crowed moved quickly under the balcony. Maybe there was someone from her own synagogue. Could she ever march in a parade like this?

She'd never marched in any parade. Not her style. She sent checks: antiwar movement, civil-rights groups, women's movement, peace groups, food banks. But she'd never marched.

Her back hurt from leaning over the camera. She stood up, stretched, and waited for the band. She felt dizzy. Probably the mimosa and the heat, she thought. But she knew better. She wanted to run back to her kitchen or the closet in her bedroom. Go back to the closet? Was she out? Could someone be sort of a lesbian?

Anna knew she didn't have to decide anything. She wanted to respect her own feelings and trust them. Listen to her inner voice. Nothing more. No agenda.

Then why was she so nervous? Like a bird released from a cage, burdened by doubt and fear. She knew the parade was marvelous. Thousands of people gathered to manifest their pride, to honor their uniqueness, and to demonstrate their personal freedom. Could she ever fly among them? Did she want to?

Anna felt proud of herself, that she was there, documenting the parade, and that she had developed the skills to do it. She realized, too, that she was also taking part in something that felt right to her. Strange as it was, she felt proud to be a part of this, all of this uniqueness, even in a small way.

Then, marching music in the distance. Anna recognized the sound of the band.

With her camera ready, Anna waited. Amidst the drumming that was getting louder and louder, someone along the curb yelled, "Play something for us!" Then she heard the first strains of "YMCA," and saw the crowd shaping their arms to the letters of the song. The band headed her way. She managed to get a long shot of the entire band as it became visible to her, and then Anna switched quickly to a close-up of the drum major.

She panned the rows of marching band members until she found Carla at the back. Anna focused tightly on her face, then quickly down to her strong, tanned arms beating the drum. Carla sweated and laughed and banged away on her drum. Anna felt her heart expand, a lightness filled her body, a feeling of joy. She had no idea what that meant exactly, but she knew she loved watching her, loved having Carla in her life. No doubt in her heart.

The band disappeared under the balcony and then out of her line of sight. That's it, she thought. Hugs all around, and she was off the balcony, out of the building. Quickly, she walked three blocks to her car. She needed to meet Ken at the parade's end to catch random band members to interview as they broke rank. Carla would be waiting for her there. They had a date.

Chapter 35

"Yo, Anna! Over here." In the chaos at the end of the parade route, Ken's hand waved above the crowd. She could barely see him standing with the band members, amidst the hundreds of other marchers winding their way through still-decorated pickup trucks and floats. The sound of noisemakers filled the air. Dogs barked and horns honked as thousands moved on to the celebration at Volunteer Park.

By the time she made her way through the crowd, Ken had already gathered several band members to interview about their post-parade thoughts. They were mostly young, the ones she had labeled in her own mind as "Ken's groupies." Anna filmed a few band members hugging each other, high-fiving, laughing, and added a quick thirty-second interview with Kelley Wilson.

Then she noticed Carla standing with another drummer, her white shirt and khaki shorts stained with sweat. She had removed the red cummerbund that all band members wore. It, too, was wet. Carla lifted the back of her short hair, trying to catch the light breeze going through the trees and saw Anna watching. She smiled, and Anna blushed.

Carla was even older than she was, and here Anna was at fifty-four, feeling fifteen. Anna had spent time during the last several weeks reading some lesbian anthologies and learned about Natalie Barney, a famous expatriate lesbian writer in Paris who fell madly in love at eighty-four—to a straight woman of fifty-six. The story gave her hope.

Ken collected all their equipment, and she helped him load the truck. He would return it to the university while Anna would spend the week editing the day's footage. She knew Ken's film was always excellent, but she was confident that the real money shots of the day came from the balcony.

Carla poured water on a small towel she had draped around her neck, rubbed it across her face, and drank half a bottle of water in one gulp.

"I stink," Carla mumbled as she sniffed her armpit. "I've got to have a shower." People moved around them, band members, strangers, and in spite of the racket of noise and jostling, a bubble surrounded them as they talked.

"You want to shower now?"

"I really do stink. Smell me." She raised her arm and put her underarm in front of Anna's face.

"No kidding." Anna pushed her arm away, laughing, "But I thought we were going to the celebration at Volunteer Park?"

"Sure we are. I just need to shower first." Carla's eyes widened as she looked at Anna. "You still want to come with me, don't you?"

"Sure, but won't we miss it if you shower first?"

"Absolutely not—the party goes on until it's dark. I need to stow my drum, anyway. You know I stink. My sweat is sweating. Should I meet you at the park, or do you want to come home with me while I shower?" The sentences came at Anna quickly as Carla lifted her drum.

At the thought of being in the park with thousands of celebrating gay people, Anna paled. Her stomach churned, her head spun.

"Are you okay?" Carla put her drum back on the ground. "Drink some water. Are you feeling faint?" She put the back of her hand on Anna's forehead.

Anna shook her head and drank some water. "Really, I'm truly fine. Just very hot."

She looked around at the throngs of people walking toward

the park and realized she was actually okay. It wasn't that they were gay; it was just that there were so many people, so many strangers. She would likely have felt as awkward at a Hadassah convention if she didn't know anyone.

Kelley, the band director, pushed through the crowd and grabbed Carla. "You and that drum of yours—girl, what a beat! You made it happen." She looked at Anna. "Weren't we great today?" She didn't wait for an answer, but moved quickly toward another group of band members on their way to the park.

Anna leaned toward Carla and took her arm. "Don't worry. I'm really okay. Where's your truck? I'll leave my car here." Her body hummed when she was near Carla. It was more than just having someone to be with. She wanted to be with Carla.

"I wonder if the twenty-year-olds are as exhausted as I am," Carla said as she started the engine. They both were quiet as they turned away from heavy traffic near the park and went east toward Montlake. They had to stop for the drawbridge, and the wait seemed endless. Carla placed her hand on Anna's thigh as they drove. "Does the air conditioning help?"

"Too much. I'll probably freeze before we get to your house." Anna reached to the controls and lowered the fan. "It's hard to get the right temperature."

Carla glanced at her as she drove. "We'll have to work on that."

Anna placed her hand over Carla's on her thigh. She had no further need to talk, but a lot to think about. She'd watched thousands of young people at the parade, people about the age of Larry and Lily. She wondered how she'd feel if either of them were gay. There had been a huge contingent of people from PFLAG: Parents, Families, and Friends of Lesbians and Gays. Would she have been capable of supporting her children in that way? They carried banners: *Closets are for clothes not for kids. We love our gay children.* Could she ever carry one of those signs?

Anna blinked quickly when she stumbled across a related thought. Would they carry a sign for her? How would her children feel if they knew she loved another woman? If she were a lesbian?

Lost in thought, Anna hadn't noticed that they had arrived at Carla's house. The sun beat down against her back on the short walk from the truck to the door. Maybe she'd take a quick shower, too. Might perk her up. She wished she had time for a nap—lugging the camera and the tripod in the heat had exhausted her. She should have brought a change of clothing. Maybe next year, she thought with surprise. Would she be seeing Carla next year?

Carla left her drum in the living room and led Anna into the kitchen. "Coke? Beer? Water?" she asked as she leaned into the open refrigerator and looked back at Anna.

"Water's good." Standing against the kitchen cabinet, Anna followed Carla's hands as she carefully poured cold water from a bottle into glasses, her long fingers easily circling the bottle.

Carla unbuttoned her shirt, revealing a light tank top. "This tastes so good." She ran her tongue over her lips, catching every drop of cold water, and then held the glass against her cheek. Then she placed the cold glass on Anna's cheek. "Should cool you down." She held it there.

Anna's heart raced. "It will take more than a glass of cold water." She felt a flush rise along her neck.

"Maybe milk? That's cooled you down before," Carla said and put her glass down on the counter. Anna closed her eyes and felt Carla's breath near her face. "Open your eyes," Carla said.

Anna lifted her eyelids slowly when she felt Carla's fingers caressing her cheek. She raised her face toward Carla and kissed her. Softly. Whisper kisses along her mouth. And then her arms were around Carla's waist.

"You scared?"

"A little."

"We won't do anything you don't want to do."

Anna smelled the rich odor of Carla's sweat. Or was it her own? Every nerve in her body reached toward Carla. She felt a warm stirring as Carla's hands caressed the small of her back. Their clothes were damp, they both smelled, and through the kisses, Anna heard laughter, realizing it was her own as well as Carla's.

"Shower?" Carla whispered into Anna's ear. Shivers ran across her skin. Anna nodded and followed Carla out of the kitchen.

Later, they dozed on Carla's bed. Covers strewn on the floor, along with their clothes. They hadn't made it to the shower. Anna heard a gentle snore next to her. She opened her eyes, raised herself up on her elbow, and studied Carla's sleeping face.

She wondered where her glasses were. Carla's face was so close, and Anna couldn't see detail without her bifocals. She wanted to see everything and knew there would be time. For now, she was close enough to see Carla's beauty. Her peacefulness. She looked at Carla's body, her skin dark against the white sheets. Her breasts heavy and spread out on her chest. Anna could still feel their softness. Like her own softness. Familiar and yet unknown.

Carla's eyes opened and she smiled. "Shower?"

"Not quite yet," Anna murmured and ran her index finger across Carla's lower lip.

Chapter 36

Their documentary finished now, Anna and Ken sat side by side during the class screening. The small campus theater that Sam reserved seated about one hundred people. The comfortable, cushy seats and superb air conditioning was very different than their usual classroom, with its movable metal seats and windows that didn't open.

Anna had hoped Lily would be able to be in Seattle for the "premiere," but her work schedule made it impossible. Anna mailed her a copy of the doc and knew her daughter would be impressed and surprised; it would give her a new way of looking at her mother and potentially at Carla—when they met. Anna wanted them to meet.

There had been room for each student to bring four guests, but Anna came alone, as had Ken. She thought about inviting Carla, but wanted her to see it for the first time with the band. It would mean more to her than it would in this academic setting.

"Welcome everyone, and congratulations to the filmmakers. We have seven very good documentaries to view tonight. Lots of talent in the class. Lots of creativity. Everyone met our deadline, and the work is excellent. You'll see for yourselves. We'll take about ten minutes after each doc for questions and comments, and probably we'll take a quick break after the first four." Sam took his seat and motioned to an assistant.

She sat through the first two docs and scarcely absorbed anything. She could hear her own heartbeat. Ken didn't seem to notice. She saw that, as usual, he seemed unflappable, although she noticed he sat rigid on the chair next to her own. Their documentary would be third.

She heard the trumpets that heralded the beginning of their doc and watched the tape roll across the screen. She saw scenes that had taken hours to light, to film, and to edit. Hours of tape distilled into ten minutes. The final edit had taken days, she and Ken in the lab at the university night after night working to meet the class deadline.

Those hours had sped by without Mort entering her thoughts.

She had remained fully engaged with the challenge that faced her. Anna wanted to make the band's story come to life, to make an audience care about the band and the people in it. Anna spent hours editing Carla's interview, using it as voice-over for scenes of the band marching with great dignity and joy down the middle of Broadway during the pride parade. She wanted an audience to care about Carla and her story.

She knew their doc by heart. She and Ken had discussed when they could expect laughs, when they hoped for a tear. The class did not disappoint. She heard heavy applause when it was over, and she clasped her trembling hands tightly on her lap. They stood to hear comments and to answer questions.

"You guys did an amazing job. The story arc works. Camera work on the marching is great."

"I can't believe how open they were with you, so personal and revealing."

"How did you get the long shot from above?"

"What a fun doc; loved the soundtrack."

During the break, Gail, one of the young women in the class, approached Anna. "I really liked your doc. Especially the interviews. I heard you did all the interviews. I mean, the camera work was good, but you got those people to really talk with you."

A dark-haired young man—not from the class—came up behind Gail and put his arm around her. She smiled at him and continued, "I'm working on another film, not for school, but a documentary on homeless teens in Seattle. Would you be interested in helping us out? Me and Tony?" She looked at the young man and smiled.

Sam called the group together to view the remaining documentaries.

"Sure. Yes. Give me a call," Anna said as she wrote her cell number on the program and took her seat next to Ken.

No one in the band knew she and Carla were dating. Intensely dating, actually. Anna knew she had blushed every time she saw Carla in a public setting, and she continued to—even more. But now, after the parade and after the premiere, there was nothing she wanted to hide.

Ken still had no idea. It amazed her that she and Ken had spent hours together and knew so little about each other. Ken knew her husband had died. She knew he did lighting for some theater productions. *Finito*. That was about it. Even if he guessed about her and Carla, he wouldn't say anything. He was the perfect person to work with. He had done his work, respected hers, and left her alone.

Anna paid to have copies of the doc made for all the band members as thank-you gifts. No one had seen it yet. Not even Carla. One of the French-horn players had an elegant home on Capitol Hill with a deck overlooking Lake Washington. He and his partner had invited everyone over for cocktails and the screening.

Canapés were artfully arranged in the form of musical instruments. Wine was served by a beautiful young man wearing a tuxedo who spent a lot of time checking to see if Ken wanted another glass. No doubt, they considered Ken a hunk. He seemed completely at ease for a straight man. Ken teased them, and they teased him back. Suggestive, even a bit lewd. Anna watched him and wondered if maybe he was bisexual. She had developed a relationship with a band member. Maybe he had as well.

Carla gave her a quick hug when she arrived and then joined the others who were assembling on the couches and chairs in the huge living room. Anna started the screening by thanking the band for their cooperation.

"Ken and I want to thank you for inviting us into your band, for opening up to us and telling your stories. You have all been brilliant, and we know that, as hard as we tried, we couldn't fully capture the wonder that is this band. You make magic, and we feel blessed to have touched it. A special thanks to all of you who gave us extra time for interviews, and to you, Kelley—we're honored to have worked with you."

Standing in the front of the room, she looked out at the band members, at men and women from twenty to sixty, and knew she was among friends. She truly felt herself in her own body. She had worn a new outfit that fit: navy slacks and an aqua silk blouse. She had decided that, although she may have gained weight, she was complete, full. She was starting to be comfortable regardless of the size she wore or who she was dating.

The blinds were drawn, the room darkened. Anna, moving to the back of the room, couldn't see Carla from where she stood. But she heard her along with the other band members as they screamed and laughed when they saw themselves on screen. They whistled and howled through the first showing and demanded a second so they could actually listen to the words and the music.

The blinds opened, and light poured back into the room. Champagne flowed and toasts made.

"You're radiant," Carla whispered in her ear.

"Did you like it?"

"Fabulous."

Other band members crowded around Anna and Ken, hugging and laughing.

"I can't believe you got a close-up of me licking my clarinet reed."

"You got my eyes over the bell of my trumpet."

"I had no idea my cheeks puffed out like bellows when I blew my whistle."

"Have you thought about submitting this to the Seattle Film Festival? It's really great."

Anna took it all in. She felt nourished. Full. Satisfied. Whole.

She noticed Carla had moved out to the deck overlooking

Lake Washington. A gentle summer breeze cooled her flushed face as she joined Carla at the railing. Jasmine, planted in huge cobalt-blue planters around the edge of the deck, scented the air. Anna and Carla leaned together against the stainless-steel railing. The sky was still clear blue, with a few wispy clouds off to the north, and they could see Mount Rainier to the south.

"You did it. People were crying. Did you see? So moving and beautiful." Carla brushed her lips against Anna's cheek. "You've captured our spirit, and we thank you for that."

"And I had so much fun. I never expected it."

"Well, there may be lots that you don't expect. Who knows, you might end up liking my chicken mole."

More people came out onto the deck as the light began to change over the lake. Ken was deep in conversation with his friend the trumpet player. Kelley and her partner talked with the drum major. Conversations buzzed around them.

Anna squeezed Carla's hand and took a deep breath, filling her lungs with the crisp evening air. A hint of pink glided across the sky from the west, and as it reached the Cascades in the east, the shape of the mountains subtly changed along the horizon. Cars moved across the bridges that spanned Lake Washington, their lights slowly becoming visible. A tiny new moon appeared high in the sky. Twilight descended on the lake. The magical beauty of the Northwest spread before them.

Anna gathered the images together, closed her eyes, and found a still spot in her heart where she could save the moment, hold it dear, no matter what might come.